What Others Are Saying About Seasons of the Heart

Allow Martha Rogers's tender voice to transport you to another time and place. With inviting characters and relatable themes, her stories leave you with a sense of satisfaction…pure "ah" factor. Martha has become one of my favorite writers for today's prairie readers.

—KIM VOGEL SAWYER
AUTHOR OF SONG OF MY HEART

Texas, my Texas! How I love stories about my great state. Martha Rogers covers all of my favorite literary elements in *Winter Promise*—a quintessential Texas tale with a strong romantic thread, a touching family theme, and a heroine who loves books. Highly recommended!

—JANICE HANNA THOMPSON
AUTHOR OF LOVE FINDS YOU IN GROOM, TEXAS

Martha Rogers creates characters that live on once the last page is turned. Do not miss this endearing tale!

—KATHLEEN Y'BARBO-TURNER
AUTHOR OF DADDY'S LITTLE MATCHMAKERS AND THE
CONFIDENTIAL LIFE OF EUGENIA COOPER

If you enjoy romance, you'll LOVE *Winter Promise*. Martha Rogers delivers yet another excellent historical romance, full of remarkable characters and a pleasing storyline. You won't want to miss this sweet romance set in my favorite location, the Old West.

—MIRALEE FERRELL
AUTHOR OF LOVE FINDS YOU IN SUNDANCE, WYOMING

Winter Promise, the third installment in Martha Rogers's Seasons of the Heart series, continues the saga of frontier romance in the town of Porterfield, Texas. Rogers gives us a multifaceted heroine, but the reader's heart goes to the conflicted hero.

Blaming himself for a tragic medical mistake in his past, he shuts himself off from people—and God. Rogers gently leads him to acceptance and a second chance to love.

—DARLENE FRANKLIN
AUTHOR OF *LONE STAR TRAIL* AND
CHRISTMAS AT BARNCASTLE INN

Martha Rogers takes us to the heart of Texas with an inspirational plot, warmhearted romance, and characters so real you almost expect them to show up on your doorstep.

—MARGARET BROWNLEY
AUTHOR OF ROCKY CREEK SERIES

Autumn Song is a charming story of following God's call and reaping unexpected blessings. It's a feast of family and friends, with a feisty, unconventional heroine.

—VICKIE McDONOUGH
AUTHOR OF *TEXAS BOARDINGHOUSE BRIDES*, *TEXAS TRAILS*, AND
THE WHISPERS ON THE PRAIRIE SERIES

Summer Dream is a sweet, heartfelt, and well-written story about faith in action and a love that never fails. I can't wait to read the rest of this series.

—ANDREA BOESHAAR
AUTHOR OF *UNEXPECTED LOVE* AND *UNDAUNTED FAITH*

Martha creates charming stories that give her readers exciting adventure and timeless romance. If you're looking for a solid, faith-based historical, I encourage you to try Martha Rogers.

—TRACIE PETERSON
BEST-SELLING AUTHOR OF STRIKING A MATCH SERIES, INCLUDING
EMBERS OF LOVE AND *HEARTS AGLOW*

Martha has done it again, written a compelling story with a charming, no-nosense plotline. I trust you'll love Rachel and Nathan's story as much as I did.

—LYNN COLEMAN
BEST-SELLING AUTHOR

SPRING HOPE

SEASONS
of the HEART
BOOK FOUR

SPRING
HOPE

SEASONS
of the HEART
BOOK FOUR

MARTHA ROGERS

REALMS

Most CHARISMA HOUSE BOOK GROUP products are available at special quantity discounts for bulk purchase for sales promotions, premiums, fundraising, and educational needs. For details, write Charisma House Book Group, 600 Rinehart Road, Lake Mary, Florida 32746, or telephone (407) 333-0600.

SPRING HOPE by Martha Rogers
Published by Realms
Charisma Media/Charisma House Book Group
600 Rinehart Road
Lake Mary, Florida 32746
www.charismahouse.com

Scripture quotations are from the King James Version of the Bible.

The characters in this book are fictitious unless they are historical figures explicitly named. Otherwise, any resemblance to actual people, whether living or dead, is coincidental.

Cover design by Gearbox Studio
Design Director: Bill Johnson

Visit the author's website at www.marthawrogers.com.

Library of Congress Cataloging-in-Publication Data:
Rogers, Martha, 1936-
  Spring hope / Martha Rogers. -- 1st ed.
      p. cm.
  ISBN 978-1-61638-618-4 (trade paper) -- ISBN 978-1-61638-863-8 (e-book)
  I. Title.
  PS3618.O4655S67 2011
  813'.6--dc23
                          2012001077

First edition

12 13 14 15 16 — 9 8 7 6 5 4 3 2 1
Printed in the United States of America

This book is dedicated to my father, John M. Whiteman, who walked with me through some of the most difficult situations and decisions in my life. He went home to the Lord in 1998.

ACKNOWLEDGMENTS

To THE LADIES of the Serendipity Sunday School class who faithfully buy my books. You ladies are the best.

To the ACFW 19th-century writers group for all their help with research.

To Lynn Coleman and her wonderful DVD on wagons and carriages that helped me picture the vehicles I wanted.

Always to my editors, Debbie, Lori, and Deborah, for their expertise and belief in my stories.

A big thank-you to those responsible for the beautiful covers that attract readers.

To the Writers on the Storm ACFW chapter in The Woodlands for all your encouragement and support.

Now the God of hope fill you with all joy and peace in believing, that ye may abound in hope, through the power of the Holy Ghost.

—Romans 15:13

CHAPTER ONE

Porterfield, Texas
February 1891

*T*HE COLDEST NIGHT of winter thus far chilled Deputy
Sheriff Cory Muldoon to the bone as he made his rounds in the
alleyways of Porterfield. Cold wind howled around the corners
of the buildings now closed up for the night. Most everyone in
Porterfield had gone home to their families and warm homes.
This was all the winter he cared to experience, and even this
would be only a few days, as the weather in Texas could change
in a heartbeat, summer or winter.

Lights and music from the saloon rang out and mocked the
dark silence of its neighboring buildings. Friday nights found
cowboys and lumberjacks both squandering their hard-earned
money on liquor and women. Tonight would be no different

despite the cold, near freezing temperatures. Most likely at least one or two of them would end up in the jail for a spell.

Cory turned up the collar of his sheepskin-lined jacket and shoved his hat farther down on his head. When he rounded the corner of the livery, the gentle nickering and snorts of the horses boarded there broke the quietness of the night.

A cat skittered out from behind the general store, and a dog barked in the distance. Ever since the bank robbery last fall, he or the sheriff had roamed the alleys behind the main businesses every night to make sure everything remained locked tight and secure. So far he'd seen only a typical Friday night, with everything as routine as Aunt Mae's boarding-house meal schedule. Of course, being Friday the thirteenth, anything could happen.

They already had two men put up for the night back at the jail. Sheriff Rutherford took the night duty to keep the jail cells warm so Cory could have Saturday off for his Aunt Mae's wedding. Ole Cooter probably got drunk and disorderly just so he'd have a warm place to sleep tonight and not have to go out to his shack. Cory held no blame on the man for that. Durand, the saloon owner, caught the other man cheating at cards and had him arrested. Maybe the card shark would move his game on to some other town.

He shivered despite the warm coat and hoped Abigail and Rachel would have dinner waiting for him back at the boarding-house. What with Aunt Mae's wedding tomorrow, those two women had taken over mealtimes until his aunt returned from her wedding trip.

What appeared to be a pile of trash sat outside the back door of Grayson's mercantile. Ordinarily the store owner wouldn't leave a heap out in the open like that. Cory hesitated in making an investigation, but the snuffling and nickering of a horse grabbed his attention. His hand caressed the handle of his gun. No one and no animal should be here this time of night.

The horse, a palomino, stood off to one side. He wore a saddle, but the reins dangled to the ground. Cory went on alert, his eyes darting about the alley in search of a rider. He reached for the reins and patted the horse's mane, then ran his hand down its flank. "Whoa, boy, what are you doing out wandering around?" No brand on his hindquarters meant he didn't belong to a ranch around here, and Cory didn't recognize the horse as belonging to any of the townspeople.

Then the pile by the back door moved, and along with the movement, a moan sounded. With his hand on his gun, Cory approached the mound. An arm flung out from the heap, and another cry. This was no animal. He knelt down to pull back what looked like an old quilt.

When the form of a young woman appeared, Cory jumped as though he'd been shot. Every nerve in his body stood at attention as he reached out to remove more of the cover. A woman lay huddled under the quilt, and her body shook from the cold while a cough wracked through her chest, followed by another cry.

On closer inspection he realized she was younger than he first thought. Her smooth, unlined face and tangled hair were that of a young woman. She couldn't be more than twenty, the same age as his sister Erin.

He bent over her to pick her up, and she started to scream, but another coughing spell prevented it. When her blue eyes peered up at him, they were so full of fear that they sent daggers of alarm straight to his soul. This girl was in trouble.

"Don't be afraid. I'm the deputy sheriff. I won't hurt you, but tell me your name and let me take you to the doctor." He pointed to his badge in hope of reassuring her.

Instead her gaze darted back and forth as she pulled the blanket up under her chin. Her ungloved hands trembled with the cold. He removed his glove and reached out a hand to touch her forehead then yanked it back. She burned with fever.

"You're sick. We need you to get you to Doc Jensen's right away." He slid his hands beneath her to scoop her up into his arms. He almost lost his footing as he rose, thinking she'd be a heavier burden than she was. Light as a feather meant she was probably malnourished too.

She moaned against his chest. "I'm so cold."

Her voice, weak and hesitant, touched a nerve in him. He had to get her warm. Cory made sure the blanket covered her then grasped the horse's reins. A low whistle brought his own horse closer. "Follow us, Blaze. We're going to the infirmary."

He held the girl tight to his chest to transfer some of his warmth to her. The quicker he could get her to the doctor, the quicker Doc could warm her up and treat that cough.

No time to worry about drunken cowboys or lumberjacks tonight.

~~~~~

The man who called himself a deputy carried her in his arms. With his gentle touch and voice, this man wasn't like others she had known. Her body burned with heat then turned ice cold with shivers. So much pain racked her body that she didn't have the strength to resist him anyway.

The man cradled her to his chest. "We'll be at Doc Jensen's in just a few minutes. Hang on, little lady."

Little lady? Little, maybe, but certainly no lady by his standards. Another cough wracked her chest and set her throat afire with pain. Her thin jacket and the quilt had been no match for the cold, especially after she'd crossed the river. Not enough heat in the day to dry her clothes before chilling her to the bone and causing this cough. She'd lost count of the days since she left home and had no idea how far she'd come. She'd avoided towns as much as possible, only entering long enough to pick up food at a mercantile.

Pa had to be on her trail by now, or he'd have others searching for her. Either way, she didn't plan to get caught and be dragged back to Louisiana. Even now the memory of all that she had endured because of Pa made her stomach retch. She'd die before she let anyone take her back to that.

The man called for someone named Clem to go get the doc, and he'd meet him at the infirmary. Maybe he was a sheriff after all since he was sending for help. She didn't dare open her eyes, lest he'd see her fears again. Until she could be absolutely certain he meant her no harm, she'd stay still and quiet.

She inhaled the masculine scent of horses, sweat, and leather. He smelled like hard work and not a trace of alcohol. Unusual for a man, even a lawman. In the background raucous music came from a saloon. She'd recognize the tinny sound of saloon piano anywhere. It disappeared in the distance, and they proceeded down the street and up what felt like stairs or steps onto what must be a boardwalk or porch.

He set her on her feet, and she peeped with one eye while he fumbled in his pocket then pulled out a ring of keys. In the next minute he had the door open and strode through it, carrying her once again.

Antiseptics, alcohol, and carbolic acid greeted her nose. This must be the doctor's office. Not until he laid her on a hard surface did she open her eyes, half expecting him to be leering over her. Instead he had walked away to light a lamp, which filled the room with flickering shadows dancing on the walls. A glass door cabinet stood against the wall, and another bed sat a few feet away from where she lay.

He returned to stand beside her, and she almost shrank in fear at his size. Well over six feet tall, he'd removed his hat to reveal a mass of dark red hair curling about his forehead. His hand caressed her forehead, but she did not flinch, even though every inch of her wanted to. No need for him to know her fears.

"I see you're awake. The doc will be here in a minute. He'll fix you right up."

Instead of resisting, her body relaxed at the gentle tone of his voice. He certainly didn't fit her idea of a lawman or a cowboy. No one but her ma had ever treated her so kindly. Most people treated her like trash under their feet and didn't care whether she was well or sick. Still, he was a man. She had to be careful.

A woman's voice sounded, along with another man's. She turned her head to find a beautiful red-haired woman and an older man entering the room.

The one who must be the doctor stepped to her side.

"Well, Cory, what have we here?" His eyes held only concern and kindness behind his wire-rimmed glasses.

"I found her in the alley behind the general store. She must have come in on horseback and fallen there."

The woman brushed hair from Libby's face. "Can you tell us your name?"

Her heart thumped. What if Pa came looking for her? But if she lied and stayed here, she'd have to keep lying. Another fit of coughing had the woman holding her upright and rubbing her back. When the spell ended, Libby whispered her name. "Elizabeth Bradley."

The woman helped her lie back down. "Hello, Elizabeth. I'm Kate Monroe, the doc's nurse, and this fellow who brought you in is my brother, Cory. He's deputy sheriff in town."

Just having her there gave Libby a sense of safety she needed with two men in the room. Her kind eyes, a green color that reminded Libby of the fake emeralds some of the saloon girls wore, had a tender look to them.

The doctor listened to her chest with a funny-looking bell on something hanging from his ears. He frowned then pulled the contraption down around his neck. "I hear a lot of congestion in your lungs, young lady. How long have you been out in the cold?"

"I don't know. I think it's been several days. I left home in the middle of the night on Tuesday." The days and nights had run together as she lost all track of time.

The doctor shook his head. "This is Friday night, so you've been out at least three days. No wonder your lungs are so congested." He turned to the one called Kate. "Get a bed ready for her. She's staying the night and maybe longer."

Libby tried to sit up but began coughing again. She couldn't stay here. Pa would find her. Her plan had been to head west then south, where the winter temperatures were not as severe. She'd lost all sense of direction after the first night and had no idea which way she'd come.

Kate's warm hands pushed her back down gently but firmly. "Lie still, Elizabeth. The doctor is right; you have to stay here."

Tears welled in Libby's eyes, and she squeezed them tight to keep the tears from falling. Though hard, this bed was so much better than the ground where she'd slept the past nights. Hospitals and doctors cost money. That's why Pa wouldn't go for the doctor until Ma was too sick to recover.

The doctor gave her something that tasted bitter, but she swallowed it and then lay back against the pillow Kate had placed beneath her head. The low murmur of voices ran together in a blur. One of the men said he'd stay, but the other one said something about a wedding. Who was getting married? Maybe they'd forget about her.

The tension ebbed from her body as the medication took over. Someone, most likely the deputy since the doctor was an old man, picked her up and took her into another room, where he laid her on the bed. She almost sighed at the cotton softness of the mattress beneath her. So much better than pine straw and hard-packed dirt.

Kate's voice followed behind then shooed the man from the room. "I'm going to help her get settled for the night, so she doesn't need you. Go on back to the boardinghouse. I'm sure you'll find Abigail has something for you to eat."

A few minutes later Kate had removed Libby's still damp and dirty clothes and slipped a warm gown over her head.

When Libby slid her arms into the sleeves, she realized it was her own gown. "How did you get this? It's mine."

"Cory brought in the satchel you carried on your horse, and I found the gown in it. I warmed it by the wood stove in the other room."

That warmth, along with the medication earlier, eased away the pain, and Libby let her eyes drift closed. Perhaps this was the place she should stay after all. She pulled up the covers and turned on her side. She'd think about that tomorrow. Tonight she'd sleep warm and dry for the first time in too many days to count.

CHAPTER
TWO

*C*ORY MADE HIS way home to the boardinghouse, his mind roiling with questions about Elizabeth Bradley. He didn't recall seeing any wanted posters with her name, so she most likely wasn't wanted for any crime. That is, unless she didn't give her real name. She had to be running away from something because of the fear he'd seen in her eyes when he found her. Fear like that only came when trying to escape someone or something.

Doc had been able to warm her up with blankets, and Kate planned to get her something to eat as soon as Doc permitted it. Despite her bedraggled appearance, her helplessness spoke to Cory's heart. Her youth led him to fear the worst, especially because he had already experienced a case where a man had kidnapped a young woman to sell her into prostitution. At least he'd been able to rescue that young woman. The kidnapper now served time in prison, and his saloon belonged to someone who would obey the law. This time the results may not be so good.

When he entered the boardinghouse, Abigail greeted him. "Well, I'd about given up on you. Your supper's still warming in the kitchen."

His heart still did a flutter step whenever he was around her, but she belonged to Elliot now. "I had a little delay. Found a young woman no older than Erin out behind Grayson's store. She was shivering with cold and burning with fever. Never seen her around these parts before. I took her to the infirmary, and Doc's taking care of her."

Abigail's eyes opened wide. "Oh my, how terrible. Was Kate there? Does the girl need something to eat? Is she going to be all right?" She shot questions at him as she went about getting his supper plate.

He sat down at the kitchen table and reached for the coffee she'd just poured. "Kate was there, and she'll probably be over for something to eat as soon as the doctor says it's OK, unless Mrs. Jensen brings something for her. From what Doc says, she's lucky not to have pneumonia. They'll get her warmed up and treated. Then we can see where she's from and what she's doing here."

Abigail shook her head. "I know you, Cory, and you go easy on her. No use in grilling her like a criminal, especially if she's scared."

Cory stabbed a piece of roast beef and shoved it in his mouth. Abigail did know him too well. With her brother being married to his sister, she'd become a part of the family. She'd learned a lot about him from Kate, and it probably wasn't all good. Although petite, Abigail didn't mind speaking her mind and letting people know what she thought. Maybe it was a good thing he hadn't become involved with her last year after all.

He swallowed the meat and washed it down with coffee. "I did find out her name, if it's her real one. Elizabeth Bradley, she said, and she was riding an old horse that stayed right with her instead of running off when she collapsed behind the store. That leads me to believe the horse belongs to her."

"Hmm. Sounds like she may have been running away. I think Kate will most likely have more success getting information from her than you or Doc ever could. If she doesn't trust men, then she's not going to tell you a thing."

She had that right, but still he needed to check Miss Bradley's background and make sure she hadn't broken the law somewhere. His instincts and her behavior told him she was in trouble, and it was up to him to find out what kind it was. "I got the impression she was running away too. I will let Kate handle the questions for now, but I do intend to get some answers."

He looked around the kitchen. "You and Rachel have done a good job here. What with Aunt Mae at Erin's getting ready for the wedding, I wondered how we'd manage."

Abigail swatted him with a dish towel. "I'll have you know I was one of the best in our domestic science class at the academy in Connecticut. There are lots of things I can do that you don't know about, Mr. Muldoon."

"If you say so, but I know Aunt Mae appreciates your stepping in while she gets married and takes a little trip to visit Mr. Fuller's family." He sat back and swiped across his face with a napkin. "It's nice for Aunt Mae to have a family now. I always thought it kinda sad she never had children of her own. She can be a grandmother to Mr. Fuller's grandchildren and get all the joy she's missed these years since Uncle Patrick's death."

"Kate and I thought the same thing." She stood and gathered Cory's dishes. "I know Elliot has said he's looking forward to being a part of a family like the Muldoon and Monroe clans. He and I are getting in the back door of the Muldoon family, but both of us are so happy with the way you've welcomed us."

Cory was glad of that, because he did like Elliot in spite of a little jealousy left over from a few months ago. He attacked the apple pie she'd made, marveling at the taste. It was even better than Aunt Mae's. He'd never expected such skill from a girl who had servants back home to take care of her needs. Elliot was one lucky young man. "Mighty good pie. Did you serve it at supper?"

"Yes, and you're lucky there was a piece left. Rachel made it. I did the rest of the meal, but she makes the best pastry around."

Cory agreed and sipped more coffee. Even if Abigail hadn't made the pie, she was still a good cook, and Elliot would benefit from it. Without many unattached females in Porterfield, Cory might have to resort to a mail-order bride like the Dawes brothers and Frank Cahoon. Those marriages had turned out well, but he saw no sense in taking a chance on something like that, sight unseen. If God wanted him to marry, He'd bring a young woman around to win Cory's heart. Until that happened, he'd be happy being a deputy sheriff with Rutherford.

He thanked Abigail again for the dinner and made his way up to the second floor and his room. He'd have to do some investigating on that girl in the infirmary, but it would have to wait until after the wedding tomorrow. Even so, he couldn't help but want to know why Miss Elizabeth Bradley, if that was her name, had come to Porterfield in the dead of winter.

~~~~~

Kate stood by the bed until the girl fell into a deep, restful sleep. Her concern for the young woman grew after seeing the bruises and welts on her back and arms. Someone had beaten her, not only recently but also numerous times in the past. Kate had started to ask about them, but then said nothing. Questions might only frighten the girl more.

From the looks of her clothing, she didn't have much money, and what had been in her satchel had not been any better. Only one skirt and another shirtwaist, plus the nightgown and an undergarment. The felt pouch on her waist had contained only a pittance and wouldn't take her very far. It lay safely clutched in Elizabeth's fist even as she slept.

The nurturing instincts that developed in Kate with her patients jumped to the forefront for this young woman, no more than a girl. If Aunt Mae were not getting married tomorrow, Kate would take the girl to the boardinghouse. As it was, she would say nothing to her aunt, who took in every stray human or animal showing up on her doorstep. Erin was just like her and would want her at the parsonage, but this young woman needed to be somewhere outside of town. From the looks of those injuries, she needed protection along with nursing, but she couldn't stay in the infirmary indefinitely.

With Rachel's baby so near delivery time, Kate couldn't bother her, and her brothers' wives had their hands full with their own families. The best place for Elizabeth would be at the ranch. Ma would take good care of her, but with the

wedding tomorrow, going out to the ranch wouldn't be prac-
tical for a few days.

Kate stuffed Elizabeth's soiled clothes into a bag for Mrs.
Jensen to take home and wash. Doc's wife would want to
do that because of her own love and concern for people like
Elizabeth. Because of the wedding Kate would have no time
for the care she liked to give her patients. Sometime tomorrow
she'd have to talk with Ma about moving Elizabeth to the
ranch. A debate skittered back and forth in her mind concerning whether or not to tell Cory about the injuries and suspected beatings. If she didn't, Doc would, because he'd seen
them when he'd examined her earlier.

A hand grasped her shoulder. "Kate, it's time for you to go
on home. Margaret's coming in to sit with Miss Bradley for the
night. You want to be well rested for the festivities tomorrow."

"Bless you, Doc. I'd be willing to stay any other time, but
tonight I'm glad your wife is coming." She glanced at the girl
on the bed. "She's sleeping peacefully now, but she'll jerk and
cry out then be quiet again. Sure wish I knew what troubles
her and why she chose to travel in this cold weather."

Doc felt the girl's pulse. "From the looks of her body
during my examination, she's been beaten severely, and more
than once."

"I saw the same thing. What should we do about it?"

The doc's bushy eyebrows knit together, and he stroked his
chin. "We'll just have to wait until she's ready to tell us what
happened. The tonic will cure the sore throat and fever, but
it'll take a lot more to take care of her otherwise."

The compassion in the doctor's voice reassured Kate. She'd
wait and let Doc decide what to do for now. "I'll leave and check

in on her again tomorrow. With her here, I guess you won't be able to attend the wedding, unless Doc Elliot comes in."

"No, he's planning to go with Abigail, and that's all right. I've wished Mae a happy marriage and paid my respects to Cyrus, so with all the others there, Margaret and I won't be missed."

"Thank you again, Doc. You and your wife are certainly a blessing to this town." She kissed his wrinkled cheek before heading back to her own warm home and her husband, Daniel. The Jensens were loved in this town not only for their medical expertise but also for the way they cared about people in general. Yes, indeed, Miss Bradley would be in good hands tonight.

Libby's eyes strained to open. A soft bed lay beneath her, not the cold, hard ground, and warmth surrounded her. She couldn't be home because of the comfortable bed and warm clothing. A strange clicking noise that sounded vaguely familiar filled her ears.

Finally her eyes cooperated, and she opened them to see a figure sitting in a chair close by an oil lamp. The clicking sound came from the knitting needles she held in her hands. That was why they were familiar. Ma could sit for hours knitting a shawl or throw for the bed. Libby gazed about at her unfamiliar surroundings. Where in the world could she be? She wore her own nightdress, but who could have put it on her? The last thing she remembered clearly was falling off Yellow Boy in a heap near a building.

She stirred, and the woman jumped from her chair to stand beside the bed. "Are you in pain? Can I get you anything?"

Libby shook her head. "Where am I?"

"You're in the infirmary in Porterfield, Texas. The deputy sheriff found you and brought you here. I'm the doctor's wife, Mrs. Jensen."

So, she had made it to Texas, but where was Porterfield? Bits and pieces returned of a man with a badge standing over her, someone asking her name, and a red-haired woman talking to her. Then it all became clear from the time the sheriff found her until now, but the hours before that were still a blur. "What day is it, and what time is it?"

"Well, it's nigh unto daylight, and it's the fourteenth of February."

Valentine's Day. What a laugh to be found on a day for lovers. Many men had loved her body, but no one since Ma had really loved her for just being Libby. She'd left on a Tuesday night, late, and now it was Saturday. Three days she'd traveled, but was she far enough away to truly escape her pa?

"Doc Jensen is coming in a bit so I can go home and make you breakfast. I'm sure you're plenty hungry after your ordeal."

Libby nodded and closed her eyes. She had to get her strength back and get on the road again. The farther west she went from Louisiana, the better were her chances of putting more distance behind her than her pa would want to track.

Mrs. Jensen smoothed back Libby's hair. "Whatever you've been through, and whatever it is you're running from, let us help you. People here in Porterfield are more than willing to help people in distress or need. God loves you, and I believe He led you here to us for a reason. Please trust us, Elizabeth."

The woman called her by her real name, not Libby. She searched her brain for what she could have told them. Then she remembered. Here she would be Elizabeth Bradley. Pa wouldn't think of looking for her under that name. No one here would know Libby Cantrell.

God had nothing to do with why she ended up in Porterfield but everything to do with why she had to leave. If God loved her, why had her life since Ma's death been so miserable? Now after all that had happened, God couldn't love her anymore. She'd broken every rule she'd ever heard about in church when she went with Ma all those years ago. God had no use for the likes of Libby Cantrell, but maybe as Elizabeth Bradley she could stay here and pretend. After all, she wasn't really lying. Elizabeth was her real name, and Bradley was Ma's name before she married Pa.

A man entered the room and came to stand beside the woman. He leaned down and kissed her on the temple. "Elliot's up already. He'll bring breakfast here to you and Miss Bradley, and after you eat, you can rest awhile at home."

"Thank you, dear. I know Elliot plans to go to the wedding with Abigail, so I'll come and sit a while with her this afternoon."

The doctor patted Libby's hand. "We'll see about a place you can stay for a few days after you leave here. I don't want you traveling until your throat is absolutely clear."

A few days? That could mean anywhere from one to four or five. She had to get back on the road again and put distance between her and Louisiana.

CHAPTER
THREE

*C*ORY TUGGED AT his tie and centered it under his collar. He'd been asked by Cyrus to stand with him at the wedding today, Valentine's Day. The only time he wore a suit he attended either a wedding or a funeral, and thankfully, Aunt Mae's wedding meant a happy occasion for all the Muldoon family. He'd known Cyrus ever since the man had come to Porterfield with his wife fifteen years ago to work with Mr. Weygandt at the bank. When his wife died five years ago, Cyrus had moved into the boardinghouse.

Aunt Mae's cooking and good humor led to the courtship and ceremony to take place today. One good thing in Cory's estimation was that his aunt would still run the boardinghouse, and he'd still have a place to live.

After he determined his clothes were in order, he made his way downstairs to the dining area, where Abigail had placed a cake for the wedding in the center of the table. Miss Perth and Mrs. Bennett stood beside the table and admired it. He had to admit it was a beautiful creation. Abigail had proven to be a woman of many talents in the months since her arrival in Porterfield.

Mrs. Bennett clasped her hands against her ample bosom. "Look at those fancy curlicues and borders. How did she do it?"

"I don't know, but it's the most beautiful cake I've ever seen. Don't you think so, Cory?" Miss Perth grasped Cory's arm.

"Yes, ma'am, I do." He held out his other arm to Mrs. Bennett. "Now, if you ladies care to join me, we have a wedding to attend."

At the doorway they separated then waited by the carriage for Cory to assist them in boarding. After they were settled in the backseat, Cory climbed up to sit behind Danny Boy and picked up the reins. While the two ladies chatted away, he let his thoughts turn to the girl he'd picked up last night.

He hadn't told anyone about her as yet, and since neither of the women with him mentioned her, most likely her presence had not been found out. He still doubted her name was actually Elizabeth Bradley, but until he learned otherwise, that was the name he'd have to accept. He'd been tempted to run by the infirmary this morning to check on her but decided to wait until later in the afternoon while everyone else enjoyed the celebration party after the wedding.

When the carriage arrived at the church, buggies, wagons, and vehicles of all sizes and descriptions drove onto the grounds. The abundance of people attested to the love the people in town had for his aunt. Her big heart and great cooking endeared her to everyone she met. Even the sun had decided to shine today after days of low cloud cover, and early narcissus and hyacinths pushed their way from the earth to add a little greenery to the barren winter landscape.

Henry Wilder hailed Cory as he assisted the ladies down from the surrey. "Beautiful day for a wedding, and it couldn't happen to two nicer people." He offered his arm to Miss Perth. "May I escort you inside?"

Miss Perth's cheeks turned pink. "I'd be delighted, Mr. Wilder. I know you'll write a wonderful story about this for the newspaper."

"Of course I will. Mr. Parsons wouldn't allow anything else for Mae Sullivan. Our newspaper editor and his wife are very fond of Aunt Mae."

When Henry had first come to Porterfield, Cory had called him a nosy reporter trying to find stories where there were none. After the way Wilder had told Doc Elliot's tragic story, Cory had changed his mind. The man had a heart after all. What would the reporter have to say about the woman lying now in the infirmary? They couldn't keep her a secret much longer, but he didn't want her bombarded with questions until he could ask a few of his own.

Aunt Mae wore a dark green dress, and Cory had never seen her look so radiant and happy. He took his place beside Cyrus, who stood tall and proud as he and Aunt Mae exchanged vows. The ladies of the church had outdone themselves with the strands of ivy, pine branches, and white satin bows on the pews and altar. Dozens of candles lent their glow to the ceremony. What with Abigail and Elliot's wedding next month, and Philip and his mail order bride Sophia's at Thanksgiving, that'd make three weddings right close together. Since the male population of Porterfield far outnumbered that of its women, three weddings so close together did attract attention.

Reverend Winston finished the ceremony, and Mr. and Mrs. Fuller turned to leave the church and head for the town hall for their wedding feast. Cory didn't intend to miss the opportunity for good food, but before he followed them, he decided to make a stop at the infirmary and check on Miss Bradley.

He spotted Henry outside the church and hailed him. "I have a stop I have to make before going to the party. Would you escort Miss Perth and Mrs. Bennett for me?"

A grin spread across the reporter's face. "I'd be delighted. Annie's helping with the food for the party, so I'm free. I'm sure the ladies will have a few words to say about the wedding. Maybe I can use some of it in my story."

Cory shook his head and turned to hunt for Kate. She stood next to Rachel, and they were deep in conversation, most likely discussing Rachel's fast-approaching motherhood. He tapped his sister on the shoulder. "Kate, I need to have a word with you. Would you excuse us for a minute, Rachel?"

"Of course, Cory. Nathan's waiting for me with the buggy." She smiled and hugged Kate as close as she could.

She spoke so softly, Cory barely heard her words. "I'm thrilled to hear your news. We'll talk more at the party."

Cory shook his head. Women and their secrets. Whatever it might be, Kate would tell him soon. Then he grimaced. Surely she hadn't told Rachel about Miss Bradley.

When Rachel had walked a good distance away, Kate put her hands on her hips. "Now what's so important that you had to interrupt our conversation?"

"I just wanted to know how Miss Bradley was when you left her last night. She seemed pretty weak to me." He narrowed his eyes at his sister. "You weren't talking about her with Rachel, were you?"

"Talking about her with...Oh, my, no. Not at all. That was something else entirely. To ease your mind, none of us have said a word. I don't think anyone has really noticed Doc and Mrs. Jensen aren't here. They're with Miss Bradley now, and I did check this morning. She's awake but not talking much about anything. If you ask me, she's scared to death about something."

Cory had figured that much out for himself, but if she were awake, he could question her. "Probably she is. I'm stopping by there on my way to the party." He waved at Daniel across the way. "I see your husband is waiting for you. I'm going on now."

Kate grabbed his arm. "Cory, be nice. I know how you can be when you want information someone doesn't want to give."

He shook his head. "Kate, I have to get some answers, but I'll try not to scare her any more than she already is."

She sighed and let go. "I'm just saying watch your tone of voice."

Kate needed to mind her own business. He'd question Miss Bradley in whatever way necessary to get the answers he needed. He backed away just as Daniel arrived. "See you two later. Don't have too much fun before I get there." He strode away while Kate tried to explain his statement to Daniel.

Cory pulled his wide-brimmed hat down on his head. Higher temperatures today replaced the cold air of last night, but even so, his buckskin jacket would have been warmer than the suit he wore, which was not the most comfortable attire in his estimation. No wind blew to stir up dust, but the many wagons and buggies headed for town did. Good thing he had only a few blocks to walk.

Men and women waved and called out to him on his way. Being a deputy made his face well known by everyone. Although the town didn't have all that much crime, they'd had their share of lawlessness in the past year or so. Kidnappings, a bank robbery, cattle rustling, a shooting, and Abigail being taken hostage by the Clanton gang had given everyone enough crime to last a while. He could only pray that Elizabeth Bradley hadn't brought more with her.

~~~❦~~~

Libby snuggled under the blanket Mrs. Jensen had pulled up around her shoulders before she left the room. She and the doctor had been so kind. Even that woman named Kate had stopped in this morning to ask about her. No one had paid Libby Cantrell that much attention since she'd been a little girl reciting a poem for a school program.

Porterfield was a lucky town to have a nice infirmary like this one. The doctor back home had nothing this nice, although his office was big enough for a bed or two. This was the cleanest place she'd seen in a long time too. Of course, it smelled like medicine, but she preferred that to breath laced with liquor any day.

Mrs. Jensen had mentioned something about a wedding today, and all the townspeople would be at the church for it and at the town hall later. How nice it would be to be a part of a town where people did things together and watched out for each other. If it was farther away from Louisiana, she could see herself staying here and becoming a part of the town.

Sunlight streamed through the window and warmed the room with its golden rays. How different from the past four days of clouds and cold winds whistling through the trees and whipping up under her clothes to chill her bones. If today was Valentine's Day, then that meant spring was less than five weeks away.

Warmer weather meant faster travel for her and Yeller Boy. She knit her brows in concentration. No one had mentioned her horse. She bolted up in bed. Where was Yeller Boy? He was her only hope of getting anywhere.

She pushed the covers back and swung her legs to the side of the bed. The door opened, and she jerked back to grab the covers. That sheriff fellow stepped through the door as she hurriedly arranged the blanket around her body. From the look on his face, she faced some questions ahead.

"Good morning, Miss Bradley. I'm glad to see you awake and feeling better. It's a wonder what a little tonic, a good night's rest, and some warm food will do for you."

"Hmm, yes, the food and warm bed helped a lot." She crossed her arms and grasped her upper arms. She had to keep her mind clear to make sure she didn't reveal too much. The less he knew about her, the safer she would be.

"Doc tells me you'll be released in a day or so. Do you have a place to go?"

His sharp eyes and set jaw told her not to lie, but what else could she do? She had no set destination in mind and no one to meet her wherever she ended up. "Not exactly, and unless you have my horse, I can't go anywhere."

"Your horse is at Cahoon's Livery, but he looks a little worn out. Your saddle is there too. How far did you ride him?"

"I'm not sure. It depends on where I am now." As long as she could evade direct answers, perhaps he'd quit asking.

"Porterfield is just west and a little south of Carthage, Texas. Do you remember any towns you passed through on your way here?"

Libby shook her head. She didn't remember any names, but Carthage was much closer to Louisiana then she would have liked to be and wasn't in the direction she had planned to travel. How had she managed to come north instead of south? With the way the Sabine snaked its way around, she could easily have lost the trail.

The sheriff narrowed his eyes and peered at her from behind half-closed lids. No way to tell anything about what he thought with an expression like that. "As soon as you're released, you can go down, saddle up, and be on your way since you seem to be in such a hurry."

He wasn't about to let her go just like that. She didn't trust lawmen. They always took her pa's word against hers. Of course, Pa wasn't here to tell the sheriff anything, but he still wouldn't believe her. "Thank you. I appreciate that."

"Nobody knows you're here except the doc and his wife and Kate. There was a wedding a little while ago, and everyone is in town for the party at town hall. Might be a good idea to postpone your leaving until the town has fewer people."

His statement didn't make sense. He spoke as if she could leave now, but the doc told her several days. What was he trying to do? The sheriff was up to something, and she didn't want to stick around to find out. "Thank you, but I'll take my chances in a crowd. If you'll excuse me, I'd like to get dressed now."

He pursed his lips in a way that made a shiver run up her spine. She could tell he didn't want to let her go, but he had no reason to hold her. She could get to another town by nightfall if she left soon.

"Sure you don't want to tell me where you're going or why you're riding alone? It's dangerous for a young woman to be riding without an escort."

Not nearly as dangerous as what she'd left behind. No man could do any more to her than what had already been done. The only thing would be if a thief took her money, for then she'd have nothing left to help her escape.

Before she could come up with an answer for the sheriff, Mrs. Jensen came in with a tray. "I've brought you lunch, dear. Doc and I have decided you're to stay here until Monday. You need another good night's rest, and since tomorrow is Sunday, we don't want you traveling on the Lord's day."

Libby choked back a laugh. Lord's day indeed. It was just another day of the week and one for traveling with fewer folks on the road. If she could get her things together, maybe she could sneak away from here later this afternoon.

"By the way, dear, I took your clothes home to wash them. They'll be ready for you to leave bright and early Monday morning."

Libby swallowed a groan and let a fit of coughing keep her from having to respond right away. She'd be stuck here. Why did Mrs. Jensen have to be so nice? She didn't like the smirk on the sheriff's face either. If no one except these few knew she was in town, then maybe she'd be safe until Monday. She had tried to cover her tracks by staying in the shallow water near the banks of the river, but even then, if her father had enough determination he might be able to track her.

When her cough subsided, Mrs. Jensen placed a hand on her forehead. Doc Jensen wandered in. "Sounds like you still have congestion. Just as well we keep you here. If you go out in the cold for any length of time, you may contract pneumonia."

Mrs. Jensen nodded. "I was just telling her that. If she's well enough by Monday, I told her I'd have her clothes ready so she can leave. Now, eat some of your lunch. It'll give you strength."

The sheriff stepped to the bedside. "Mind if I ask her a few more questions?"

Doc raised his eyebrows. "Yes, I do. Go on over to the party and join the fun. After all, it is your aunt's wedding."

Libby hid her grin by popping a chunk of cornbread into her mouth. That ought to take care of the lawman for a while. Then she swallowed. The cornbread tasted very good, and her stomach let her know it appreciated the food she sent its way.

The sheriff didn't look too happy, but he turned and left the room. Doc and Mrs. Jensen did the same with a reminder to enjoy her meal. That she would have no problem doing. Roast beef and gravy along with potatoes and cornbread would fill her up good.

In the quietness of the room she contemplated the white walls and the other two iron beds in what must be a ward of some kind, like in a hospital. A white, glass-fronted cabinet sat against one wall and held supplies, from what she could see. It also had a lock on it. As if she'd steal anything from a hospital room. At least the smell of anesthetic and disinfectant wasn't as strong as it had been earlier.

She finished her meal and set the tray aside on a chair by the bed. Even with the window closed and shuttered, gay strains of music and laughter drifted in from somewhere down the street. That must be the party the Jensens mentioned. She settled back against the pillow. As long as she was alone, she'd rest. Monday she'd be on the road again.

Kurt Cantrell stumbled through the door and kicked debris out of his way. He waded his way through tin cans, papers, and garbage littering the floor and sank into a chair at the table. The stench of rancid fat, decaying meat, and rotting food filled the room and sent his stomach rolling. He controlled the urge to add the contents of his stomach to the mess all around him.

It was all Libby's fault. If she were here, the place would be clean and food would be on the table. He spat out words of hate and disgust as he dumped a few coins on the table and counted them. At this rate he'd never have enough to take out after that girl. No telling where she might be now, but he'd search the entire country if he had to.

He stuffed the money into his pocket and headed out again. The lure of the saloon pulled him that direction, but this time his willpower kept him on track to the livery. When he arrived, the stable man came outside and snarled at Kurt.

"May as well turn around and go home, old man. You know I ain't gonna loan you no horse, and until you have the money to rent one, you ain't gettin' one. Thought I made that clear."

"Aw, Bernie, I gotta go look fer my girl. She may be out there hurt and needin' her pa. Jest loan me one for a couple a days. I'll bring it back." Bernie was his last hope. He couldn't take out after her on foot, especially if she crossed the river anywhere near here.

"Can't do it, Kurt. You oughta leave that girl alone anyways. Let her find herself a new life out there somewhere."

"I cain't do that. She's all I got." Nobody in town cared about him or Libby. Nobody wanted to help him find her. Those men who had enjoyed her favors wanted no part of any hunt. They were afraid they might get themselves all dirtied up.

"Go on home and get something to eat. And you might consider lookin' for a job. Do an honest day's work for an honest day's pay. Do that, and you can rent any horse you want."

Kurt waved his hand at Bernie and shook his head. Get a job indeed, and what kind of job would that be? Mucking out the stalls for Bernie? Sweeping floors for one of the businesses? No, sir, he was too good for that. Maybe it was time to pull up stakes and sell everything, then get a horse and take out after Libby. Once he caught up with her, he'd settle in a new town and put her to work there. Then he'd have money to play a few card games. His luck would change, yes, it would. All he had to do was find Libby and bring her home.

CHAPTER
FOUR

*C*ORY SAUNTERED DOWN Main Street and passed town hall without stopping. He planned to go through the wanted posters in the office before he joined the party. He'd seen a few women among them the last time he'd browsed. If Miss Bradley was one of those, he planned to arrest her tonight.

The music and laughter from the party would go on for another hour or so, since the train going to Dallas and then on up to St. Louis didn't arrive from Houston until after three. Aunt Mae's and Cyrus's baggage stood ready on the station platform, so all they had to do was leave the party and board the train.

Although he'd miss her the two weeks she'd be gone, his heart filled with happiness for his aunt, who would be visiting more of Cyrus's family, including grandchildren who hadn't been able to come to the wedding.

He left the party music behind and headed to the courthouse and Sheriff Rutherford's office. Ever since they'd moved into the new building last year, the jail had been more secure than when it was located on Main Street across from the hotel. An extra thick brick wall and smaller windows meant fewer attempts at escape, and the locked iron door separating the office from the cells gave added security.

Sheriff Rutherford glanced up when Cory walked through the door. "Thought you'd be down there celebrating with your aunt and Cyrus. What brings you here on your day off?"

Cory hooked his hat on the rack behind the sheriff and strolled to his desk. He had no real excuse to be here except for curiosity about a strange runaway girl. "Thought I'd look through some of our posters of wanted men and women. I picked up a girl last night not from around these parts. She's tight-lipped about where she came from, so I thought I'd check to see if we had anything on her."

The sheriff frowned. "Why didn't you tell me before now?"

"Too busy with the wedding, I guess. Anyway, she says her name is Elizabeth Bradley, which probably isn't real, but there might be a description of her somewhere in that stack of posters."

"Be my guest, but you most likely won't find anything. Not many women are wanted for any crimes around here."

Cory sat down at his desk and pulled the stack of papers toward him. "I know, but I just want to give them a look-see."

Sheriff Rutherford made no comment and returned to the paper he was writing. Most likely he had to finish up his report for the week. The only people they'd had in the cells were a few drunks and a couple or three men arrested for disorderly conduct in the saloon. Nothing really exciting had happened around town since the bank robbery last fall.

He laid aside any poster that mentioned a woman and continued through the bunch. When he turned over the last one, he had four female outlaws wanted for robbery. One was even suspected of being with the gang that robbed the train out near Fort Worth last year. Never did catch that gang, but the description didn't fit the girl at the infirmary. In fact, none of them did.

Despite her ragged appearance and fear, he had a difficult time believing she might be involved in anything illegal. Maybe she was running from a husband who beat her. Various scenarios galloped through his mind. How far had she come, and whom was she running from? He suspected she had no destination in mind when she left here, and her statement confirmed it. If only he could find some reason to keep her in town beyond the days allotted by the doctor, then he might have time to find out more about her.

Her blue eyes had pierced him straight to the soul, and he wanted to know everything he could find about the girl, no matter how bad it might be. He gazed up at the posters pinned to the wall by Rutherford's desk. No pictures of women showed on any of them. Even if her picture wasn't here, Elizabeth Bradley hid something behind her delicate features. Not quite as small as Abigail, she still stood inches shorter than Kate or Rachel. Even his sister Erin stood a little taller than Elizabeth. It seemed his destiny lay in rescuing the smaller of the female species.

New determination filled him to probe until he learned why she ran in the first place. If not for the party he'd go back and question her again, but his absence for so long probably drew frowns from his ma even now. Might as well go on down to town hall and make the most of what time he had left.

"I didn't find anything, so I'll be down at the party if you need me." His hand rested on the handle of his gun. He always wore it and his badge, no matter what the occasion. "I'm prepared if there's any trouble."

"Didn't think you would be, but I'm glad to know you're available. Give my regards to your aunt and Cyrus, and I don't want to see you back here until Monday morning. I'm looking forward to spending Sunday with my family, so you do the same."

Cory nodded and headed out. With no prisoners, the sheriff could take off for a much-needed day of rest. He and his wife and twin daughters attended the same church as the Muldoon clan, so it would be nice to see them together as a family tomorrow.

The music still resounded from the town hall. Cory glanced up at the clock tower. Another hour and the party would be over, and Aunt Mae and Cyrus would board the train. If his luck held out, he might find some food left. But with his three brothers and Daniel, as well as many other men, the pickings most likely would be little to none. He had no one but himself to blame for that.

Before he headed inside, his gaze landed on the infirmary down the way. Since no wanted posters bore her picture or information, perhaps it might be in the girl's best interest for her to stay in Porterfield. If anyone could convince her, it would be Kate. Besides, if any news came in later, she'd be where he could find her.

Aunt Mae and Cyrus held court at the back of the room, where guests from all over town and the outlying ranches and farms offered their congratulations. He could talk to them later. The spread of desserts and other foods called him first. Two six-foot tables sat loaded down with food. One held three different

meats, platters of homemade bread and cornbread, various vegetables, and bowls of homemade pickles and canned tomatoes.
All this in the middle of winter, thanks to home canning, as
well as tin cans from the store. Pies, cakes, and pastries filled the
other table. As he filled his plate, Kate joined him.

"Glad you finally made it, big brother. What kept you
away so long?"

He stabbed a slice of roast beef and laid it on his plate.
"Stopped by to see Miss Bradley and then went to check to
make sure she wasn't running from the law."

Kate narrowed her eyes. "And?"

"She's not wanted, and that's what bothers me. If she's not
running from the law, she's running from something that has her
too scared to tell anyone about it." Then he grinned. "And I was
nice to her. I didn't ask a lot of questions. She'll be here at least
until Monday, because Mrs. Jensen took all her clothes to wash."

Kate laughed and shook her head. "Trust Margaret to do
something like that to keep the girl over Sunday." She glanced
around then leaned over and said, "I wish we could do something else to keep her safe. I hate to see her take off again all
alone. No telling what might happen to her."

Cory placed a chunk of homemade bread on his plate and
gazed about the room. "I'm thinking the same thing. Let's head
over to that corner. I have an idea to run by you."

Kate turned to Daniel. "Cory and I are going over there to
talk in private for a minute."

Daniel smiled and nodded his head then continued his
conversation with Nathan Reed and Mayor Tate.

Cory led her to the corner and sat in one of the chairs

there. "I'm glad to find a place to sit so I don't have to juggle this plate in my hands."

Kate sat beside him. "Now, what is your idea?" She held up her hand. "No, wait. I can guess. You're going to suggest I tell Ma and see if she'll take Miss Bradley out to the ranch."

Cory almost choked on a piece of meat. He'd never been able to keep ahead of Kate. She knew him so well. Of course, the two of them had been close growing up and discovered that many of their ideas coincided. "You're right. What do you think?"

"I had the same thoughts. Soon as Aunt Mae and Cyrus leave, we can talk with her. Ma will probably want to take her out to the ranch tonight."

"I'll leave the telling to you, and then we can both talk to the girl. We'll have a lot more convincing to do with her than we will with Ma. It's about the safest place for her far as I can tell." Of course, he'd never tell either Ma or Kate his real reason for keeping her in town. Something didn't add up right with Miss Bradley, and Cory wanted to make sure he found out why before he let her leave.

As soon as the train pulled out of the station, Kate sought out her mother and pulled her aside. "Ma, Cory and I have a situation we think you might be able to take care of for us."

Ma raised her eyebrows. "You and Cory have a problem? What kind of problem? Does it have to do with that young woman in the infirmary?"

Kate gasped, and her mouth gaped open. How in the world had Ma found out about Elizabeth Bradley?

Ma laughed. "Dear, not much in this town escapes me. Besides, I saw Margaret Jensen, and she told me. She thinks it might be a good idea for the girl to come out to our place for a spell. Margaret thinks she's running away from somebody."

Kate couldn't decide whether to be angry or glad, but Cory would most likely take the angry route. Still, it saved having to explain to Ma the circumstances. "That's what Cory and I were going to ask you do too. He's checked, and she's not wanted by the law, but I could see that she's frightened to death about something. If someone is chasing her, he may not be far behind. We figured the ranch would be a safe place."

"I agree. Let me tell Callum, and then we can walk down there and talk to her."

Kate waited for her mother to return. Ma had always been an amazing woman, and this type of concern proved it. She didn't like to see anyone suffer at the hands of another, and she'd made a tremendous difference in the lives of many a young man or woman. Elizabeth Bradley would be no different.

Kate told Daniel she needed to run by the infirmary and that she'd meet him at Erin and Seth's house before her brothers and their families returned to their homes. Fifteen minutes later, she and Ma arrived at the infirmary.

Kate led her mother into the room, where Elizabeth sat up in the bed eating her supper. Margaret Jensen sat nearby. "Elizabeth, I want you meet my mother, Ada Muldoon. We have something we want to talk with you about."

Elizabeth patted her mouth with a napkin and narrowed her eyes at Ma. "I thought no one else was supposed to know I'm here. I trusted you and your brother not to tell anyone."

Kate recognized the veil of secrecy that fell over Elizabeth's eyes. She'd seen it in Doc Elliot only a few months ago when she had questioned him about his past. Whatever this girl hid, it must be uncovered so they could help her.

"I'm sorry, Elizabeth, but we're hoping this will be a good thing for you. You see, Ma and Pa live on a large ranch a few miles outside of town. They have a big house and only the two of them in it for now. They also have a full bunkhouse of cowboys who would protect Ma and Pa if trouble comes hunting. We thought you could go out there and stay with them and be safe. No one else will know you were here or that you've gone out there except the ones in this room and Cory and the doctor."

Elizabeth said nothing, but her gaze darted between Kate and her mother. She bit her lip then glanced over at Mrs. Jensen, who smiled and nodded.

"Why…why would you do this for me?"

Ma stepped closer and brushed Elizabeth's hair from her cheek. "My dear, I can sense you're in trouble, and I want to help you with whatever is troubling you. We've done this before, and you'll have all the Muldoon men protecting you if it comes to that. Even if you've broken the law, we want to help you."

Tears glistened in Elizabeth's eyes. "I didn't know I'd be so cold and hungry when I ran away, but I'd do it again just to…" Her eyes opened wide, and she clamped her lips shut as though afraid she'd said too much.

"Whatever it is troubling you, we'll find an answer. Now, this is what we'll do. Erin and Seth, with Daniel and Kate, are hosting the family Sunday dinner here in town, so when we're ready to head home, we'll come get you and take you with us."

Mrs. Jensen stepped over to the side of the bed. "I'm taking her to our place for tonight. Doc thought maybe that would be better. Elliot is there, and the two of them can watch out for her."

"Good, then it's all settled." She patted Elizabeth's hand. "It'll all be OK, sweet child."

Ma and Mrs. Jensen headed to the door to finish discussing the details, and Kate stayed with Elizabeth a few more minutes.

"You'll see. Ma and Pa will take really good care of you. If anyone comes looking for you, Cory won't say anything until he can be sure they mean you no harm." She squeezed the girl's hand then followed Ma and Mrs. Jensen out.

Libby waited for the women to leave before she let the tears stream down her cheeks. People hadn't been this kind to her since Ma's death. Then Pa started drinking, and people looked down on him and expected nothing good from the Cantrell family. Maybe she would be safe at the ranch. Maybe she could make a life here. Sounds of people outside calling to each other and talking only served to emphasize her loneliness and increased the desire to want a normal life in a small town. The sheriff had been kind to her, as had his sister and mother, but what would be their attitude when they learned what kind of person she really was?

The front door to the hospital sounded again, and Dr. Jensen greeted Cory. She grabbed the edge of the sheet and dried her cheeks and eyes. He mustn't see her tears. She turned over to face the wall.

His footsteps echoed on the floor, and she sensed his nearness.

"Miss Bradley, I need to speak with you."

Her hands trembled, and she blinked her eyes to make sure no tears remained before turning to face him. "Yes, deputy, what is it you want?"

"Ma and Kate tell me you've agreed to go out to the ranch with them."

Libby gulped and nodded her head. "That's right."

"I just wanted to let you know that you will be safe from whatever it is you're running from out there. If anyone comes looking for you, only a few people in town know about you, and we won't be revealing your whereabouts. But it would sure help if we knew what to be on the lookout for so we can help you better."

His bluish-green eyes pierced her soul, but she couldn't reveal the truth to him. She closed her eyes against his scrutiny, and her heart pounded in her chest. Any lie to get him to leave. "Thank you, but you needn't worry. I was going somewhere and just got lost crossing the river and couldn't find my way."

"I see. We'll keep watch anyway just in case somebody does come looking."

The disbelief came clearly through his words and tone of voice. She didn't have to open her eyes to know what she'd find in his. At least he'd stay busy trying to figure out who she really was, but that suited her much better than all the questions.

"If you don't mind, I'm rather tired and would like to get some rest now." She looked him in the face and lifted her chin to let him know she had finished talking.

"All right, but I'm not through with you yet. I want to know just who it is going be staying out at the ranch." He turned and with long strides left the room.

Libby let her breath out in whoosh. That had been close. Let him search all he wanted. As long as he didn't keep questioning her, she didn't care what else he did.

CHAPTER FIVE

LIBBY STRETCHED AND yawned then opened her eyes. At first nothing registered. The blue floral wallpaper, white lacy curtains, and comfortable bed confused her for a minute until she remembered this was her bedroom in the Muldoon home. She lay back on her pillow to soak up the dawn peeking through the window and the warm feelings of acceptance experienced yesterday when Mr. and Mrs. Muldoon picked her up and brought her to the ranch. The size of the house had surprised her, but then she remembered how many people made up the Muldoon family. Mrs. Muldoon had shown her around before bringing her up to this room, which would be her own for now.

Everything was so different from what she had at home. She could grow to like this kind of life real quick. Then the pain of all she'd endured under Pa's thumb came crashing back. She blinked back the tears. No matter where she went to hide, he would come looking for her. The memory of the stench of liquor, unwashed bodies, and foul breath overpowered her senses even in this clean bedroom. Hadn't he told her enough times that she would never get away from him, no matter how hard she tried?

The ugliness of her past would follow her, no matter where she lived. Even if Pa never found her, she'd be a prisoner. If only she could have met someone like the deputy and the Muldoon family before Pa started hurting her, she would have been spared the pain and humiliation. They could have rescued her. She pounded the mattress with her fists. Why was God so cruel to her? Why hadn't He saved her?

Despite her hopes Saturday night of staying in Porterfield and beginning a new life, reality demanded she get on the road again as soon as possible. More than a day or two here meant the closer she might be to Pa's finding her.

The aroma of frying bacon drifted into the room and created a rumbling in Libby's stomach. Although she'd had good meals since Saturday, they hadn't made up for the many days and nights she went without food so Pa would have something to eat. If he didn't, he beat her because she wasn't doing her job. She'd never been able to please him with cooking, cleaning, or fulfilling any of his demands.

After taking care of her morning routine, Libby closed her eyes and hugged her arms about her chest. If she had been born into such a family as this one, she wouldn't be on the run. She had loved her mother, but illness had kept Ma in bed the last few years of her life. Pa had never been attentive or seemed to care whether Libby was there or not. He only cared about Ma. After Ma died, he looked at Libby with different eyes and decided he could use Libby's pretty features to make money, which he promptly gambled or drank away.

The cabin back home had fallen into shambles. As long as she made the money and Pa had a bed to fall into every night and a little food on the table the next morning, he didn't care what happened to the rest of the place or to her.

Time to forget *if-onlys* and *what-ifs* and face reality.

Libby followed her nose to the kitchen, where Mrs. Muldoon stood at the stove frying bacon. The Irish woman had none of the brogue she'd heard in others from that country, but she explained she'd been born in this country and had never really picked up the language of her family. A few streaks of gray ran through her auburn hair, and her waist had thickened with middle age, but Libby saw the beauty of a woman who loved people.

"Good morning, Mrs. Muldoon. Whatever you're cooking smells wonderful." Even with all the weight she'd lost in the past months, she'd fill out her clothes soon with their cooking. "Can I help you with anything?"

Mrs. Muldoon stooped to pull out a fresh pan of biscuits from the stove. "No, you just have a seat. Callum will be in shortly, and we'll eat. And please call me Ada, dear. Everyone calls me that or 'Ma.'"

"Ada" would do just fine. She'd call no one else by "Ma" except her own. Libby made note of the fact that only three places sat at the table. Where would the others eat? Kate had said they had a number of ranch hands, but so far Libby had seen no sign of them.

The back door opened, and Mr. Muldoon entered the kitchen and took off his hat. He then peeled off his gloves and slapped them into the hat. He removed his jacket and eyed Libby. "Did you sleep OK, Miss Bradley?"

She ducked her head to avoid eye contact with him. "Yes, sir, the bed was very comfortable." She sat down at the table when Ada placed the platters of bacon and eggs on it.

Ada poured a mug of coffee for herself and Mr. Muldoon. "Would you like coffee, Elizabeth?"

She blinked her eyes, forgetting for a moment she hadn't told them the name people usually called her. "Uh…yes…please." She'd have to start thinking of herself as Elizabeth to keep from slipping up.

The rich aroma of the coffee filled the room. She'd never learned to make it so it smelled like this. Pa had thrown it back at her more than once when what she prepared didn't suit him.

Libby picked up her fork to stab a slice of bacon, but Mr. Muldoon bowed his head to offer thanks. The fork fell to the plate with a clatter, and heat rose in her cheeks. She hadn't said a blessing over a meal since before Ma died. It'd never done any good for them, but if that's what the Muldoons did, she'd have to wait, although her stomach rumbled in anticipation of the fare set before her.

After the prayer Mr. Muldoon spread his napkin over his lap and peered across at Libby. "That horse of yours has seen better days, but he appears to be in good health. Had one of the boys brush him down for you and give him a bag of feed."

"Thank you, Mr. Muldoon. Yeller Boy has been a good horse." She ducked her head again and filled her mouth with scrambled egg. The less she had to talk with them, the less they would ask prying questions, and the less she would have to lie.

Neither of them paid much attention to her but discussed the ranch instead, and for that she was grateful. More of the family had found out about her, and she had learned a great deal about the family from conversation. The only ones she actually met besides Kate and her brother were Erin and her husband, the preacher, when they came with her parents to the Jensen house. Their coming had surprised her, but Erin had been so nice and was even close to Libby's own age. Then the reverend had prayed for her before they left. They sure weren't like any family she'd ever known, but just for safety's sake she might stay clear of the deputy. She didn't want to end up in a jail cell.

After breakfast Libby offered to help Ada with chores, but she declined and told Libby to just sit and talk. Talk was the last thing she wanted to do, but neither did she want to appear rude to this woman who treated her like her own daughter.

While Ada worked, Libby took note of the organized kitchen. She'd never seen anything quite like it. Cabinets with glass doors held dishes and glasses that looked like crystal, and countertops held various containers for cooking meals. Pots and pans hung on hooks beside the stove, which was bigger than any Libby had seen. Some kind of plant that looked like a sweet potato filled a jar in the window and trailed its leaves across the sill.

An ache started down deep inside her. A longing for a real home and a family to love her and take care of her rose up and threatened to send a flood of tears. This is what it might have been like if Ma hadn't gotten so sick and Pa hadn't taken to his sinful ways.

Ada finished putting away the dishes and came to sit across the table from Libby. She poured them both a cup of hot tea with a minty aroma. "Herb tea always helps me to think and soothes my worries."

Libby blinked her eyes and swallowed her tears. The warm tea did soothe her throat, but her problems and worries were still there. Ada reached across and grasped Libby's hands in hers.

"My dear, I know something is troubling you deep inside. You don't have to tell me anything about it, but I do want you to know I'll be praying for you every morning and night. God can resolve the problem for you, but it may take time and patience on your part. If you ever want to tell me what's wrong, I'll be here to listen."

Libby gazed into Ada's eyes and saw nothing but kindness and concern there. The women back home had turned their noses up at her in judgment and called her all kinds of names Libby didn't want to repeat. She had no friends, because none of the mothers wanted their sons or daughters to associate with her. Oh, the sons had wanted to, but Pa made sure the young ones without much money stayed away from her.

She shoved those thoughts aside. "Thank you for your concern, but I'll be OK. I'd best be traveling on in a few days so as not to bring trouble down on you and your family."

Ada waved her hand. "Nonsense. There's no trouble you can bring that the Muldoon clan can't handle. We've about seen it all, child. I've got one son who is a lawman, and my Kate's husband is a lawyer, and Nathan Reed is a lawyer too. We can help you. Besides, if you wait two or three weeks, spring will set in, and you'll have better weather for traveling if you still want to go."

That sounded so good, but could she afford to wait that long to put more distance between her and Pa? Maybe she could stay a week and then decide what to do. The idea of staying here appealed to her, but the fear of them learning the truth about her outweighed the good.

Cory glanced up from his reading to find Erin coming through the door of the office. She carried little Connor in her arms. He jumped up from behind his desk and held out his arms to hold his nephew. "What brings you down here with this little one?" He cradled the baby in his arms and rocked him back and forth.

"I declare, Cory Muldoon, you need to get married and have yourself a passel of young'uns. You're so good with them."

That may be true with his nieces and nephews, but Cory was in no hurry for children of his own. Being a lawman put him in danger, and he wouldn't wish that on any woman. Besides, he'd struck out with Abigail, so who was there left? He grinned at his sister. "You didn't answer my question."

"It's about that young woman we met at the Jensens'. The one—"

"Wait a minute. What were you doing at the Jensens'?" How could they keep Elizabeth's presence a secret if everyone in the family knew about her?

"Ma told Seth and me about her and her situation. Seth wanted to meet her, so we went with them when they went to pick her up. We had a nice prayer for her safety before they left."

Anger rose in his gut. Ma shouldn't have done that. He opened his mouth to respond, but she held up her hand to silence him before he had the chance.

"I feel so sorry for her. I saw the fear in her eyes and know she's running from some danger. What if someone wants to kill her?"

Cory shook his head. Erin made the perfect minister's wife. She worried more about everyone else than she did herself.

"I can tell you that she's not on any wanted posters we have, so I don't think she's running from the law, but something had her out on that old horse in the dead of winter without proper clothing and very little money. You haven't said anything to the others, have you?"

"No, Seth and I keep confidences, and you should know that. Besides, I think it's a shame, and I want to help her. Seth and I talked about it with Ma and Pa before they left with her. If Libby stays here, we'd like for her to live with us. She can help me with Connor so I can again take on some of the duties of the church. She'd be safe at the parsonage. Ma thinks it's a good idea and plans to discuss it with Elizabeth before we all go out there on Sunday."

"Erin Winston, what in the world are you thinking? We don't know a thing about Elizabeth Bradley, or if that's even her real name. I'll not have her putting you and Connor in danger by letting her stay at your house." He'd never heard such a wild idea in his life.

She drew her hands into fists and placed them on her hips. "Cory Muldoon, you may be my big brother and a sheriff, but you can't tell me what I can or can't do in my own home."

Her eyes held fire that Cory recognized. When Erin set her mind on something, not much—if anything—could change it.

"Does Seth know what you want to do?" he asked.

She blew out her breath in exasperation and shook her head. "You're so stubborn and mule-headed, just like some other men I could name in our family. You don't listen to a word I say unless you think it's wrong and want to correct it. I told you we talked about it and both decided it was the Christian thing to do."

That still didn't make it right, but he could no more change Erin's mind than he could play a fiddle. Maybe he could talk with Seth later and show him the danger of letting Miss Bradley stay with them.

Erin reached for Connor. "Now, if you'll hand me back my son, we'll be getting out of your way."

He handed the now sleeping child back to his mother. "Just think about it awhile longer. You don't need to do it right away. Let me do some more investigating."

She tucked the blanket up under Connor's chin and sighed. "Oh, all right, but I don't think you'll find anything criminal in her background." She turned toward the door. "With Rachel's baby not long to be born, I'm going to be helping Abigail at the boardinghouse while Aunt Mae is gone, so I'll see you at noon."

She marched out the door mumbling something about a pig-headed mule, whatever that was. He didn't care what she called him. His only concern was her safety, and if she couldn't see that, then he'd have to take measures to make sure Seth understood. Until he could know more about Miss Bradley, he didn't want her around any of his family except Ma and Pa. From the years on the frontier they knew how to deal with trouble. Besides, they had plenty of ranch hands for protection.

He tried to go back to his work, but a blue-eyed young

woman with shining gold hair kept getting in the way. Finally he tossed aside his pen. Saturday, seeing her cleaned up and with her hair combed and pulled back with ribbon, had been a surprise. She resembled nothing of the heap of girl he'd found back of the store.

Her beauty haunted him. Somehow, someway, he had to find out more about this young woman he didn't really trust.

CHAPTER SIX

*T*HE MORE DAYS Libby spent at the ranch, the harder it was to leave. By Friday she had decided to give the time here a few more days. She enjoyed helping Ada with the chores around the house, even if they didn't take very long to finish. Watching Ada cook gave her some good pointers for the time she would be on her own.

If Pa had come looking for her or sent men after her, they'd be here by now. A comfortable bed, good food, and no responsibilities appealed to her much more than making her way on the road alone.

She had discovered the ranch to be much larger than she had first believed. Ada had taken her out for a ride, and it seemed that the land went on forever. Pine trees and open pasture beckoned her, but she resisted for the time being. Until the time came when she must leave, she'd take advantage of all Ada and Mr. Muldoon had to offer. They had become the parents she had longed for over so many years.

Although she'd met only Kate, Cory, Erin, and Seth,

she understood the Muldoon family consisted of three more brothers and their families. The only real family Libby ever had died with Ma. Little Jonah had gone before in a typhoid epidemic that left Ma sickly the remainder of her life. Pa's spirit and will to live died when Ma did. After that everything in life went downhill faster than a sled on a snowy hill.

Libby gazed out the window of her second-floor bedroom at the Muldoon house. A barn with a stable for the horses, a corral, a pen for the chickens, and a plot of ground that looked like it would be a garden made a picture she longed to call home. How nice it would be if Ada and the others never had to know about her sordid past, but the truth always had a way of showing itself. She could tell them she ran away because all her family had died and she had no place to go. That was true, or at least most of it was.

She stood and brushed her hands down the brown wool skirt Ada had given her. In addition, she added a dark blue cotton skirt and two more shirtwaists. They had belonged to Erin, Kate's younger sister, when she lived at home. They were in much better condition than Libby's own clothes had been. She straightened her shoulders and held her head high. She mustn't go soft. Being alert and aware of everything going on was the only way to keep herself out of trouble and to protect Ada and her family.

Ada called to her from downstairs. Libby realized that time had gotten away, and by the slant of the sun it must be almost noontime. She hurried down to the kitchen and grabbed an apron. "I'm sorry, Ada, I must have been daydreaming. What do you need me to do?"

"If you'll set the table, I'll get the stew ladled up and the cornbread sliced. It'll be just you and me today since Callum is out on the range with the boys."

The rich aroma of beef stew filled the air as Libby set two places at the kitchen table. She'd learned that they used the big one in the dining room only when all the family gathered. This house had so many rooms that Libby could hardly believe it belonged to one family. The four bedrooms upstairs gave the house the feel of a hotel, but the cozy kitchen and wonderful room with a fireplace where they sat at night while Ada sewed and Mr. Muldoon read gave proof this was indeed a home.

Mr. Muldoon had even suggested Libby call him Callum, but Libby couldn't do that. Ada was different and more like a friend, whereas Mr. Muldoon was a man, and she'd never called an older man by his given name. Nor did she ever plan to get close enough to any man to call him by his first name.

After a short blessing Ada spread a napkin on her lap and reached for a square of cornbread. "Callum and I have been talking about what you can do. You haven't told me your age, but you can't be much older than my Erin, who just turned twenty a few weeks ago."

So that's why the clothes had fit so well. Libby chewed a piece of potato longer than necessary to give her time to think of a response. Her age wouldn't reveal anything to do her harm. "I will be nineteen my next birthday in April."

"Just as I thought. You'd make a perfect companion for Erin. By the way, the family is all coming here to dinner on Sunday. We figured it was time to introduce you to the rest of the Muldoon clan."

This time Libby almost choked on a piece of meat. The last thing she wanted to do was meet all the others, but she couldn't stay here any longer and not meet them. Ada had already talked about their Sunday gatherings for dinner after church. "I...I thought we were going to keep my staying here a secret."

"That's still the plan for a little while longer. Callum and I will go into church on Sunday like always and then come back out here for dinner with the rest of the family. You can stay here or go with us to church as a visiting friend. We go to a different home for Sunday dinner each week, and this Sunday happens to be my week."

"But won't you have to stay at home and prepare the dinner for all of them? I can stay and help you." Church was definitely out of the question. Not only had she not attended church since her mother died, she had no use for God anymore. Ada and Mr. Muldoon may be different, but all the churchgoing people back home had looked down their noses at her and pretended she didn't exist after she started working in the saloon.

Ada laughed and waved her hand. "Land sakes, child, I do all my cooking on Saturday, and the girls bring the rest. The only work on Sunday is serving the food and cleaning up. Of course, keepin' up with those young'uns might be considered work, but if it is, then it's a labor of love."

Never had Libby considered any of those as a labor of love. Cooking and cleaning for Pa had been true work, for which she never received a thank-you or acknowledgment unless it was done wrong or not on time, and then most likely she received a beating. She didn't know about children except Jonah, and he'd been young when he died. The only other children she knew had been in school. By the time she was fifteen, she had to quit because she had no decent clothes to wear that would hide the marks Pa made with his belt when things didn't go his way. A shudder ran through her body from head to toe. She'd die before she went back to that.

Ada reached over and grasped Libby's arm. "I see fear in your eyes again, honey. Please tell me what's scaring you so bad. With two lawyers and a deputy in the family, we can help you."

Libby wanted to laugh at that notion. Lawyers and lawmen only meant trouble for her. No one could help her but herself, and if it meant running away from here, then she'd have to do it. "I'm OK, Ada. I guess it's just the fear of meeting so many people on Sunday and worrying if they'll like me or be angry with you for hiding me here."

"Now that's a good one. A pretty little thing like you, what's not to like? They'll accept you because Callum and I have. They know how we take people in and take care of them. And if one of them says a word to the contrary, they know they'll have to deal with me or their pa, and that's not something any of them wants to do."

Libby had to keep the truth from them at all costs now. She couldn't risk bringing the wrath of the entire Muldoon family down on her when they found out what she really was. "A pretty little thing" would be the last thing on their minds if that happened.

~~~·❦·~~~

No matter how fond of Miss Bradley Ma had become, Cory wanted to make sure the girl wouldn't bring trouble to the family. Kate and Erin both defended her and said it was not Christian to condemn a person before one knew all the facts.

Well, he wasn't condemning anyone, only being careful to make sure his family was safe and not being hoodwinked by someone on the run from the law.

Nothing had shown up in the new batch of posters that had come in the mail earlier in the week. When Marshal Slade had come by, Cory asked him about women on the run, but even he had found nothing concerning a woman named Bradley. If that was her real name, then she appeared to be clean. Still, she ran from something or somebody, and he was bound and determined to find out what it was.

He had to admit he'd been impressed by her youth and beauty the last time he'd seen her at the hospital on Saturday night. He still knew no more about her than he had then. At least she'd be in good hands with Ma, and perhaps Ma could even get Elizabeth to open up to her and tell her the truth. Although his lawman instincts kept him from trusting her completely, her deep blue eyes drew him to want to know her better. The memory of how she looked when he first discovered her haunted him. In the week since that time he'd been torn in his feelings toward her.

Just meeting her had created a raw ache in his gut that he couldn't understand and sent shivers of fear through his veins. When Abigail Monroe had come into town he'd been attracted to her charms. He'd even begun to harbor hopes she might be attracted to him, but then Doc Elliot captured her heart.

He had to be more careful around Elizabeth Bradley until he could learn the truth. He'd kept his feelings for women in check until Abigail, and that had not ended well for him. Now Miss Bradley, with her fears and vulnerability, threatened his heart again. This time he'd make no mistakes until he found out exactly who Elizabeth Bradley really was.

The door opened, and Cory glanced up to find Pete Davis coming in. The boy had a minor scrape with the law once, but he was growing up to be a fine young man.

"What brings you in here on a Friday afternoon, Pete, and why aren't you in school?"

"Whizzers, Mr. Cory, school's done out. I jes' want to talk with you a bit."

"Oh, you do? Why is that?" It must be important from the way Pete's cheeks burned red and the way he crushed his hat in his hands. "You aim to mash that hat to pieces there, boy?"

Pete reddened further but smoothed out his hat. "No, sir, but I want to talk to you about being a lawman."

Cory eyed the boy, who had grown considerably in the past couple of years. He'd just had his fourteenth birthday and now stood almost as tall as Cory. He'd filled out too. Gone was the scrawny twelve-year-old Kate had watched over when their house burned down a few years back, and in his place Cory faced a boy on the edge of manhood.

"Being a lawman is a dangerous job, Pete. You have to be willing to sacrifice a lot of time and effort." If the boy was really serious, then Cory would help him. He remembered his own ambition at that age. Sheriff Rutherford had been a good mentor until Cory reached the age he could be deputized.

"Yes, sir, I know that. I know I have to learn to use a gun and learn a lot of laws and stuff, but I can do it."

The earnest expression in the boy's eyes touched him. "And why do you want to be a lawman?"

"I seen the way you hunted down those outlaws what took Miss Monroe hostage. I also remember how you and that lawyer Monroe rescued that girl Mr. Darnell kidnapped. I want to help people like that. I want to catch the bad guys and put them behind bars."

"Those are good reasons, Pete. I tell you what I'll do. You stay in school, make good grades, and help Miss Miller keep order in her classes, and I'll show you the ropes, but only if you keep up your grades, and only if it's OK with your pa and ma. If it is, you can meet me tomorrow afternoon for some lessons in handling guns."

Pete's eyes lit up like the candles on a Christmas tree. "Yes, sir. And Pa thinks it's fine. Wait till I tell him you said you'd help me." Pete backed toward the door, his face beaming with a smile as wide as the Texas plains. "Umm…thank you, sir." He smashed his hat back on his head and raced out the door.

Cory chuckled at Pete's enthusiasm. He would enjoy mentoring the boy. In his line of work Cory didn't get much of a chance to bring the good out in people, only to punish the bad. Looking for the best in others didn't happen automatically for him, nor was it part of his deputy job, but perhaps it was time he learned, especially when it came to Miss Bradley.

CHAPTER SEVEN

*K*ATE CAME OUT of one of the examining rooms wiping her hands on a towel to find Erin coming in with the baby. "Erin, what are you doing here on a Saturday? Is Connor sick?" She strode over to Erin and reached for the baby.

Erin handed the baby to Kate. "Connor's fine. I couldn't get the young girl at the ranch off my mind. The whole family will be going out there for dinner after church tomorrow, and I wanted to talk with you about what Seth and I want to do."

Kate crinkled her nose at the baby and kissed his forehead. She glanced up at her sister. "And what is it you want to do?"

"Seth and I have decided we want to take her in as a nanny for little Connor. She can watch after him and help me with all the things I need to do as a minister's wife."

"Erin Muldoon Winston, whatever gave you such a wild idea?" She positioned Connor on her shoulder and frowned at Erin. "This little fella needs his mama to watch after him, not some unknown young woman running from who knows what."

"You're as bad as Cory. Neither one of you thinks I have

a lick of sense. I'm not a baby anymore. I have one of my own and am quite capable of making decisions about what Seth and I want to do. I expected opposition, but I'd like to have your support."

Kate narrowed her eyes for moment and pressed her lips together. She could understand Erin wanting to help, but not in this way.

"I don't really think it's a good idea to bring her back to town where others will see her and perhaps someone looking for her will find her, but let's give her a choice. If she wants to stay in Porterfield, the parsonage might be a good place for her. I don't think Cory will agree, though, because he still thinks she might be running from the law."

Erin clasped her hands to her chest. "I'd hug you if you weren't holding Connor, but thank you. I need your support, because Cory has already told me he doesn't approve. There's something about Elizabeth that grabs my heart and won't let go. Whatever she's running from has nothing to do with the law."

Kate grinned and handed Connor back Erin. "I sense the same thing, sweetie, and I'll help make sure we keep her safe from whatever it is she fears. Cory is right in that you are just like Ma in the way you want to take care of everyone. Maybe because you're the baby of the family and we always took care of you."

Erin snuggled Connor close to her shoulder and kissed his cheek. "I guess having this little one has made me want to mother the world, especially someone like Elizabeth, even if she is my age."

Kate slipped an arm around Erin's shoulder. "You are the perfect minister's wife. Seth is very lucky to have you." She gave Erin a squeeze. "We'll do this together, and between the two of us and Ma I bet we find out what Elizabeth is running from."

"Seth can handle whatever we find out. He's so good with people." She pulled the baby quilt up over Connor's head. "I have to run now. I promised to help Abigail get things ready for noon at the boardinghouse. At least no one expects the place to be open to anyone other than the boarders while Aunt Mae is gone."

After another hug from Kate, Erin headed out the door and over to the boardinghouse. A few minutes later Kate followed her. The clinic had no patients, and she wanted to talk more with Erin about this plan.

When Kate entered the boardinghouse, she found Erin had already placed Connor in the basket Aunt Mae kept there for him. He made a few sucking noises, but his eyes stayed closed in peaceful sleep. What a precious baby. Then she caressed her own belly. She'd know the joy of one of her own next fall. She and Daniel hadn't told anyone except Rachel and Nathan, but they wouldn't tell until Kate told the rest of the family.

Before she left for the library this morning, Abigail had set out the menu for the noon meal and had chopped the vegetables to be cooked. How that young woman could be so organized in the kitchen baffled Kate. She found Erin slicing potatoes to boil and making the coating for the steak she planned to fry.

"I see you have things under control. Looks like a good meal." She sat at the kitchen table and watched Erin. She'd certainly inherited all the housekeeping skills in the family. Good thing Daniel didn't mind having a cook and housekeeper take care of their home. Domestic pursuits had never been Kate's strong suit.

"Now tell me, Erin, just how will this work with Elizabeth coming to your house?"

Erin scooped the chopped vegetables into a large pot. "The parsonage has four bedrooms, so Elizabeth will have a room of her own. With the nursery between the two larger bedrooms, the arrangement will be perfect. With Elizabeth there, I can leave Connor at home to attend meetings at church.

"When I became Seth's wife, I had no idea how many groups our church has, but Seth explained he didn't want any lady to be left out of planning things at church, and the more committees they had, the more women could participate."

She reached over and punched down the bread dough. "I'm making Parker House rolls that Aunt Mabel showed me how to do from that place back east."

Kate said nothing but let her sister talk. Erin had her mind made up about what she wanted to do. Although barely twenty, her sister possessed more skills than Kate could ever hope to have. When had her little sister grown up and become so responsible?

Finally she spoke her thoughts. "I know you're set on doing this, but I say talk it over with Ma and see what she has to say. I'll support you all I can."

Erin reached over and hugged Kate. "Thank you, my big sister. We have to stick together against those brothers of ours, or we'd never get anything done."

Kate returned the hug then stood. "I'm going before Cory gets here. No need to start an argument today." She slipped out the back door and headed for home. Erin most likely would put up a good case for Elizabeth, but Cory could be stubborn and stand his ground. This may be one of those times.

~~~❦~~~

All remained quiet in the sheriff's office. Rutherford had returned from taking a prisoner up to Dallas, where he was wanted for armed robbery. He'd picked the wrong town to visit, and Rutherford had noticed the stranger right away. Cory picked up his hat and sauntered out the door. With the rest of the day off he could spend time with Pete Davis teaching him how to handle guns.

First though, a good, hot meal would take away the chill in his bones. He unhitched his horse and swung up into the saddle. All along Main Street people greeted him with smiles and waves. Annie's Kitchen had a full crowd of people waiting in line to eat, and he suspected the hotel did too. Families had taken to eating together when they came to town on Saturday from the outlying ranches and farms. He spotted his cousin Jim Lowell going into the library and grinned. He'd bet his last nickel that Miss Miller was in the library waiting for Jim. From the looks of things there'd be another wedding come late spring or early summer.

Weddings and babies had sure made a leap in number this year. Most were in or connected to his family. That was fine with him as long as it happened to somebody else.

Ernie the barber waved at Cory. "When you coming in for another haircut, sheriff? Gettin' kinda scraggly lookin', ain't ya?"

Cory's hand went to the back of his neck. His hair had grown somewhat shaggy since his last cut, but he didn't really have any need to spend the money on a haircut. "I'll get it done eventually, Ernie. See you around."

He rode on past the bakery, Mrs. Bennett's dress shop, the saloon, and the infirmary. Seeing the infirmary brought Elizabeth Bradley to mind. Nothing had turned up on her so far, and his doubts about her had lessened. He hadn't been out to the ranch since she'd gone out there with Ma and Pa, but he'd be there tomorrow. He planned to observe her much more closely but without being obvious. That is, if he could pull that off in front of Ma.

When he reached the boardinghouse, he swung down from his horse and greeted Henry Wilder, who doffed his hat and nodded to Cory.

A broad grin spread across the reporter's face. "I see you're right on time for the meal. No criminals to catch today?"

Cory laughed and slapped him on the back. "Nope. Our town is safe. But why aren't you down at Annie's?"

"Too big a crowd on Saturdays. I'll go there this evening when the place is closed. Get to spend more time with her that way."

Cory started to ask why Henry didn't just marry Annie but thought better of it. He didn't like it when others asked him why he didn't do things, so he wouldn't do that to Henry. Cory followed Henry up the steps and into the parlor. Wonderful aromas filled the room, and Cory sniffed. "Hmm, smell that? Erin's made bread." He strode over to Connor's basket and picked him up.

"Say, little fella, you're wide awake. Are you as hungry as I am?"

The baby gurgled and waved his arms. Then his little

tongue stuck out, and his face turned red. Cory's eyes opened wide. That wasn't fresh bread. He held Connor away from his body and yelled for his sister.

Erin burst through the door from the kitchen. "What is it? Is something wrong with the baby?" She hurried over to grab him then wrinkled her nose.

Cory released his hold. "Nothing wrong that a clean diaper won't fix. You do that, and I'll see if Abigail needs help."

Erin grabbed a diaper from the basket and headed for the bedroom. He tossed his hat to the rack and strode into the kitchen. "I'm here if you need any help."

Abigail dropped the wooden spoon she'd just picked up and squealed. "Cory Muldoon, you scared the living daylights out of me. Be glad I dropped that spoon and didn't whack you over the head with it. Don't you know better than to sneak up on a woman in the kitchen? She might have a knife in her hands, and then where would you be?"

Cory laughed and shook his head. "Sorry, Abigail, I just came in to see if you need help. Erin had to change Connor's diaper." He gave the pump a few strokes then washed his hands.

Erin thrust a bowl of potatoes and a bowl of beans into his hands. "Then make yourself useful and put these on the table, then come back and get the meat. I'll get the bread and bring in the tea and coffee."

"Yes, ma'am. I'm at your service." He grasped the bowls and headed for the dining room. Henry Wilder and Slim Jenkins, Frank's new hand at the livery, were already seated. Mrs. Bennett scurried in like a bunny across the field, her cheeks bright pink from the chilly air.

He set the bowls on the table then pulled out Mrs.

Bennett's chair for her. "No need to rush so to be on time. Erin made plenty, and besides, Doc Elliot isn't here yet."

"Somebody call my name?" The doctor strolled in rubbing his hands together. "Hmm, smells like the women have something good cooked up for us. I imagine they'll be glad when Aunt Mae returns."

Henry bobbed his head, his bald pate shining bright. "It'll be good to have her back, but I can't say as I've missed her all that much. Good cooks must run in the Muldoon family. I haven't had a meal yet from one of them that wasn't excellent."

Cory laughed. "Not that you eat that many meals here these days." He seated himself by the man. "But not all Muldoon women cook. You haven't eaten one of Kate's meals." His sister cooked better now than when she helped Aunt Mae in the kitchen, but she still had a long way to go to be a Muldoon cook.

Henry grimaced. "I do remember a few of those attempts."

After the boarders said grace, conversation abated while they ate. Cory itched to talk more with Erin about her idea of having Elizabeth come into town, but this wasn't a good time. She had to see what a bad idea that would be. If someone came looking for the girl, he might not take kindly to whomever had her. No, she belonged at the ranch where Pa could protect her.

After dinner he headed out to find Pete and talk with him about gun safety. Shooting could come later after he learned the rules. Maybe he'd take a ride out to the ranch after he worked with Pete.

Libby helped Ada clean up after dinner. She cooked for the ranch hands on Saturday when they didn't go into town.

Having a large meal in the middle of the day still seemed strange to Libby. She barely ate anything at this time of day, and then only if lucky enough to have something left over from the night before. She had been aware that other people had plenty but had never been invited to eat with any of them.

Everything about the Muldoon family and their home spoke of love for each other. That proved harder to understand than having plenty to eat. Tomorrow would mark a week since she'd come out to the ranch, and it had turned out to be the best one of her life.

Ada had regaled her with tales of all her children and their antics when younger. She learned how close Kate and her brother had been growing up. That must be why they got along so well and seemed to really care about each other now. How she would have liked to have had a big brother like him. Maybe he could have protected her from Pa and his demands.

Ada said something, and Elizabeth jerked her head around. "What did you say?"

"I said with the whole family coming here for dinner tomorrow, we need to talk." She dried her hands on a towel. "Come over to the table, and let me tell you about an idea that Erin proposed."

Libby laid her dishtowel on the rack to dry and joined Ada. They'd had a number of talks this week, and each time Ada had tried to find out more about the past and what Libby had run away from. So far she'd been able to skirt around the reasons and turn the focus back to Ada's family. She hoped that would be the case today.

After they were both seated, Ada reached across and grasped Libby's hands. "I know you're afraid of something, but you've been reluctant to share. I won't ask you what it is, but I'm worried about you."

The sincerity in Ada's voice caused a lump to rise in Libby's throat. Why couldn't she trust this woman to help her? Because she was a lawman's mother, that's why.

Libby gazed across at the fire blazing on the hearth, lending its warmth and comfort to the chilly day. The big dining table bore the marks of many years of use by both children and adults. Everything in the house, from the curtains at the windows to the pictures on the wall, spoke of love and caring by this family. Still, her fears wouldn't allow her to trust any of it.

Ada patted Libby's hand. "There's one more item we need to discuss. Last Sunday you met my daughter Erin and her husband, the minister. Well, Erin has an idea."

Libby remembered the young woman and her husband, but why would they be concerned about her? His prayer had been kind, but it didn't mean anything. "Yes, and she's a nice woman."

"I'm glad you liked her, because she would like for you to come into town and live at the parsonage and be Connor's nanny."

A nanny? Live in town? Libby sat back and swallowed hard to allow the idea to sink in. Living in a parsonage might provide some safety. If Pa came to town, he still had enough respect for the church not to cause trouble there, but she wouldn't be completely safe. "I don't really know much about being nanny, and I wouldn't want to bring trouble to your daughter and her family."

"I don't think you have anything to worry about there with Cory in town watching out for you. Taking care of Connor at his age is easy. All he needs is food and clean diapers. Erin will take care of the feeding, so all you have to worry about is keeping him clean."

She made it sound so easy, but taking care of her brother hadn't been. Of course, he was older when she had to start watching out for him. Maybe a baby would be less trouble. "I'll think about it. But what if the baby doesn't like me?"

"We'll know that soon enough tomorrow when they're all here. You can hold Connor then and get a feel for who he is and what he needs."

"All right. I'll wait to let you know then."

Ada leaned her forearms on the table. "One more thing concerns me. Why don't you want to go into church with us tomorrow? Is it truly because you don't want to be seen by others, or is there some other reason?"

"I'd just prefer not to go yet." What could she say to Ada, who wore her Christianity like no others she had known? She couldn't tell her that all she knew about church was the bunch of hypocrites in the church back home. They said they loved God and God loved everybody, but that's not what she'd seen. Even God ignored her cries for help. Ada could worship God all she wanted, but Libby wanted no part of religion now or ever again.

~⚜~

Kurt Cantrell pounded the sheriff's desk. "Look here, my girl's been gone almost two weeks, and you ain't done nothing to find her."

The sheriff hooked his fingers into his belt, which sat well below his bulging waistline. "I'm sorry, Cantrell. Libby's of age and can go wherever she wants to go. I know it's hurting your pocketbook, but just let it be."

Cantrell's eyes narrowed, and his lips pursed. "What about her taking Yeller Boy? She stole my horse and took her ma's quilt."

"Seems to me that those things belonged to her anyways. Go on back to your cabin, and get on with your life. Libby's gone, and there ain't nothin' I can do about it. You need to sober up and get your head on straight." He sat down at his desk and began thumbing through a stack of papers there.

"Well, I aim to do somethin'. I jest don' know what yet." He turned and staggered out of the office. Dumb sheriff. Kurt didn't know why he'd come to the man in the first place. He should'a knowed he wasn't going to do anything about it. He needed a drink so he could think better.

He headed over to the saloon, jiggling the few coins in his pocket. If Libby hadn't run off, he could be making some good money with her. A few new gamblers had showed up at the Lady Slipper, and he could have set her up with them.

He stumbled into the saloon and up to the bar, where he laid a coin down. "Gimme some whiskey."

"I don't think so, Mr. Cantrell."

Kurt whirled around and almost fell. He grabbed the barkeep's lapel and cursed him. The man removed Kurt's hands and straightened his coat. "Without Libby you're just another drunk who can't afford to gamble or drink. I think it's best you go on back home and sleep it off."

"My money's jest as good as anybody else's." Kurt swayed but held tight to the bar.

"Not tonight it isn't." He jerked his head to the side, and two men jumped to Kurt and lifted him from his feet then escorted him to the door. They swung him out onto the street, where he landed with a thud.

Anger burned through Kurt at the loss of Libby and his income, as well as the humiliation of being kicked out of the saloon. He wasn't so drunk that he didn't notice the looks of the men at the tables. They thought he was dirt and trash under their feet. He swiped at his mouth. He'd show them. He'd have income again, and he'd get out of this lousy town and start over somewhere else. But first he had to find Libby.

He scratched his head, thinking. At the sheriff's office he'd seen the wanted posters tacked up on the wall. Maybe he could make up some wanted posters of his own and mail them out to neighboring towns. Someone had to have seen the girl.

Then another idea occurred. If he stopped drinking and saved what little money he could pick up by selling some of that furniture and stuff stored out in the barn, he could get a horse and go looking for her. Even old Bernie might be willing to give him a job if he cleaned himself up and stayed sober. Mucking stalls and sweeping floors didn't sound so bad now. Kurt straightened his shoulders and headed home to make up his posters.

Chapter
Eight

*L*IBBY FINALLY CONVINCED Ada to go on to church with Mr. Muldoon without her tagging along with them. The house's silence after they were gone wrapped around Libby in a blanket of peace. The last time she'd experienced such love and care had been four years ago, before her mother died. She had never expected to find it on this journey.

The roast beef simmering on the stove sent its enticing aroma throughout the house. The loaves of bread sat ready to place in the oven at the set time, and a huge berry cobbler covered with a dish cloth waited on the counter. She and Ada spent a busy day on Saturday making sure everything would be ready for today's dinner with the Muldoon family.

Libby sat down at the kitchen table with a cup of tea flavored by the mint Ada grew under the kitchen window. She perused the list of family members that Ada had given her. Only the brothers and sisters would be here and not the aunts and extended family. For that she had to be thankful, as it would be bad enough to meet this many new people without all the others added in too.

Her count showed fourteen adults, including herself, plus the children. She would be most comfortable if Ada sat by her, but she had no idea how the family arranged itself around the table, especially with the children.

She rose and sauntered out to the dining room. Fourteen places were set around the big table, plus high chairs for the younger ones. The glasses shone in the sunlight beaming through the window. Libby picked up a pottery plate glazed in a nice umber tone. The dishes at home had been tin and had become dented and out of shape over the years. How nice it would be to have a home with new things that weren't bent, cracked, or chipped.

The big clock in the larger sitting room chimed the noon hour. That meant she should start getting things ready for the family's arrival. Her palms became moist and warm despite the chill skittering up and down her spine, and she fought back the impulse to bolt and run off on Yeller Boy. Swallowing her anxiety, Libby headed for the kitchen.

In half an hour the bread sent its yeasty aroma over the room, and delicious smells coming from the roast sent Libby's stomach to rumbling. Ada had said they'd be back before one o'clock, and the clock showed that time to be near.

She raced upstairs to check her appearance one more time. Shivers of fear filled her body, and her hands shook as she smoothed back her hair. She pinched her cheeks to add a little color, moistened her lips, and checked her skirt for any stains or spots. Not that it would do a bit of good.

One last look into the mirror, and she sucked up a deep breath. Today would be the first real indication of her welcome or rejection. If the other members of the family didn't agree with Ada and Mr. Muldoon about keeping her here, she had no choice but to leave.

When she reached the bottom of the stairway, sounds of the family arriving drew her to the front door. Ada and Mr. Muldoon burst through first, and Ada rushed to Libby's side and wrapped her arms around Libby's shoulders.

"Put on that pretty smile of yours, and don't worry about trying to remember everybody at first. Let them get over the surprise of seeing you, and then they'll remind you who they are as they talk with you. Remember, you're our guest, and I won't stand for rudeness from any of them."

Ada clapped her hands together as a little boy raced through the door and into her waiting arms. "Why, my goodness, Rory, you're so strong you almost knocked me over."

"I'm almost nine now, Grandma, and I learned to rope a calf."

Then the other children swarmed in. Libby's eyes misted at the sight of so many happy little faces with smiles as big as the sun brightening the room. She glanced up and away from them to find six adults staring at her with more than curiosity filling their faces.

Kate smiled and stood beside Libby. "Family, this is Elizabeth Bradley. She's a newcomer to Porterfield and has been ill. Ma and Pa decided to bring her out here to recuperate in the fresh air and sunshine of the ranch."

Libby's heart jumped with gratitude. Kate made it sound as if Elizabeth Bradley was truly someone worth knowing.

The men all began talking at once to their mother, but the women came to Libby and surrounded her with smiles of welcome. She recognized the minister and his wife, as she had met them last Sunday. The others introduced themselves as Megan, Sarah, and Jenny. Libby tried to remember which wife belonged to which son but came up blank. She would just smile and answer questions until she learned the families.

Even as the women of the Muldoon family welcomed her, doubts intervened. Libby envied their status, but the dream of a loving husband and a family faded with the cold light of the truth of her life. How would it feel to have a man love her and want her for herself and not because of greedy desire? She'd most likely never know.

All the ladies departed to the kitchen, and the men continued talking with their father. As she stood there uncertain what to do next, the glances from those around Mr. Muldoon warned her to be careful how she behaved for the next several hours. Men didn't scare her in surroundings like this, but right now she wished she could be out on the road again and not in this room with all these people.

Cory stood to one side while his brothers talked to Pa, observing Miss Bradley from the corner of his eye. In one of Erin's old dresses and with her hair styled, Miss Bradley proved to be a very pretty young woman. She bent over the table, pretending to straighten a fork, then turned her head in his direction. Uncertainty screamed from her eyes, and the need to rescue her overwhelmed him.

He separated himself from the others and strode to her side, not sure if she'd wait for him or scurry off to hide somewhere. She stood still until he reached her side. "I'm glad to see you looking well, Miss Bradley." He grinned and inclined his head toward the fireplace, where his nieces and nephews gathered to play until dinnertime. "Let's go meet those young'uns over there."

He led her to the circle of children. "Hey, I want you to meet our special guest. This is Elizabeth Bradley, and she's visiting with Grandpa and Grandma for a while."

The oldest, Patrick, jumped up and took charge. "Hi, my name's Patrick, and I just turned eleven. This here is my sister Jeanie, and she's seven." He placed his hand on his youngest sister. "And this one is Mary. She's four. That there is Rory. He's eight, almost nine, and his brother Eddie, and he's six. They got a sister named Elizabeth just like you."

Miss Bradley grinned and held out her hand to Patrick. "It's nice to meet you, Patrick, and all of you."

Cory bit back his chuckle. "Very well done, Patrick."

Patrick pulled on Cory's sleeve. When Cory bent down, Patrick whispered in his ear. "You gonna be sweet on her like you was Miss Abigail?"

Heat infused Cory's face, and he bit back an angry retort as he stood. His nephew was teasing, that's all, but it didn't help that Miss Bradley looked so pretty today. Suddenly he wished he'd taken old Ernie up on the offer of a haircut. "Miss Bradley is our guest for a few days. Be nice to her."

He waved at the children then ushered her back to the dining table, where Ma had just set a large platter of meat.

"All right, everyone, it's time to gather 'round the table," Ma announced. "Patrick, will you take charge of your cousins today at your table?"

Cory shook his head and winked at Patrick, who stood even taller and prouder than he had a few minutes earlier. He sure wouldn't let his cousins forget who was the leader at that table. Cory stood beside Miss Bradley, and the fragrance of lavender wafted his way. Ma must have loaned some of hers, and it sure fit the girl next to him.

When his pa stood to say grace, Cory closed his eyes, but his mind filled with the image of the girl at his side. He had to get his thoughts back on the right path. She could be a fugitive from some outlaw gang or running from her husband. Whatever the reason, he couldn't afford to let his guard down and allow her to slip into his heart.

During dinner his brothers kept to their manners and didn't embarrass Miss Bradley, but from the looks on their faces, they had a few questions for later. They wouldn't have any better luck than he had. So far she'd managed to evade every one he asked. Erin glanced at him a few times, and worry niggled at his innards. He prayed his sister didn't still plan to go through with her idea of asking Miss Bradley to come into town to live in the parsonage.

Kate poked his side. "Where are you, big brother? I asked you to pass the gravy this way."

Cory blinked and grabbed the bowl of gravy. "Sorry, Kate, had my mind on other things."

She snickered and leaned toward him while she ladled gravy onto her plate. "Could it be a pretty girl is sitting beside you? Still worried she's going to bring trouble?"

Cory clenched his teeth. First Patrick, now Kate. That was one of the problems with a big family: everyone took note of each other's business. "No, I mean yes. I don't know, but keep your voice down. No need to embarrass her."

Kate ignored him as she took a bite of mashed potatoes

and gravy. "Hmm. Ma, this gravy is delicious. Something about it is a little different."

Ma grinned proud as a mother hen over her new brood of chicks. "That's Elizabeth's doing. She finished up with everything while we were at church."

So she knew how to cook too. Everything he'd observed about her so far had shown her to be everything but someone being chased by the law. Even if she ran away from a mean husband, she could still be trouble. He couldn't let her get to him until he knew the truth.

When the meal finished, the older children went out to play, and Ma stood to call the family to attention. "Miss Bradley has been a guest in our home for the past week, but she has agreed to go back to Porterfield with Erin and Seth to be a nanny for Connor and a housekeeper for Erin."

Immediately his brothers and sisters murmured among themselves. At their response Miss Bradley's eyes opened wide, and fear settled there. Had Ma and Pa not anticipated the negative response of the family? That certainly wasn't fair.

Then the questions began, but Ma shook her head. "I don't want to hear any of it. The decision has been made. If you boys want to discuss it, then do so on your own."

Everyone at the table went about their business, knowing better than to speak right now. Cory avoided the discussion of ranching and headed outdoors to watch the older children. He sat on the porch and grinned at the scene before him. The girls sat under a tree and played with their dolls while the boys engaged in a game of tag. At one time in his life Cory had wanted a passel of young ones just like his parents, but since he'd chosen keeping the law as his profession, that idea disappeared to the recesses of his mind. Then the image of Elizabeth Bradley holding a young child and rocking it eased into his thoughts. He blinked his eyes and shook his head. Best not go down that path.

The door burst open, and three mothers stepped through the door to claim their children. Erin and Miss Bradley followed them and headed his direction. He stopped the swing and sat still, his eyes riveted on the girl he'd rescued.

Erin sat in one of the nearby rockers, and Elizabeth sat next to her. Cory sucked in his breath. All she needed was a baby in her arms to look just like the picture he'd imagined only a few minutes before.

Erin's voice broke the thought. "Cory, please tell Elizabeth that she'll be perfectly safe at the parsonage. She's worried about coming back into town."

And well she should be. Tongues would be wagging faster than a coon hound's after treeing a coon. Why couldn't Erin leave well enough alone? He wanted to argue with Erin, but with that determined look in her eyes, he may as well be talking to the wind. He shrugged and agreed with his sister. "You'll be safe there with Erin and the reverend, and Connor is a good baby."

Elizabeth nodded. "Yes, I fell in love with the baby as soon as I held him and he reached up and touched my cheek."

Erin stood. "Now, that's settled for sure, and I think I hear a baby crying, so I'll leave you two here to talk about it."

Cory had no desire to discuss the move, but he'd talk about anything to keep Miss Bradley on the porch.

When the clamor of mothers and children heading back into the house ceased, Cory's tongue thickened. So many questions and so few answers, but today he'd stay clear of any mention of her past.

"How do you feel about moving in with Seth and Erin? The idea seemed to unsettle you a bit."

"The reaction of your brothers startled me. That's all."

"I see. So...um...what do you think of the family so far? They can be quite noisy and intimidating."

"The women are very friendly and welcomed me with open arms, and I loved the children. Patrick stood so tall and proud when he introduced the others."

"Yes, he's getting to be quite the young man." He had to find a better topic than his family.

At that moment Kate and Daniel stepped through the door. "We're headed back to town, so we'll see you there, Cory."

Then all the others exited the house in preparation for returning to their own homes. Cory's heart thudded in his chest. He didn't want the afternoon to end, but he had no real excuse to stay behind, even though he'd like to visit with Miss Bradley a while longer. Why did she have such an effect on him?

He retrieved his hat and returned to the porch to say good-byes. After he had hugged his mother and shaken his father's hand, he turned to Miss Bradley. "Now that you'll be moving into town, perhaps we'll manage to see each other more often."

The stricken widening of her eyes and deep swallow told him all he needed to know. Miss Bradley had secrets, and she had no intention of revealing them. Still, he planned to find out what they were.

CHAPTER NINE

*L*IBBY PLACED THE last of her belongings into the flowered satchel she'd brought with her. Three of Erin's discarded dresses as well as a new nightdress and skirt filled the bag. Now that she was going into town to live with Erin and Rev. Winston in the parsonage, Libby wanted to be the person they all believed her to be. Still, second thoughts about going into town plagued her this morning. Ada had seen the bruises that were not quite healed, but she had not pressed for answers. Of anyone, Ada deserved to know the truth, but shame kept Libby silent. What would Erin say if she saw the marks?

She didn't have to be a genius to guess the deputy's disapproval when Ada made her announcement that Erin had invited Elizabeth to come into town to live. He didn't trust her, plain and simple as that, but he had every right not to trust her, just as she didn't trust him. At least he hadn't brought up her past. Still, she couldn't keep her heart from beating a little faster when he stood nearby or even now just thinking about him.

She shook off those thoughts and closed the satchel. Ada and Mr. Muldoon planned to take her into town and have supper at the parsonage. Mr. Muldoon had been working out on the range all week and wanted them to wait until he could escort her and Ada into town. Just why she couldn't be sure, but Ada said he didn't want them riding into town alone.

What little she had seen of Porterfield had whetted her desire to find a place and settle down to call home. Although still close to the state line, the town sat just far enough west that Pa would probably not venture this far. At first she'd feared he might send the law after her but then realized the law considered her to be an adult, so the sheriff at home couldn't charge her with crime and most likely wouldn't waste time hunting her. And the more time passed with no signs of her pa, the more she could relax.

She set the bag on the floor and strolled to the window. The sun cast golden rays slanting through the glass to create squares of light on the floor. The warmth through the window filled Libby with a peace she hadn't experienced in too many years to count. The only thing to mar these past days at the ranch had been Ada, who kept bringing up God. Libby had closed her ears and simply smiled and murmured a few words of agreement, which served to keep Ada from expounding further.

Libby turned from the window and its view of the pastures and barn. Leaving the ranch was not her first desire, but Erin was her age and would be a good friend to have. Erin had married and had a child of her own, while Elizabeth had been given to one man or another like a toy doll.

Then she gasped and plopped on the bed. Her hand went

to her mouth. Whatever was she thinking? Going to live at the parsonage meant she'd be hearing about God every day and would be expected to go to church on Sunday. God had sure played a cruel joke on her. Well, she didn't have to go along with anything except to sit and listen. A million other things could fill her mind so she would not have to listen to sermons and lectures about God's love.

With her heart steeled in resolve to ignore religion and its teachings, she picked up her bag and headed downstairs.

Ada met her at the bottom of the stairway. "I see you're all packed. You did include those things of Erin's I gave you, didn't you?"

"Yes, ma'am, I did, and I thank you for altering and fixing them to fit me. Are you sure Erin won't mind my wearing them when I'm with her?"

"Of course not. Erin has a whole new wardrobe we made when she married. I was going to give these to the church to use for handouts in case of something like the fire at the Davis place a year or so back. We like to have things handy to help people make a new start when such a tragedy strikes. I'm glad they'll get some good use now."

"I appreciate them, as well as the shoes and night-clothes." Libby set the satchel down and bit her lip. "Ada, I know Cory doesn't like this idea, and your other sons didn't appear too happy either. I don't want to cause trouble in the family."

Ada laughed and waved her hand. "They're just being over-protective. Kate was way too feisty and independent for all of them except Cory, so they've always looked after Erin. Kate and Cory would take on the three older ones any day of the week and come out on top of the pile."

Once again the love in the Muldoon family struck Libby and filled her with a longing for a home and family of her own. Living with Erin and the reverend would be as close as she would ever probably come to a normal family life again.

Ada hooked her arm with Elizabeth's. "Let's go and have a cup of tea and some of those cookies we made this morning."

Once they were seated with steaming cups of hot tea and a plate of cookies before them, Ada leaned on her forearms. "Before you go, I want you to know that Callum and I will do anything and everything we can to make sure you're all right. I do wish you'd tell us why you're running and let us help you."

"That's very kind of you, Ada. I know I should have explained before now, but I just couldn't. Please understand." Libby fiddled with her teacup, turning it around and around between her hands.

"I'm trying to, honey." She paused a moment then tilted her head. "Would you tell me one thing? Are you running from an outlaw gang?"

Libby almost choked on the bite of cookie she'd just put into her mouth. "No, no, nothing like that." It had never occurred to her that might be what they were thinking. No wonder Cory didn't trust her and kept eyeing her like she'd robbed the stage. In his eyes she most likely had done just that. Perhaps she ought to give just a little bit of the story.

"I'm not running from the law, and I'm not running from a husband. I'm not married, but I lived with my pa, and I just couldn't live with him anymore." That's all Ada needed to know. The rest would stay a secret.

"Oh, my. I'm so sorry. I figured it had to be something like that. You're too pretty and sweet to be an outlaw anyway. And as soon as Cory sees that, the better off he'll be." She reached over and patted Libby's hand. "Enjoy these last minutes of peace. Knowing my Erin, she'll have you so busy helping her with the house and taking care of Connor that you won't have much quiet time to yourself."

That Libby wouldn't mind at all. Hard work never hurt anybody, especially when it involved taking care of a child. Besides, nothing could be as hard as what she'd endured for the past four years.

Cory hit his fist on the desk. Still nothing on Elizabeth Bradley. That should give him some comfort, but it didn't. That girl held more secrets than Ma around Christmastime. He pushed the papers aside. He should've been able to find something on the girl by now.

Sheriff Rutherford strolled through the door and hooked his hat on a peg near his desk. He stared at Cody and shook his head. "I've seen that look on you before, and something's stuck in your craw. Have anything to do with that little gal you found in the alley?"

"Yeah, I hate not knowing who she is. What if she is wanted and some outlaw comes looking for her?" He'd asked himself a dozen times if that feeling came out of knowing she might be a fugitive from the law or from the way she'd worked her way under his skin. His heart wanted to be attracted to her, but his common sense warned him to be careful and get the truth first.

"Buck up, boy. We'll handle it. Couldn't be much worse than when Miss Monroe was taken hostage by those bank robbers last year. Her life was in danger every minute she stayed captive in their hands."

"True, but if this involved Miss Bradley only, it wouldn't be so hard to accept. Trouble is, Miss Bradley is moving in with my sister Erin to help with the baby. If anyone wants Miss Bradley bad enough to shoot, their lives could be in danger."

"What do you expect to do now, son, besides keep your eyes and ears open to any trouble?"

"I don't know, but I'm worried that Erin might be putting her family in harm's way." Cory glanced across at the sheriff. He'd been married over twenty years, and yet he still took care of Porterfield and upheld its laws. "How do you do it? How does Mrs. Rutherford do it? You've been shot at more times than I like to think about, and so have I. Aren't you afraid something will happen to you? Isn't she afraid for you? And what about your girls?"

The sheriff scratched his chin for a few minutes and seemed to ponder the questions before he gave an answer. Finally he leaned forward with his forearms resting on the desk. "If I let the fear of being shot or killed keep me from doing my job, I'd been either be dead or retired by now. That doesn't mean fear isn't there, but it doesn't keep me from doing my job. Millie knew I was a lawman when she married me, and she does fret and stew sometimes, but she does a lot of praying. And that's what I want her to do. As for the girls, I don't think they really understand the danger yet."

"I don't know. It just seems it's not fair to a woman to have her constantly worried about what might happen to her man when he goes after an outlaw."

Rutherford chuckled. "Don't you know it goes against the Lord to worry? The Bible tells us to cast our cares on the Lord. That doesn't mean to cast them out then pull them back. It means to leave them out there and let Him take care of the problems. Millie knows God will protect me until it's my time. She gets all frazzled and on edge at times, like when we chased the Clanton gang, but she gets over it when I come home."

That chance of not coming home bothered Cory the most. The Bible did say he shouldn't worry about tomorrow, because tomorrow had enough worries of its own, but that didn't make *not* worrying any easier.

He pushed away from his desk. "Ma and Pa should be here with Miss Bradley by now. I'm going down to check on things."

A grin spread across the sheriff's face. "Gotta check out that young lady again too, I imagine. Just be careful, son, and I don't mean because she might be wanted. I think she's dangerous and might steal something, but it won't be money."

Cory shook his head and grabbed his hat. Once outside he mounted his horse and headed for the parsonage. Before he'd gone a block, the implication in Rutherford's words hit Cory. He groaned. Why did that man have to go and read something into nothing? Or was there something there that he didn't want to admit? Either way, Rutherford meddled where he shouldn't.

When Cory arrived at the parsonage, Pa had just helped Ma and Miss Bradley from the carriage. Ma beamed a welcoming smile at him. He made a mistake coming here. His arrival made it look like he changed his mind and accepted the move. At least Ma would think that, but the only reason he'd come had nothing to do with Miss Bradley, or at least he didn't think so.

He swung down from his horse and strode over to the porch, where Erin waited with Connor. Seth stepped out onto the porch and shook Cory's hand.

"Glad you came, Cory. I want to talk to you a little later, but now we want to get Elizabeth settled."

Cory stood to the side while Ma cooed over her newest grandson, who would have that honor only a little longer until Sarah's new one arrived in a few months. Erin welcomed Elizabeth and hooked arms with her to go into the house. It made a pretty family picture, and to passersby it would appear as a simple gathering at the parsonage.

He leaned against the doorjamb and stared at Miss Bradley and forced down the tug she pulled at his heart. In Erin's clothes and with her hair hanging loose down her back, she looked no older than a schoolgirl, but the hardness in her eyes said differently. His heart reached out to her, but his brain said not to trust her.

Certainly, once the single men in town discovered her, she'd have suitors competing right and left. Single women were a rare commodity, and Miss Bradley was too attractive to escape notice. What a laugh. Even if she looked ugly as a broken-down barn door, they'd take note of her as a single woman.

"Mr. Muldoon, why do you keep staring at me like that?"

"Like what?" He jerked himself to stand straight. When had she come so near? He caught that lavender scent about her again and swallowed hard to keep from saying something he'd be sorry for later.

"Like I was some monster. You don't seem to like me much, and your brothers don't either. Well, I can tell you this, I'm not a murderer or a thief, and I won't do anything to hurt Erin, Rev. Winston, or little Connor."

She glared at him a moment longer then swirled around with a swish of her skirts and headed for the kitchen.

A snicker sounded behind him, and he turned to see Seth standing there with a grin as broad as the back side of a cow. "Looks like she set you in your place." He then shrugged. "Look, Cory, I'm a pretty good judge of character, and I see a hurting girl in Elizabeth. I don't see someone who has broken the law, but she is a girl with troubles in her past. We intend to love her and help her get beyond the hurt and pain."

Seth didn't judge people at all. He saw the good in them until they proved him wrong, and that hadn't happened very often. Cory prayed Elizabeth wouldn't be one who would.

"Then I withhold my judgment. We'll see how it turns out." Cory followed Seth into the house.

In the sitting room Elizabeth and Erin stood at Connor's cradle talking about his care. Cory tapped Elizabeth's shoulder. "I'm sorry you thought I don't like you."

Pink tinged her cheek, adding to her beauty. "It's difficult for me to think otherwise."

Erin picked up the baby. "He needs a diaper change. I'll be back in a moment." She turned to Seth. "Be a dear and bring the cradle upstairs for me."

Seth frowned as though puzzled but then grinned. "Of course, I'm right behind you."

Elizabeth bit her lip, and Cory's tongue worked in his mouth as he searched for something to say. "Hmm...I think my sister will keep you plenty busy."

"I...I won't mind that all. Connor is a precious baby, and so good." She picked up a baby blanket from a chair and folded it.

Cory swallowed hard. "It's not that I don't like you, Miss Bradley. It's just that I...we don't know that much about you. Have you had experience taking care of children? Do you have brothers and sisters of your own? Are you running from a vengeful father or perhaps former suitor?"

With each question her face had grown tighter until the last one, when she narrowed her eyes and clenched her teeth. "I can tell you this, Mr. Deputy Sheriff, I'm not running from the law or a husband. Think what you want about me and try to find out whatever you want, but it's my business. Your parents and Erin and the reverend trust me, and that's enough for me."

Cory bit back a retort. It wasn't enough for him, but if he stayed much longer, he'd be sure to say something he'd end up regretting later. He could talk with Seth later. "Then I take my leave, Miss Bradley." He turned and all but stomped to the door, where he shoved his hat down on his head and headed out.

CHAPTER TEN

ON FRIDAY LIBBY picked up baby Connor from his cradle and held him. The scene with the deputy wouldn't leave her head. He'd apologized and then started in with his questions again. She could understand his lack of trust, but fear kept her from trying to gain it. Even if she could trust him and his family, she had to keep the truth from them at all cost.

She stroked Connor's cheek and marveled at his beauty and innocence. A longing stirred deep inside. She hadn't held a baby since her baby brother when she'd been just a little girl herself, but she'd never forget that feeling of his tiny body in her arms. If she closed her eyes tight, she could still picture him, all fair-haired and blue-eyed, just like her and Ma. She'd been fourteen when the typhoid had come and taken his life, but she'd never forget his bright smile and playful eyes.

A tear slipped down her cheek, and she quickly brushed it away. She couldn't let Erin see her crying, and Seth would be here in a few minutes ready for dinner. Libby placed Connor back in the cradle and turned to Erin. "Anything I can do to help before Rev. Winston gets here?"

"No, it's all ready, thanks to your help this morning." Erin dried her hands on a towel and picked up a platter of meat. "It's been really nice having someone my age to talk to and work with these past two days." She reached over and hugged Libby. "I'm glad you're here."

Not as much as she was. Not once had Erin or the reverend asked questions about her past. Oh, they'd probably get around to it eventually, but that gave her time to come up with a good story.

The reverend's voice preceded him through the kitchen doorway. He reached down and picked up his son then grinned at her and Erin. "Something smells mighty good in here." He leaned over and kissed Erin's cheek then cuddled Connor to his chest.

Libby's throat tightened, and she fought the sadness that threatened. Seeing the love the reverend had for his wife and son tore at her insides until she could barely stand it. This was the way families were supposed to be, and she could enjoy it as long as she kept her secret. She didn't think of it as lying but as self-preservation.

After the reverend said grace over the meal, he and Erin talked about the dinner planned by the church ladies for after church on Sunday.

Erin passed the potatoes to Libby. "Sunday is the first day of March, and we want to usher in spring. I know officially spring is still three weeks away, but what with Rachel's baby due and Abigail's wedding, the rest of March will be pretty busy."

"Exactly what do you do at these things?" Libby had no idea what church activities entailed, as she'd never attended anything but the church services with Ma and Pa before her brother died.

"All the ladies fix the food and bring it to share with everyone else. We'll go over later tomorrow afternoon and set up all the tables outdoors. Then on Sunday morning we'll cover them with cloths and have them ready for the food to be brought. We have some great cooks here in Porterfield, so you'll have some good eating on Sunday."

Then Libby remembered her family had attended something like that when she was a young girl. It had been fun then, but now it meant more people she'd have to face. Maybe she could get out of it, but how? She didn't care to experience what she had faced at home. If all Christians were like Erin and her family, going to church might not be too bad, but she couldn't count on that.

"You can help me with some of the cooking I want to do tomorrow. Ma and the other ladies will do their share, but I want to contribute too."

That Libby could do, and she looked forward to it. Having all the necessary ingredients for the things Ma had taught her to cook brought pleasure to her heart. She even remembered a few of Ma's favorites. Perhaps Erin would let her make one of them. "I'd like that. I haven't had much chance to cook in the past few years."

Maybe if the deputy learned that she could truly be a help to Erin, he'd be more pleasant. Libby dreaded seeing him because of his dislike for her. The only man who had been kind to her besides the doctor now appeared to have turned against her. Of course, as a lawman he just did his job and took care of his business.

His questions had grown more probing, but up until now she'd been able to avoid them or skirt around them with vague answers. Soon he'd stop being nice and demand to know the truth, and what would she do then?

Reverend Winston rose from the table. "I hate to leave the company of such beautiful ladies, but duty calls me back to the church. The Ladies Missions Society is meeting this afternoon, and I promised to be there." He kissed Erin then rocked Connor's cradle and caressed the baby's head. "Good-bye, little fella. Be good for your ma." He stopped at the door. "If the meeting runs long, I'll meet you at the station."

When the door closed behind him, Libby frowned. "What did he mean by that? Are you going somewhere?"

Erin laughed and stacked a few dishes. "Oh, no, we're meeting my aunt Mae and her new husband. They're coming back from their wedding trip. They'll be here on the afternoon train."

That must be the lady who got married the day Libby lay in the hospital. More family to meet and smile at and be nice to. The longer she stayed, the harder it would be to get away from this family.

Libby glanced over at Connor, who had begun to fuss and fret. "Why don't you take him upstairs and feed him while I take care of cleaning up. After all, that's why I'm here."

"Thank you. You do make my days easier."

When she had gone with the baby, Libby pumped water into the sink then filled a pot to heat more water for rinsing.

All the while she worked she imagined this to be her house and her kitchen. Someday she'd have one just like it.

She stopped and shook her head. No one would want her as a wife, and right now, as much as she wanted a family of her own, she couldn't bear the thought of what the Muldoon clan would say and how they would act when they learned the truth about her. What a foolish and hopeless idea to think she could stay here and live with her secret. The time had come to pack her bag and get out of Porterfield.

⚜

Cory finished the paperwork on the week's activities. After the hearty meal at the boardinghouse the afternoon loomed long and boring. Then he remembered Aunt Mae and Cyrus were due to arrive on the afternoon train from Dallas. It'd sure be good to have her home again and taking care of her boarders. Not that Abigail hadn't done a good job, but Aunt Mae added something no one else could—her wisdom and humor.

Rutherford looked up from the stack of papers on his desk. "This looks interesting. It's some kind of wanted poster for a woman named Libby Cantrell. It's not a regular wanted poster and looks like it was done by hand. Came in the mail this morning. Probably a husband hunting a runaway wife."

"What?" Cory strode to the sheriff's desk and grabbed the paper. "Let me see that."

WANTED
Libby Cantrell
Horse theef and rober
Return Kurt Cantrell, Bayou Point, Lousana

Cory snorted. "Whoever made this didn't know what he was doing. There's no description of her, and no reward. Oh, well, better check this out."

He folded the paper and stuffed it into his shirt pocket. Never hurt to be cautious about things like this. Cory left the office and mounted his horse. He removed the poster and studied it again. Something didn't seem right about it, besides the crudely done work. Still, it contained a lead he'd been looking for the past few weeks.

When he reached the parsonage, Cory swung down from his horse and hitched it to the post by the walk up to the porch. When he started up the steps, he heard laughter and stopped. He strode across to a window and leaned down to peek inside. Erin and Elizabeth sat together folding diapers with Connor's cradle nearby. Erin said something that caused Elizabeth to laugh again. The two could have been sisters. This girl couldn't be a thief of any kind, horse or otherwise. Still, he had to make sure.

He cleared his throat and knocked on the door. Erin jumped to greet him, but he saw Elizabeth's eyes open wide, and fear, not surprise, filled them. If she had nothing to hide, she had no reason to fear him.

Erin hugged him. "Why, Cory, what a nice surprise. I sure wasn't expecting to see you this afternoon. What's going on?" Her eyebrows raised, and her hand went to her chest. "Nothing happened to Aunt Mae, did it? I was going down to the station to meet her when we finished here." She waved him inside.

"No, nothing is the matter with Aunt Mae. Her train should be on time, and I plan to be there to meet her myself."

He glanced over at Elizabeth. "Fact is, I've come to talk with Miss Bradley."

"Oh." She turned toward Elizabeth. "I'll take Connor upstairs to get him ready to meet the train."

He sat down in the chair across from the sofa where Elizabeth folded a diaper. Her hands trembled, and she kept her head bowed. How could he approach this and not scare her? He needed to know the truth, but did he truly want to hear it?

He rolled the brim of his hat in his hands. Why did this have to be so hard? "Miss Bradley, I remember you saying you crossed the Sabine River. Did you come from Louisiana or from northeast of here in Texas?"

She raised her eyes and bit her lip. Terror replaced the fear he'd seen earlier, and it cut him to the core. He hadn't seen fear like that since Abigail's face when Clanton held her captive. This girl had either been badly hurt by someone or had hurt someone else and run from it.

Her eyes blinked, and she took a deep breath. "I came from Louisiana."

So she admitted being from there. Now for the next question, and her reaction. He kept his gaze glued to her face. "Did you happen to know a man by the name of Cantrell where you're from?"

The slightest jerk of her chin told him more than any words, but he waited to hear them.

"No, I don't." Her head bowed with her chin almost touching her chest.

She wasn't telling the truth, but a gut feeling told him to leave it. Things didn't add up. He stood with his hat in hand.

"That's all I wanted to know for now. I'll leave you to finish your work." He turned and strode from the room.

He faced hardened criminals many times in his work, and he'd questioned many a suspect for various crimes. Most times, when a man lied, he didn't look the sheriff straight in the face, and if he did, a slight twitch or movement in the eyes or mouth indicated a lie, which is what just happened. People telling the truth held their heads high and their shoulders back, denying all allegations. The only drawback came because he'd never seen pure terror in anyone's eyes like he'd seen in Elizabeth Bradley's.

Seth met him coming up the walk. "Hello, Cory. You headed for the train station to meet Aunt Mae?"

"Yes, I am." Cory shoved his white hat onto his head and reached for his horse's reins.

"What brought you out for a visit?"

"Had to talk with Miss Bradley." He turned his horse and trotted away before Seth could ask more questions. The time would come when he had to seek more information, but it wouldn't be today. She had sounded too happy with Erin, and her laughter had touched a nerve deep in his soul. He couldn't explain it, and he wasn't sure if he wanted to even try.

One thing he had to do but dreaded. Before going to the station to meet his aunt and her new husband, he had to make a stop at the telegraph office. May as well check out the information on the poster.

After he sent the telegram, Cory arrived at the station and met up with his parents and the other members of the family come to welcome Aunt Mae and Cyrus home. By the time the whistle blared out its warning, all the Muldoon family stood on the platform waiting. Even Elizabeth had come with Erin and Seth. Abigail and Nathan arrived just before the train. What a welcome home for a wonderful woman everyone in town loved.

After Aunt Mae and Cyrus stepped down, they were surrounded by family. Elizabeth stood off to the side and watched. Cory stepped back from the family circle and observed the girl from his spot.

No matter what she'd done in the past, it couldn't be as bad as that wanted poster made things sound. He wanted to help her, but at the same time his instincts warned him to be careful until he knew more about her. In only two weeks she had worked her way into his life in a way no other girl had. Not even Abigail had caused feelings like this, and no matter how he fought them or denied them, they were still there.

A hand landed on his shoulder. He turned to find Ma standing beside him. "I see how you're looking at our girl. She's a pretty little thing."

Heat rose in Cory's cheeks. "Yes, she is, and I wish I could get the truth from her about where she's from and why she's running."

"Be careful what you do, because I know the girl is running from abuse."

Cory shook his head and blew out his breath. "Now, how do you know that? Did she tell you?" Ma always could get more out of a person than anyone else.

"Didn't need to. I saw the evidence, and so did Kate. She has bruises on her body and welts that don't come from an accident. She's taken a beating, and more than once if the old scars say anything."

Cory blinked and gulped. How could he deal with that? Any man or woman who beat another person, especially a young woman, like the way Ma said, needed to be strung up. "If that's true, there's even more reason I need to know where she's from and who did this to her."

"Then earn her trust and let her tell you when she's ready. Abuse is not something anyone, especially a woman, wants to reveal. Whether it came from a parent or some other relative, we have to love her and let her know how much God loves her. We have to make her feel safe."

Of the two evils, he'd rather she be a victim than one accused of a crime. Victims he could help, but the criminals must be punished. Once again he turned his attention to the young woman. Their gazes met, and the pain in her eyes went straight to his heart. He sent the silent message of "trust me, Elizabeth" with his, but hers sent back the same one of fear she'd worn since he met her. Could he gain her trust and help her? Right now he could only hope and pray.

CHAPTER ELEVEN

Sunday morning as Libby dressed, she tried to think of a way to get out of going to church with Erin. Every excuse she thought of, from faking a headache to flat telling the truth that she no longer went to church because God didn't care what happened to girls like her, fell flat and sounded either too lame or revealed too much about herself. With a sigh she finally twisted her hair up in the back and pinned it in place. No one in Porterfield knew her, so they had no reason to shun her.

No matter. She'd be ready to leave tonight. Her satchel sat ready to go, packed with a few of the things Ada had given her. Now she only had to figure out a way to get Yeller Boy saddled and ready for a middle-of-the-night ride. She didn't know how the deputy found out her real name, but it could only mean that Pa wanted her back.

When she went downstairs, Erin waited for her. "Seth has left to make sure the church is ready for services."

Libby had tended Connor yesterday when Erin had gone

over to arrange flowers for the altar table. "I thought you did all that yesterday." What would there be left to do today?

"Oh, he likes to make sure all the songbooks are in place and that it's warm when the weather is cold and cool with the windows open in warmer weather." Erin wrapped a lightweight blanket around Connor then handed him to Libby. "Hold him while I get my bonnet and shawl. He's been a little fussy this morning."

Libby held the baby and smiled at his perfect little mouth and pink cheeks. His eyes already held the color of his mother's, but the peach fuzz of his hair grew in dark like his father. Then his mouth scrunched up, and he began fretting. She leaned close and kissed his head. "Shh, little one. Your ma will be right back."

She swayed back and forth with him, and he settled back down in her arms. How wonderful it would be to hold a new life in her arms, knowing it came from her. But then an icy shudder of guilt and pain replaced the warmth. She swallowed hard. Why did she have to keep reminding herself of her sordid past?

If he was fussy as Erin said, maybe staying home with him would be an option for her not to attend church. Erin returned and reached for the baby.

"Perhaps I can stay home with him so you won't have to worry with him in church."

"I don't think that will be necessary. He's been fed, so he'll settle down and sleep. If he doesn't, others will understand if I leave with him."

She waited for Libby to put on a shawl and bonnet. "You know, I had an idea this morning, and I'm going to put it before Ma. With so many babies born in the past year and so many coming this spring, we need a special place for them during church services. Maybe we can use one of the back rooms for a little nursery-type area where they could be, and the mothers can take turns caring for them during the services."

Libby shook her head. She'd never heard of such a thing, but it sounded like a good idea. She remembered crying babies and fussy children as being a part of church when she was child. Ma had scolded her more than once for fidgeting and wanting to talk.

Once Libby donned her hat, she followed Erin through the door, all excuses for staying behind lying useless in her mind. She braced herself for stares and whispers when they approached the lawn where buggies, wagons, and carriages unloaded their passengers.

Ada walked over to greet her first. "Oh, Elizabeth, I'm so glad you decided to come."

As if she could have done anything else. Dread settled like a stone at the bottom of her stomach. It took all her strength to stand still and not bolt back the way she'd come.

Ada hugged her then grasped her arm. "Come, I want you meet some of our friends."

Held by Ada's firm grasp, Libby had no way of not following along. At least she recognized Kate and that lady they called Aunt Mae. She was the one who got married on Valentine's Day and then returned this past Friday. Everyone seemed to love her, so she must be a special person.

Ada nodded to a group of women by the steps. "Ladies, I want you to meet a friend of ours from Louisiana. She's staying at the parsonage and helping Erin with the baby."

Libby waited with clenched teeth for their curiosity to kick in and the questions to begin. But it never happened. Instead, sincere smiles beamed at her, and words of welcome poured over her like warm summer rain. She forced a smile to her lips, but it couldn't reach her eyes, which still darted about for signs of her trouble.

Pa couldn't be in town without her knowing it, but she could not afford to let her guard down and not be on the lookout at all times. Ever since Deputy Muldoon asked about a man named Cantrell, she'd been on edge. Her pa must have sent a letter or flyer asking after her.

Her attention drew back to the women when one of them invited her to drop by the town library while in town and fill out a card so she could borrow books. She turned to the woman. "I'm sorry, I didn't catch your name. You said you have a library?"

"Yes, and I'm Abigail Monroe. I run the library and have a lot of books you might enjoy reading. You can have a temporary loan sheet while you're visiting with us. Any idea how long that will be?"

Libby's voice stuck in her throat, and she coughed to try to clear it. She had no idea how long she'd be here or anywhere else, but Miss Monroe deserved an answer of some kind. "I'm not sure just yet. The reverend and Mrs. Winston have been so kind to let me stay with them."

A lady named Mrs. Grayson smiled and patted her arm. "Well, you stay and enjoy yourself. Porterfield is a nice town."

As all the four ladies agreed and nodded, hurt grew deep inside Libby. They were so nice today, but what would they think or say if they knew her background and the way she had lived?

The group proceeded up the steps and into the church

with their husbands. Abigail stayed behind. "Please do drop by the library. I've only been here since last August, and having another young person to visit and chat with will be most welcome. Mrs. Grayson was so right, because the people of this town are wonderful. I don't feel like an outsider anymore."

Appreciation caught in Libby's throat. "Thank you for the invitation. I'll try to come in and check out a book. I enjoy reading." And that was the truth. She'd just never had time for it taking care of Pa.

But her plan to leave that night grew stronger. If she stayed here any longer and became a part of the town, it would be that much harder when someone bared her secret and forced her to leave. Being shunned by the women she'd met thus far would be more devastating than the remarks of the women she'd left behind.

"Good morning, Miss Bradley."

Her heart jumped straight up, and she sucked in her breath. The deputy sheriff stood right beside her with a grin as big as the Texas sky. "Good...good morning." She ducked her head and stared at her toes.

A giggle sounded beside her, and Abigail patted her arm again. "I'm going on in with Elliot. You two don't tarry long. Wouldn't want to miss the sermon."

Libby wanted to shrivel up and disappear right on the spot. Not only was she about to go into church for the first time in many years, but a lawman escorted her. This had not been in her plans when she'd run away from her father.

Something certainly made Elizabeth Bradley nervous this morning. Whether it was because of the questions earlier in the week or because he was a lawman, Cory didn't know. He hadn't been able to get what his ma had told him out of his mind. Seeing Elizabeth here now clad in one of Erin's dresses and shawl delighted him in one way and alarmed him in another.

He followed her toward the front to sit with Erin and the baby. Out of the corner of his eye he spotted the raised eyebrows of Ma. She'd have plenty to say about him sitting up front in church this morning with Elizabeth and Erin instead of his usual spot nearer the back. Of course she'd read more into it than she should, and if he knew Kate and the other women, they'd take it and gnaw it like a bone. With that thought he made an about-face and returned to his regular place by the back door. He could always use the excuse he had to be ready to leave in case of trouble.

He didn't need their help if he wanted a mate. He could make a mess of things all on his own. At least, that's what he'd done with Abigail. Not that he had been in the marrying frame of mind, but the librarian had come close to getting him there. Just as well Doc Elliot had her love. They were much more suitable for one another.

Seth's sermon this morning must be having some effect on Elizabeth Bradley. From his vantage point he watched her lean forward and focus on the preacher. It set Cory to questioning again where she had come from and who had abused her. Just the thought of someone deliberately hurting her caused his blood to boil.

When the service ended, he joined Erin and Miss Bradley on the porch. His sister lifted Connor to her shoulder. "Elizabeth, if you'll watch Connor for me, I can go out and help the ladies get the food ready to be served. You are to eat with our family group, of course, and I don't want to hear any excuses. Right, Cory?"

He nodded. "Of course you'll eat with us. Let's go find a place where you can sit and hold Connor until the ladies are ready to serve."

Erin handed off the baby then scurried across the lawn to help the women setting out food. The church now stood nearly empty, with only a few lingering members. Most already gathered outdoors, ready for the fun.

Elizabeth's face paled, and her eyes grew dark with fear. "I'm not sure I want to stay. There'll be so many people." Elizabeth's hands trembled as she clutched Connor.

"It'll be all right, Miss Bradley."

Finally she nodded. "All right, I'll go to dinner." Cory knew she couldn't turn down Erin's request and not appear rude, especially since the reason for her being here was to take care of the baby.

Cory grasped her arm, and she flinched so that he let it go and simply stood back for her to pass. Whatever tormented Elizabeth stayed in her eyes and the way she walked across the lawn. Even after Ma's hug and Pa's hearty greeting, the fear remained.

Flags of warning cropped up all through him, but Cory chose to ignore them today and concentrate on giving Elizabeth a good afternoon of fun and feasting with the members of the church and the Muldoon family. Perhaps they could all make her forget her fears for the afternoon.

He led her to a grove of trees where tables stood ready for people to bring their plates and enjoy their meal. Cory thanked the Lord for the balmy weather typical of approaching spring in East Texas. Next week they could very well have another freeze. He selected a table and held a chair while Elizabeth seated herself and the baby. He searched his brain for a topic of interest for conversation with Elizabeth until the serving began.

"Now, where did you say you were headed when you came to Porterfield?" Where had that question come from? She'd never said where she was going or exactly where she'd come from. Her eyes clouded over like the sky before a storm, and her lips formed a straight line across her mouth. He'd chosen the wrong thing to ask.

"I didn't say, Mr. Muldoon, and it's really none of your business. If you'd rather I get on with my trip, just say so, and I'll leave." Her words dripped ice even in the warm sunshine.

"Of course it isn't my business. I didn't intend to be nosy. You can stay here in Porterfield as long as you want. Erin certainly enjoys having you around."

Her hands clutched the blanket around Connor, but still they trembled. Cory remembered his mother's words about the wounds on Elizabeth, but why would they cause fear in her today? Then it dawned on him. Most likely she and the Libby Cantrell that this Kurt person was looking for were one and the same, and she now knew that he hunted her. Could this Kurt be her abuser?

Laughter from children and other adults rang in the air, but the silence between them remained thick enough to slice. Seth appeared with a plate in each hand.

"Erin suggested I bring these over to you so you wouldn't have to stand in line with the baby. She'll be over soon as she's finished with the serving." He set the plates on the table. "I'm off to make the rounds. We really appreciate your taking care of Connor for us. He looks quite contented there in your arms."

Elizabeth's cheeks bloomed a bright pink. "Thank you, reverend. I don't mind at all."

Seth left, and Elizabeth remained silent. So much for getting to know more about her. She answered yes or no to most questions and didn't offer any further information. Even after other members of the family arrived and settled around, she didn't contribute to the conversations going on around her. Twice Cory noted her eyes darting about from person to person, and it wasn't from curiosity about the man or woman. What did she expect to find?

Toward the end of the meal Erin gathered Connor in her arms and smiled at Elizabeth. "I've been telling everyone what a wonderful help you've been to me already. I've been able to get so much more done at the church knowing someone is watching out for Connor while I fulfill my duties."

Red crept into Elizabeth's face again, but still her reply consisted of only a few words. "Thank you, but it's been a pleasure."

Kate clinked her knife on her glass, and all eyes turned toward her. A huge grin spread across her face and danced in her eyes as she reached down and grasped Daniel's hand. "We have a wonderful announcement of our own to make today. Come early fall, Daniel and I will become parents."

Cory sat back with a slump. Another sister becoming a mother. An exciting announcement, but it only reminded him of his age and the fact he had no family of his own. He had vowed not to marry, but for a moment he regretted that vow. Envy for what his brothers and sisters had filled him with a longing he couldn't fight. Would he ever find a love that would lead to marriage and children?

Ma and the others all gathered around Kate and Daniel. Cory could give his congratulations later and tease Kate about her lack of household expertise. She'd make a wonderful mother though. Her treatment of the children in the infirmary attested to that.

A flash of color beside him caused him to snap around as Elizabeth pushed back her chair. "I have to leave. I'm not feeling well."

A gasp sounded around the table, and questions of concern rose in the faces of those there. Kate started to go after her, but Cory caught her arm. "No, you stay here, I'll go."

He hurried after her and reached out to grab her arm. She jerked away with such force it knocked the breath out of him. Her eyes filled with something he couldn't quite determine. Could she be that afraid of him or dislike him that much?

"Please, just let me go. I don't belong here with all this family talk."

"Let me at least walk you back to the parsonage."

"No." She bit her lip. "I...I really need to be alone right now. Stay with your family, and tell Erin I've gone back to the house."

Cory followed her to the edge of the church lawn, but she didn't look back and almost ran away from him. Determination filled him to find the cause behind her fears and that strange look she'd just now given him. For once the stubborn will of the Muldoon clan would come in handy, because he wouldn't rest until he found the truth about Elizabeth Bradley.

CHAPTER
TWELVE

*L*IBBY STOOD OVER her bed and packed her satchel for the second time in four days. The urge to slip away in the night filled her once again. Sunday night Erin had been up much of the night with a colicky Connor, so Libby abandoned her plan to leave. Today, more family would be arriving from Connecticut for Abigail's wedding. With so many people around, no one would notice her absence until she could be well on her way, possibly as early as this afternoon.

A sob caught in her throat as she folded a dress on her bed. She had recoiled at Deputy Muldoon's touch on Sunday when she had wanted to leave. He meant her no harm, but she couldn't rid her mind of how men had grabbed at her before. Shudders shook her body so that she clasped her arms around her middle to try and stop them. Would she ever be able to forget?

She remembered the night the deputy found her and how safe she'd felt in his arms as he carried her to the doctor. In the dark of night and in her weakened state, she could accept his assurance that he wanted to help. In the cold, hard daylight of reality she saw it for what it had been—the simple rescue of a girl in trouble. The deputy would do that for anyone he found in her condition.

He had not attempted to see her in the days since Sunday, and she had stayed close to the house to avoid seeing him on the streets. His attention on Sunday had only served to bring back all her fears and distrust of men. They were all polite, but so had been the others at first. She had learned that men were interested in only one thing once they had her alone.

She closed the satchel and secured the lock then shoved it under her bed. Everything would fall into place, and she'd be out of here tonight. She had to get farther away before Pa tracked her down and before Deputy Muldoon found out who she was and sent her back to him.

She trusted Rev. Winston only because of the minister back home, who had tried to help her several times. The pastor had been kind when Ma passed away, but the members had been so rude and cruel after Pa had become the town drunk that Pa had promised to never darken the door again. She couldn't and wouldn't believe that God would take care of her, nor could she believe the people here would be any different once they learned about her past.

A knock sounded on the door frame, and Erin stepped through. "Elizabeth, I'm getting ready to go to the library to help Abigail. She's due over at Mrs. Bennett's for a fitting for her wedding dress, and then her parents are coming in on the afternoon train. I've put Connor down for his nap. When he wakes up, you can bring him down to the library if you'd like."

"Didn't I hear that the reverend's family is coming too?"

"Yes, they'll all come together. With Rachel's baby due at the same time as the wedding, they decided to all make the trip now. Seth's parents haven't seen Connor, so this will be a joyous time for everyone."

It also meant more people around. Erin would need this space for some of them to sleep. The parsonage had four bedrooms, but Erin wouldn't need help with her family here, and Libby would only be in the way of the family gathering. The request to tend to Connor offered the perfect solution for her leaving, this time in daylight.

"I'll bring Connor to the library when he wakes up, and you can take him to the depot to meet his grandparents." Then she'd come back here and leave. Her saddle lay ready to put on Yeller Boy in the carriage house and stable behind the parsonage. She could finish packing and get the horse ready while Connor napped. With the help of daylight and the mild weather, she should be able to make good time before anyone noticed her absence.

"That will be perfect. Ma and Pa are coming in to meet the train. Micah and Noah, Rachel's brothers, will be staying out at the ranch. Seth thought they'd enjoy seeing how a ranch is run and riding horses out there." Erin wrapped a light shawl about her shoulders and pinned a hat atop her head.

Libby walked downstairs with Erin with plans to see what food she could take with her that would not be missed too much. Some might call it stealing, but for her it meant survival.

Once Erin left, Libby checked on Connor then went about getting ready to take her leave. She must write a note and let Erin know not to worry and to enjoy her family's visit.

By the time Connor awakened, she had everything ready in the coach house. Soon as she delivered the baby to his mother, she could get back here and be gone before the train even arrived.

Libby changed Connor's diaper, dressed him in the outfit Erin had laid out, and wrapped him in a lightweight blanket. The baby cooed and made gurgling sounds in his throat and moved his head as though taking in everything he could see. She caressed his cheek and head, and he smiled at her. Oh, how she would miss this baby. He'd been the light of her life the past week.

She could do nothing to change the past, and she must stop thinking about it. After pinning her shawl and getting her hat, she placed Connor in his basket and headed the six blocks to the library.

Cotton puff clouds drifted across the blue sky. Suspended in space, they appeared as though one could reach right up and pull one down. Sunshine warmed her shoulders and gave her hope for a safe journey. This time she'd have daylight to guide her way, and she wouldn't become disoriented and lost among the trees. The sun would tell her which direction to go.

Satisfied with her decision, she made her way to the library. Several people she had met at church waved to her and spoke a greeting. She would miss the town, the Muldoon family, and especially the baby, but they would all be better off without her.

The bell jangled when she opened the door, and Erin looked up from helping a woman with checking out books. She turned, and Libby recognized the doctor's wife. "Good afternoon, Mrs. Jensen."

A smile lit up the older woman's face, and her brown eyes

twinkled. "Hello, Elizabeth. It's so good to see you healthy and happy. Such a vast improvement over the first time I saw you."

Heat rose in Libby's face. She may look healthy, but she was a far cry from the latter. She wouldn't be happy until she was as far away from here as she could get and had found a way to make a living for herself. "Thank you, Mrs. Jensen."

Mrs. Jensen left after she admired the baby and patted Libby's shoulder. Erin took the basket from Libby. "I didn't even think about it, but you could have ridden into town with Seth. He's bringing the carriage so we can take Miriam back to our home. You'll really enjoy Rachel's sister. She's sixteen and a very pretty girl. From what I remember, she loves to talk, and she's as sweet as Rachel is."

So that's why the carriage hadn't been in there when Libby had gone to saddle Yeller Boy. Miriam was a lucky girl to have such a wonderful family at her age. At seventeen Libby had already seen a side of life no young girl should ever have to see or be a part of. Good thing she planned to leave before anyone knew that.

"I'm sure I will. If you don't need me for anything, I thought I'd go back to the house and make sure everything is all ready for your guest."

"You'll do no such a thing. We'll all go to the station together to meet our family. After all, you're a part of us now."

Before Libby could open her mouth to protest, the bell jingled, and Deputy Muldoon walked through the door. Her heart leaped to her throat. He looked so handsome in his light brown shirt and brown leather vest. His boots, shiny and waxed instead of dusty, peeked from beneath his trousers. He'd left his gun belt somewhere else for this afternoon, and he held his white Stetson loosely in his hands. Why did he have to come in and spoil her chance to get away?

He strode across the room to the checkout desk, where he plopped his hat and hugged his sister before bending over Connor. "Hey, little buddy, you all ready to meet your grandparents? They're going to think you're the best-looking kid they've ever seen."

Then he straightened and ran his hand through dark red curls. "I saw Seth headed this way with the carriage, but I'd call it a privilege to walk down to the depot with you, Miss Bradley."

Her blood turned to ice in her veins, and she trembled in spite of her attempt to control her feelings. "No, I plan to go back to the parsonage and wait there."

Erin pursed her lips and shook her head. "I told her she didn't have to do that. We want her at the station with us. You'll have to convince her to stay."

When he turned his smile toward her and gazed at her with those green eyes, all resolve began to melt. She had to get away before it completely thawed in a puddle about her feet. "I really don't need to be there with all the family. There'll be so many people."

"Nonsense. Erin wants you there, and that's where you should be."

"That's exactly what I told her. Now, you go with him, Elizabeth. I see Seth at the door, and we're ready to close up and head that way." She shooed them toward the door. "Now go, so I can lock up."

Against her will, Libby left with the deputy. How in the world could she get out of this?

Elizabeth's facial expression and her posture shouted her
displeasure with him, but she had no choice. Erin could be
quite the boss when she wanted to be. Remembering the
way Elizabeth had flinched when he reached for her arm last
Sunday, he kept a bit of distance between them, although they
were side by side.

"I still don't see why Erin thought I should be at the station to meet these families. I don't know them, and they don't
know me. I could be back at the house making sure everything
is ready."

Cory laughed and shook his head. "Knowing my sister, she
has the house spotless and all she needs prepared in advance.
I've never seen anyone so organized as she is. Even Kate gets a
scolding every now and then for not keeping things straight."

"Your sisters both seem to be careful women. Erin said
that Miriam, Seth's younger sister, would be staying with
them. Don't they need my room? I could go somewhere else."

Maybe that was what really bothered Elizabeth. "No, the
boys will stay at the ranch, Rev. and Mrs. Winston will be at
Rachel's to be there when the baby is born, and Abigail's parents are staying with Kate and Daniel." One good thing about
large families all in the same town: they always had room for
visitors.

They walked past the bakery, and the aroma of fresh
bread made his stomach rumble. Heat rose in his face, and he
shrugged. "Sorry about that. Sam makes about the best bread
you can buy. His pies are excellent too." Sam had brought pie

to the sheriff's office more than a few times, and if Cory didn't watch it, his waistline would match that of the baker.

Miss Bradley sniffed the air, and the aroma forced a smile from her. "Hmm, it does smell good, and if my nose is right, Annie's serving corned beef and cabbage to her guests today."

"You're right, and it's one of my favorites. Aunt Mae and Annie make good corned beef, but it can't hold a candle to Ma's. She makes it like her grandmother did in the old country. You'll have to go out to the ranch sometime and try it."

Her face became serious again, and she turned away from him. What could be so wrong about going out to the ranch again? Whatever the reason, he wanted to take back the words and return to the pleasant conversation they had begun. Being around Miss Bradley and trying to talk with her had him walking on eggshells all the time. But he'd keep trying until she decided to tell him whatever it was that kept her so wary of her surroundings.

Even as they strolled down Main Street, her eyes darted about as though on the lookout for someone. If someone had followed her or hunted her, they certainly should have found her by now, but then again, if that person had no idea in which direction she'd gone, it may be months before he or she found her. He hoped to know a whole lot more about her before then. He should have an answer from his wire in a day or so.

A blast from the train whistle split the air, and Cory picked up his pace. "Come on, Miss Bradley. The train will be here any minute." He started to reach for her hand to pull her along but stopped just in time as she stepped back.

"I'll...I'll just stand back and watch."

"Erin would hang me if I let you do that. Please help me stay alive." He tilted his head and grinned in hopes that a little teasing would break out a smile. He almost shouted when her lips curved, only slightly, but the smile still came through.

"Now, I suppose I can't let that happen." She side-stepped him then strode toward the station.

Cory hurried to catch up. So many people milled about on the station platform that he had to stop at the steps leading up to it. A good number of them were there for the Winston and Monroe families, but a number of men from the sawmill were there, as well as several other families from town.

When the train arrived, he noted that it carried an extra passenger car, and people spilled out of the brown-trimmed green cars like bees from a hive. At the sight of so many people, Miss Bradley cringed beside him and visibly shrank back from the noise. The instinct to protect her from whatever or whomever she feared sprang to his heart. He stepped closer to her to act as a shield against the throng.

He'd never been around a woman so skittish about large groups of people. The more he saw of her and her behavior, the more curious and anxious he became about her background. Would she ever trust him enough to tell him the truth about herself?

CHAPTER
THIRTEEN

*O*NCE AGAIN LIBBY put aside plans to leave until after Abigail and Elliot's wedding on Saturday. With so much going on and so many visitors, Erin needed all the help she could get. Erin's greatest worry at the moment involved Rachel Reed, who was already several days past her due date. Erin told Libby to pray extra hard that the baby didn't decide to arrive in the middle of the wedding.

Pray? That brought a laugh now as Libby dressed to attend the late afternoon wedding ceremony. She hadn't prayed about anything for a very long time. God probably didn't even remember her name, so He certainly wouldn't listen to her prayers. He had too many others to care about.

Abigail wanted to be married just before dusk so that the sunset would be part of her wedding. She said something about the sun setting on her old life and the sunrise on Sunday being the beginning of a new and wonderful life with Elliot. Such high hopes and wonderful dreams brought an ache to Libby's heart.

Would she ever experience what Abigail, Kate, and Erin had in their lives? Although drawn to the deputy because of his care and concern for her, she grew tense every time he came near. Except for the night he carried her, his touch had sent a shudder through her bones. His closeness did things to her that she didn't understand. Between her father's beatings and other men's attention, she had no time to understand anything but fear of men.

When things settled down after the wedding, she planned to leave and get as far away from Porterfield as she could with what little money she managed to save. How close she'd come to being found out last week. As soon as she could leave the Monroe house, she had run back to the carriage house and unsaddled Yeller Boy. Then she raced up to her room with her satchel and hid it under the bed to be unpacked later. Knowing Ada, she'd worry herself sick about Libby's disappearance and would send her son Cory searching for her, and the family didn't need that distraction with the wedding and a baby due all at the same time.

A knock sounded on the door, followed by Miriam's voice. "May I come in, Elizabeth?"

"Of course." She turned to face the girl. "Oh my, you are certainly elegant in that green dress, and it makes your eyes shine bright." Thick, curled eyelashes accented Miriam's brown eyes and would be the envy of other young women as she grew older.

"Thank you, and you are beautiful. I wish I could wear my hair curled and up on the back of my head like that. I love your dress too."

Erin had given Libby another one of the dresses she no longer wore, and the dark blue complemented her coloring.

She ran her hands over the lustrous fabric trimmed with rows of ecru lace on the bodice from shoulder to waist. Never had she worn such an elegant dress. It had taken three petticoats to keep the skirt from looking limp and lifeless.

She bounced one of the curls on Miriam's shoulders. "Someday you'll be old enough to wear your hair up. Don't rush it, and enjoy these years you have with your family." How she envied Miriam and the love she had from her parents and her brothers and sister. To have a mother and father who took care of her and brothers and sisters to play with was a blessing Miriam probably took for granted.

Miriam twirled around, causing her skirt to billow out in a balloon of silk. "I'm supposed to go to Bainbridge Academy next year like Rachel did, but I'm not sure that's what I want to do now that I've visited Texas again."

Libby picked up the feathery-light shawl that matched her dress then wrapped her arm around Miriam's shoulders. "You're but sixteen, and going to school is important for young women today." And Libby would give anything to have had that opportunity. "Texas will be here long after you finish your schooling."

Miriam let out a long, lingering sigh. "I know, but it's just so romantic out here in the west—cowboys and marshals and lots of horses and cows and open land everywhere. Noah and Micah are so lucky they get to stay out at the ranch."

They reached the bottom of the stairs to be met by Seth. "And you don't enjoy staying with us?"

Miriam's cheeks flushed a bright pink. "Of course I do, and I love being around little Connor. It's just that I'd like to see more of the country around here."

Seth winked at Libby and smiled at his sister. "Then we'll have to do something about that this week. I imagine we can find you a horse to ride so you can explore—not by yourself, mind you, but with a riding companion."

Miriam reached up and hugged Seth. "Oh, thank you. I should have said something before now, but I guess we've been too busy for that."

Seth kept his arm around Miriam, but the beam of joy remained as he gazed at Libby. "I must say that you look stunning yourself, Miss Bradley. I know one deputy sheriff who won't be able to take his eyes off you."

Heat filled Libby's face. That's the last thing she wanted to have happen. She'd much rather fade into the background and not be noticed. "Thank you, Rev. Winston. Isn't it time to be at the church?" She had to draw attention away from herself in any way she could this evening.

With the big party planned at the town hall after the ceremony, all eyes would be on the bride and groom, not her. For that she could be thankful, but if she had her way, she wouldn't be at the party at all.

Erin entered carrying Connor. "Well, it looks like we're all ready to go." She tilted her head to one side and grinned at Libby. "I must say that dress looks nicer on you than it ever did on me. The color suits your blonde hair."

Libby murmured her thank-you and hurried to leave the house with Miriam right behind her. They walked across the wide expanse of lawn and the area where wagons, carriages, buggies, and surreys parked. Although the spring season hadn't officially arrived, the trees already sported fresh green buds, and early daffodils and narcissus bloomed at the front steps to the church.

A great crowd attested to how much the town liked the librarian. Libby had grown to like the young woman too and would have treasured her friendship, but staying in town to develop it was not an option she had.

Seeing as how this was her first ever wedding, Libby had no idea what to expect and watched the others closely to know how to act. Miriam rushed ahead to find a seat with her parents and brothers. Rachel, her stomach swollen with her unborn child, sat on a back seat with Nathan beside her. Libby didn't know much about childbirth, but it sure looked like that baby was ready to come.

Libby stood with the others as Abigail walked down the aisle with her father. Libby's eyes misted over at how beautiful the young woman looked in her ivory-colored gown with more lace adorning it than Libby had ever seen in her lifetime.

When Seth started the ceremony, she tried not to listen to the words. Instead she concentrated on how and when she'd be able to leave.

Cory sat a few rows behind where Elizabeth Bradley sat with Erin. Her beauty stunned him to the point he hadn't even been able to approach her to say hello. The elegant hairstyle set off her blue eyes and high cheekbones. He breathed deeply several times to keep his heart from bouncing right out of his chest to land at Miss Bradley's feet.

He shook his gaze away from her and concentrated on the church and Seth's words. It had looked nice for Aunt Mae's wedding, but today it was only what he could describe as elegant. The Monroe family had spared no expense in having flowers shipped in and securing enough candles and candelabras for decoration. If this was a sample of what they'd planned, his mouth fairly drooled at the thought of what the party would be like.

When Seth mentioned the word *obey*, Cory furrowed his brow. That was one word he wanted to omit from his own ceremony if he ever married. He wanted his wife to respect him and honor him, not be cowering in obedience.

True, the Bible said wives should submit to their husbands, but that didn't mean they couldn't have their own opinions and ideas. Daniel had shown that with Kate, and it impressed Cory to see how Daniel respected Kate and her desires to study medicine, and Kate had shown a great deal of respect for Daniel and his position as county attorney.

Then he shook himself to clear his head of such thoughts. He had no plans at all to be married, so it was a moot point, one he'd never have to worry about. Then his gaze landed on Miss Bradley, and all sensible reasoning went out right out of his head. He heard nothing of the remainder of the ceremony, his concentration being on the girl with the golden hair.

As soon as the couple walked back up the aisle and the guests began milling about, Cory searched for Miss Bradley. When she lifted her head and turned to see him, she leaned over to say something to Erin, then skirted around the pulpit area to the back door and disappeared. He rubbed his fingers across his chin. Had he made her that afraid of him?

He turned and greeted the Winston family, who had been seated in the row behind. "It's nice to see you again, Rev.

Winston. You must be really proud of Seth. He's grown a lot in his sermons since his arrival three years ago."

"Well, I haven't heard him preach yet, but Mrs. Winston and I are proud of both Seth and Rachel. They seem to have made a place for themselves here without any problem. Will we see you at the party?"

"You certainly will." He turned and smiled at Miriam. "And I expect this pretty young lady to save a dance for me."

Miriam's cheeks turned pink, but she returned his smile. "I'd like that, thank you."

"Then I'll see all of you at the town hall. I can't wait to see what Sam has done for the refreshments."

A few minutes later he swung up onto his horse and headed toward town. All the way he kept an eye out for Elizabeth Bradley, but either she didn't plan to come or she was already there helping get things ready. His hopes lay with the latter.

When he dismounted at town hall, lively music already rang in the air. Porterfield's musical ensemble had a workout this past month with two weddings and a birthday party dance for the Grayson daughter a few weeks ago. Now that the weather turned more toward spring, they'd be busy with the town socials again. Maybe... no, he wouldn't go there.

He entered the building already filled with folks wishing the couple good times and a happy marriage. He sauntered over to the table to see what good things Sam had made. There the baker had laid out an array of pastries, cheeses, breads, and cakes, along with punch and coffee. Every bit of it looked so good that Cory figured he'd try them all.

A flash of blue caught his eye, and he spotted Elizabeth

Bradley with Miriam getting a cup of punch. He filled his own plate then sauntered over to where they were both seated. "May I join you two lovely ladies?"

Miriam beamed up at him. "Oh, yes, Mr....I mean, Deputy Muldoon, please do."

He spoke to the girl but stared at Miss Bradley. How he wished to call her Elizabeth, but it wouldn't be proper. "Only if you stop calling me Deputy Muldoon and call me Cory. After all, your brother is married to my sister, so we're family."

"All right, Cory it is. I like having another brother. I bet you wouldn't be as big a pest as Micah and Noah are. Of course, since Noah is off at school now, he doesn't bother me as much. Did you know he's going to be a veteger...vetinarigen...oh, you know, an animal doctor. I never could pronounce that word."

All the while Miriam prattled on about her brothers, Miss Bradley never once looked directly at him. If he found a pause in Miriam's monologue, he'd speak to her and perhaps ask her to dance when the music started up.

"Don't you think so, Cory?"

Cory snapped his attention back to Miriam. "I'm sorry, don't I think what?"

"I knew you didn't hear me. I said Elizabeth is one of the prettiest girls here and asked if you agreed."

Miss Bradley's face filled with color, and her hands trembled so that her punch cup rattled on the plate. She set the plate in her lap and gripped the edges so tight that she might have broken them with only a little more pressure.

"Yes, I do agree with you."

The fiddler tapped his bow. "Choose your partners, here we go." Then the music filled the room. Cory didn't recognize the tune, but then he never paid that much attention to music anyway.

Cory turned to the young woman. "May I have the pleasure of the first dance, Miss Bradley?"

She raised her head, and her eyes were wide with a mixture of emotions. "No. I mean, I'm sorry, but I have to go and tend to some things." She jumped up with her plate and cup rattling and hurried away.

Miriam put her hands on her hips. "That's the strangest thing I ever saw. You'd think she was scared of you or didn't like you, but that's weird because you're handsome with your red curly hair, and you're so tall. Just like a sheriff should be."

Forget Miss Bradley and her cold-shouldered attitude. He grinned at Miriam. "I believe this is our dance then, Miss Winston." He'd take Miriam's chatter over the icy treatment of Miss Bradley any day. Well, at least tonight he would.

Even as he swung Miriam about the floor, his mind wouldn't leave Elizabeth Bradley. Whatever frightened her in her past haunted her in the present. No matter what he did, he could make no headway with her.

There he went again. He had to make up his mind. Either he planned to stay single, or he planned to get to know Elizabeth better. If he managed to get to know her or get her to pay attention to him, would she be the kind of woman he would want to court, much less marry?

After the dance he headed toward the back of the hall to hunt for her. Just then Frank Cahoon called to him. "Cory,

Sheriff Rutherford needs you. There's been a ruckus at the saloon, and I think somebody was shot."

Cory's lawman instincts took over, and he sped from the hall, all thoughts of Elizabeth Bradley fleeing from his mind.

Kurt counted his money again. Just a little more, and he'd have enough to get out and find Libby. Odd jobs around town offered some, but he still needed more. He'd abandoned the idea of selling everything and taking off. Too many men here in town asked about her, and the saloon owner said he'd be glad to have her back.

Tonight he'd be sweeping and cleaning up around the diner. Murphy, the owner and chief cook, had been one of Libby's admirers. When Kurt said he needed a job to make money to find her and bring her home, Murphy had given him a job three nights a week to clean up after everyone left.

How tempted he was to sit in on a card game and have a few drinks, but the image of Libby in her fancy clothes, her face made up, and her hair all in pretty curls kept him sober. He planned to buy a suit and dress himself like a businessman and hunt for the daughter who'd run away from home. Her age didn't deter him. She may be old enough to be on her own, but he was still her pa, and he had rights.

Kurt tucked the money away in a cotton pouch and stowed it behind a loose board in the floor. He made sure it was secure before pulling the braided rug over it. Even if someone pulled the rug back, unless he knew which board, he wouldn't find it.

Now shaven and hair combed, he made his way to the

diner just before closing time. One of the side benefits included a meal on the night he worked. The music of the saloon pulled him that direction, but he made a steadfast path to the diner, keeping the image of Libby solid in his mind.

One of the waitresses greeted him when he entered. "Evenin', Mr. Cantrell. Murphy has your supper waitin' in the kitchen for ya."

"Thanks." He hurried back to where Murphy dished up one last plate for a late customer.

Murphy grinned and nodded toward a counter. "There's your supper plate. Had a good crowd tonight with not many leftovers."

"Thanks, Murph. I'm hungry tonight." He donned an apron then picked up the plate and some cutlery and took a seat at a table near the kitchen door. Only three or four patrons lingered over dinner, with the one late diner just beginning his meal. As soon as he had his belly full, Kurt would wipe down all the tables, put on clean tablecloths, and sweep out the place. Then he'd take home any leftover food Murphy set aside for him.

Funny how he was better fed and better paid now that he'd been sober for a few weeks. People treated him differently when he was cleaned up. Maybe he'd do better business with Libby if the men knew her pa was a good man. That way they couldn't cheat him out of paying what they owed.

The stranger who had come in late approached Kurt's table. "Excuse me, aren't you Kurt Cantrell?"

Kurt eyed the man, taking in his pinstripe suit and black vest, the watch chain across his middle, and the silk tie at his collar. "Yes, I am. Who's asking?"

"My name isn't important. I heard you have a little lady who can give a man a good time for an evening." The man hooked his thumbs in his vest pockets and peered at Kurt with piercing brown eyes.

"You heard right, but she ain't here right now. Away on a short trip. You just passin' through?"

"Um…yes, I am. That's too bad. Thought I'd have a good companion while I'm here. Guess I'll go on over to the saloon and check out the ladies there." He turned and sauntered out the door.

Murphy locked the door and returned to sit by Kurt. "Sounds like Libby is gettin' famous around these parts. How soon you think you can bring her back?"

"I don't know. Depends on how far she's gotten in these few weeks. Wherever she is, I aim to find her and get her back where she belongs." At least that was his plan.

"Good, and I'll be glad when you do. I miss her. Whenever she came to get a few supplies, my Gertie tried to help her." He shoved his chair back and stood. "I'll finish up in the kitchen and let you get to work out here." He paused at the door. "Kurt, are you sure you want to bring Libby back to the old life?"

Kurt handed him the empty dishes. "I have to, and I sure appreciate your letting me do this, Murph."

The cook smiled and backed his way through the kitchen door. "Anything that will help you get on your feet, Kurt. Just remember, you don't have to live like you did before. You were a good carpenter once, and you can be again. Do it for Libby. She deserves a better life than what she had."

At first anger rose in Kurt. Murph had no business trying

to tell him what to do. He grabbed the damp cloth and began wiping down the tables. Then anger subsided, and doubt for what he had done crept in. Maybe Libby did deserve a better life. But did he have it in him to provide it for her?

CHAPTER FOURTEEN

*T*HE DAY AFTER the wedding Libby didn't have to fake an illness. The headache that began last night pounded in her temples and all but blinded her with pain. At least the headache had allowed her to leave the reception early and gave her an excuse to skip church this morning.

Libby pulled the covers up to her chin and closed her eyes against the light of the new day. Sleep still would not come to ease what seemed like horses pounding in her head. Deputy Muldoon's face at the wedding party last night kept intruding on her thoughts. He'd wanted to dance, but the idea of being that close to him troubled her. The deputy may be a Christian, but he was still a man, and she never wanted to be close to a man again.

A few minutes later Erin knocked then came into the room. Libby didn't raise her head, but she saw the tray in Erin's hands.

"I fixed you a cup of herbal tea and a few slices of toast. Ma always gave me some when I felt poorly. The toast will help keep you filled until dinnertime. We'll just have a quiet dinner here instead of going to Aunt Mae's. Connor was around a lot of people last night, and I think it's best for him to be at home with just us today."

Libby only nodded and tried to sit up. Erin helped with the pillows, and in a minute Libby sat back and raised the tea to her lips. It not only warmed her as it went down, but it soothed and relaxed the muscles that tensed up when she had a headache.

"Thank you, Erin. You are such a good minister's wife. You look after everybody, and I do appreciate it right now."

"The house will be nice and quiet in a few minutes, so maybe you can get some rest." Erin hurried to the windows and pulled the draperies closed. "There, that should be better. I know light can sometimes make a headache feel worse."

She strode toward the door then turned to Libby just before closing it. "We won't be long, and I do hope you will be able to sleep."

After Erin left, Libby finished the tea and toast spread with fresh butter and Ada's homemade blackberry jam. With the mild temperatures outdoors the house needed no heat to keep it pleasant, but sleep still eluded Libby. So much had happened in the past two weeks that her mind whirled with all the names and faces she had met.

So far every plan made for running away had been thwarted, but she wouldn't give up in her attempts. The day Mr. and Mrs. Fuller arrived back in Porterfield would have been perfect if Cory and Erin hadn't corralled her into going to the station to meet them.

Now today she'd be alone, and once again any chance to escape eluded her because of her headache. The side that longed for a home and family to love her clashed with the side that reminded her of her past. No matter how she looked at things, it always came back to the simple fact that she wasn't Elizabeth Bradley but Libby Cantrell. Every day she remained in the Winston home, that truth became more and more difficult for her to hide, because it meant one more day for Pa to find her.

Voices from downstairs broke through Libby's consciousness. She shook her head and frowned. She must have finally fallen asleep if Erin and the others were back from church. She sat up on the side of the bed and discovered her head didn't hurt nearly as much as it had earlier. Sleep must have done more than give her rest.

Her stomach rumbled in hunger, but dare she venture downstairs to find something to eat? Getting out of her nightclothes might help.

A few minutes later, dressed in a fresh frock, she combed through her hair and tied it loosely at the nape of her neck. If she went down quietly, she could listen and see if anyone besides Erin and the reverend had come back here from church.

Just as she reached the middle of the stairway, Deputy Muldoon's voice stopped her cold in her tracks. Her heart raced, and her hand trembled on the banister. What was he doing here? Why wasn't he with his parents at the boardinghouse? She turned to head back upstairs when she heard her name. Libby sank onto the steps and listened. The deputy said he had missed her in church this morning.

Seth replied, "When Erin went in to check on her, Elizabeth had a headache and didn't want to get up, so she stayed home."

"She seemed out of sorts at the party last evening as well. Too bad I had to leave when I did, or I could have walked her home."

Libby bit her lip, thankful she'd left before he had a chance to find her. Seth said, "I heard about the shooting at the saloon. Anyone hurt badly?"

"No, two men got into a fight over a poker game, and one pulled a gun on the other. Rutherford arrested the shooter, and the other man will live, so it won't be murder."

"Seems like a lot of things have happened in the past year. When I first came, not much ever happened."

"That's true. Must be because the town's growing so fast."

Libby stood to return to her room. No telling how long these men would talk. Just as she started up, Seth mentioned her name. She sat back down to listen.

"Yes, Erin really enjoys having Elizabeth around." A pause came followed by a few more words from Seth. "Have you learned any more about that girl Libby Cantrell you told me about last week?"

"Not yet. No one has answered the wire I sent to Louisiana asking Kurt Cantrell what his daughter looks like."

"He might be coming to see for himself if it's his Libby here."

Her heart shattered with those words. The pain went deeper than she could ever imagine. Deputy Muldoon had betrayed her and wired her father. Libby didn't wait to hear the rest. She tiptoed back up the stairs, but Miriam bursting through the door downstairs stopped her once again in the upstairs hallway.

"Rachel's having her baby. Nathan took her over to the

infirmary, and Doc Elliot is with them. Mama said we should all go over there and wait."

Seth shouted, "I'm going to be an uncle. Let's go. Erin, get Connor so he can meet his new cousin."

"What about Elizabeth? Are you going to leave her here?" Deputy Muldoon asked.

Erin's voice joined them. "With a headache like she described, she won't want to go anywhere. She'll be all right here. I'll leave a note in the kitchen with her plate from dinner."

A few minutes later the voices faded as they left the house. Libby hurried back to her room. What a lucky break. With Rachel's baby on the way, everyone would be tied up for hours. She'd have plenty of time to saddle Yeller Boy and make her getaway.

Her headache forgotten, Libby stuffed a few clothes into her satchel but left most of the clothes Erin had given her. She then went down to the kitchen for something to eat. The plate Erin mentioned sat covered with a napkin on the table. Libby first ate it then packed a few leftovers in a box and placed it in her satchel. She filled her canteen with water then hurried out to the stable for Yeller Boy.

As an afterthought she wrote a note to Erin and Seth thanking them for their hospitality and kindness then tacked it to the stable post, where they would find it. "OK, Yeller Boy. Here we go again, but this time we won't have to worry about being followed."

She led the horse from the stable and out into the yard. A stiff breeze whipped her hair about her face, and a chill filled the air. When had the sky become so dark and cloudy? Only an hour ago the sun shone amidst scattered clouds. Rain would come from those rolling, dark clouds now filling the sky. She remembered a slicker hanging by the back door and ran to get it. Erin would understand why she had borrowed it.

She laid the rain cloak across the saddle and hoisted herself up. With a flick of the reins, Yeller Boy turned toward the fields and trees at the edge of town. She dug her heels into the horse's flank, and he raced away toward freedom once again.

⁓⁂⁓

By the time they reached the infirmary, Doc Jensen had Rachel in a room with her mother by her side. Cory stayed out on the boardwalk, worried over the sudden change in the weather.

The sky rolled with dark clouds that turned afternoon daylight to dusk. He stepped inside, where all the family still filled the waiting room in anticipation of the arrival of Rachel's baby. Nathan paced the floor, and the others huddled in chairs near the front door.

Erin approached him. "I hope this weather doesn't get any worse. Doc Elliot and Abigail were at the Jensen place, so they came when Nathan went to get them. Elliot's with Rachel and her mother, but Abigail went to the Reed house to help Aunt Mae make sure everything's ready for the baby's arrival home."

What a way to spend the day after your wedding, but Elliot had purposely stayed in town because of Rachel. The situation made Cory even happier he wasn't a doctor. He removed his hat and addressed the group. "It looks like a major storm is headed this way. I see lightning to the north. I'll keep a close eye on the weather, because we may all have to head for the storm cellars."

Mrs. Monroe clung to his arm. "But what about Rachel and the baby? You can't move them to a storm cellar."

Cory removed her hands and held them. "Let me talk to Kate. We'll think of something."

What that might be he had no idea, but Kate and Doc Elliot would. He knocked on the door to the room where Rachel was and heard her scream out. Kate opened the door and stuck her head out. "Cory, what are you doing here? The baby will be here any minute."

Cory grabbed Kate's arm before she disappeared back into the room. "Kate, wait a minute."

Kate stared hard at Cory. "Better be a good reason for this."

"There is. A bad storm is headed this way, and we may need to get everyone into the storm cellars. Can you move Rachel?"

"Not now, but as soon as the baby comes we can move her to the cellar here. It may not be as safe as the one at her house, but that's too far to take her."

Cory blew out his breath. "All right, that will have to do. I'll let you know if the move becomes necessary. I just hope that baby gets here quick."

Kate glanced over her shoulder. "It shouldn't be long now. I have to go." She slammed the door just as Rachel screamed out again. He shuddered and glanced at Nathan, who had stopped and stared at the closed door with wide-open eyes and a face as pale as the sheets on the infirmary beds.

After explaining to Mr. Winston what they planned to do if the storm came, he strode toward the second examining room, where Doc Jensen checked on the gunshot victim. "What do you have, Doc?"

The older doctor's mustache twitched. "He'll live. He lost a lot of blood, but I stitched him up, and he'll be fine in a few days. I just changed the bandages. You want to take him on down to the jail?"

"Not now. A bad storm is coming. I spotted lightning in the south. I think it's still several miles out, but it sure looks like it holds a lot of rain. I'm going to keep an eye on it and make sure we can get everyone to safety if we have to. Mayor Tate will ring the bell in the clock tower if the storm gets worse. I fear a twister this time of year."

"Just let me know. The cellar should hold us, and this building is pretty sturdy. I think we'll be OK if we stay here."

"Good. I'll go out and see what's happening." He jammed his hat back on and headed outdoors. The wind had picked up, and the streets were just about deserted. Cory walked a block to get a better view of the sky. Swirling clouds of dust stirred up around his feet, and the force of the wind grew stronger. The way the clouds rolled and the green tint in the atmosphere spelled trouble. He turned to go back to the infirmary just as the bell from the courthouse rang out, warning the people of Porterfield to take cover.

Rain now pelted the earth, followed by hailstones that pounded the street. Then suddenly it stopped, but the wind continued. The boarders at Aunt Mae's were headed into the storm cellar there, as were others up and down the streets and roads leading from town. Fighting the wind, Cory made his way back to the infirmary.

He burst through the doors into the waiting room to find it empty except for Nathan carrying Rachel, Kate holding the baby, and Doc Elliot leading the way down to the cellar. When he entered the stairway, Cory closed the door behind him and descended the steps. Although musty smelling, the space was big enough for everyone, including the shooting victim. Mr. Winston and Seth had brought cots from upstairs for both Rachel and the other patient. Erin had already lit a few oil lamps, and they sent their glow to ease the darkness.

Cory made his way over to Rachel, who held the baby in her arms. The baby's dark eyes stared up at him. "Hello there. You certainly picked a fine night to join this world. Welcome."

The baby's eyes blinked then closed. The tiny sucking motion and sound of its mouth touched a spot of longing deep inside Cory that he'd never had before. A lump formed in his throat. Was he being too hasty in thinking he should never marry?

Rachel smiled and caressed the baby's face with her fingers. "Her name is Felicity Hope, which means 'happiness,' and of course 'hope,' and that's what we have tonight. Happiness that she's here, and hope for our future."

"Perfect." He turned to Nathan and shook his hand. The new father still appeared pale, but joy filled his eyes.

Erin tugged at his arm. "I clean forgot we left Elizabeth back at the house because she wasn't feeling well. She needs to get to a shelter."

Dread filled his heart. "Don't you think she would have heard the warning to take cover? You can hear that bell all over town and even out to the country." He almost seemed to be trying to reassure himself.

"But she doesn't know the parsonage has a storm cellar, much less how to get into it. I hate to make you go back out, but I need to know she's all right."

He needed to know she was all right too, but he couldn't

admit that to his sister. "OK, I'll check on her. You stay put until I get back."

Doc Jensen called to him. "You'll find my oilskin hanging by the door in my office. It should protect you some."

"Thanks, I'll get it." He loped back up the steps, praying that the storm would pass over with only rain and maybe hail. Hail damage was a far sight better than that from a tornado.

Once he retrieved the oilskin, he braved the elements to walk to the parsonage. Hail littered the street and the yards on his way, and the green aura remained in the sky.

When he reached the house, he entered the front door and called her name. When no one answered, he proceeded upstairs to double check. Her room stood empty, which meant she most likely had heard the warning and taken cover. If she'd run outside, anyone close by could have directed her to a storm cellar.

Once he determined no one remained in the house, he headed back outside. The twisting, turning, ugly cloud coming across the outskirts of town sent him scrambling back into the house and down into cellar, where it sounded like he had taken refuge under the train station. He'd heard that roar only a few times in the past, and each time it accompanied a tornado. With no lamp and no way to find one, he sat in the dark with the sounds raging above him. He prayed for those at the infirmary to be safe and that everyone had reached shelter in time, especially Elizabeth. He could no longer think of her as Miss Bradley. She had woven herself into his life, and despite the doubts, he cared for her. She had to be safe somewhere in town.

After what could have been an eternity but in reality was

only minutes, the noise lessened. Cory felt his way back to the stairway and went up the steps. He opened the door and surveyed the kitchen. It looked intact. Except for the broken windows and several lamps, papers, and small, loose items scattered across the floor, the living room appeared almost normal, at least on the inside. He still needed to check outside.

Cory picked up a lamp and walked around to the back of the house. He held the light high and could see where most of the back wall of bricks was missing from the house, and the chimney lay in a heap of jumbled bricks. One wall of the carriage house was down. Hay lay strewn about, and pieces of equipment littered the floor and ground outside the damaged wall. Seth had tied up his two horses in the remains of the stable, where the roof still covered it, but his heart leaped in fear when he saw there was no sign of Yeller Boy.

Just as he turned to go, a flash of white caught his eye. He held the lamp higher and spotted a piece of paper tacked to a timber. It had been ripped and torn so that only a small piece remained, but the words there sent fear coursing through his veins.

Dear Erin,
I'm sorry, but I just have to

The rest was gone. Cory clenched his teeth. Elizabeth had gone out into that storm. What desperation could have made her take such a chance? He yanked the note from the nail and crushed it in the palm of his hand. She'd never survive if she ran into that twister. Anger toward Elizabeth twisted his gut.

She had no right to do this to those who tried to help her and keep her safe. Such a crazy, foolhardy, dangerous thing to do.

Then the anger melted into concern. He had only one choice, and that was to hunt for her. With all the rain and the storm, tracking her would be nearly impossible. Even Hawkeye couldn't follow her trail in this mess. But no matter how hard it might be, he had to try.

CHAPTER FIFTEEN

*D*ARK CLOUDS BOILED in the sky and sent flashes of lightning streaking across the horizon. Libby crouched low over Yeller Boy as the wind buffeted them. If she continued this way, maybe she could outrun the storm. With a yank on the reins she kept Yeller Boy pointed southwest, or what she hoped was southwest. No roads marked the way, only trees and more trees, slowing her pace to a walk.

Yeller Boy tossed his mane, and his head reared back as the storm lit up the sky with lightning then roared with thunder. A crack and then another roar filled the air to her left, and it didn't come from the sky. A tree fell victim to the storm's fury. She needed a shelter, and quick. Trees would provide no safety from this storm, and Yeller Boy knew it better than she.

Maybe she should head back and wait for another day to make her escape. How could she have been so desperate? When she turned Yeller Boy back the way they had come, his ears perked up as though he sensed what she planned. Raindrops began pelting them both, and she stopped long enough to pull the slicker over her body, but with no hat, she had nothing to protect her head.

In only a few minutes the rain poured in torrents, and the sky became a strange greenish color. If she couldn't see more than a few feet ahead, her horse couldn't either. If they took out across the open field, she'd be a target for lightning, sure as she sat on the horse. If she kept Yeller Boy close to the trees, there was the chance of a strike among the trees, and that was just as dangerous, if not more so.

She had to stop. Nothing looked familiar, and none of her options were safe. How far had she come from town? She couldn't have been gone longer than an hour, but right now she had no idea where she was or even if they were headed in the right direction.

Her hair hung in streaks plastered to her head, and rain blinded her eyes. She loosened her grip on the reins and gave Yeller Boy the lead. She bent low over him and clung to his mane. "Take us back, take us back to Porterfield. You know the way." At least she hoped he did.

The ground beneath the horse's hoofs soaked up the water but would soon be thick mud, making travel more difficult. As if uncertain where to head next, Yeller Boy stopped by a stand of bushes with trees around it. The thunder and lightning ceased, but the rain continued to pound her body, and the wind howled around her.

Libby slid down from her horse and hunkered down in the bushes, which offered little protection, but they could stay here until the storm passed. Then the rain slowed, and another sound filled the air with a roar far louder than any thunder.

She wiped her eyes then shielded them with her hands to peer in the direction of the noise.

Her throat closed and her heart jumped. A twisting mass of clouds swept across the open field and into trees beyond, breaking them up like they were sticks and twigs. Yeller Boy pranced beside her, and it took every ounce of energy she had left to keep him from running away. Then she realized the twister moved across and not toward her. A deep awe of the power in those clouds filled her, and in only a few minutes the twister veered and sped away, tearing up whatever lay in its path.

Despite the oilskin covering her, cold settled in her bones, and wet clothing clung to her body. The grasses lay matted and soggy under her feet. Rain soaked through her shoes and weighted down her skirt. She held Yeller Boy's reins and trudged through the mud, rain still trickling down her face and neck. She should have stayed on the road, but then she might have met that storm head-on and been swept away with it. No matter which way she looked at her situation, she had made the most foolish decision of her life to leave Porterfield with a storm approaching.

She raised her eyes to the sky. "God, if You're there, You must hate me for all I've done to lead me out here and let me get lost. Haven't I been punished enough?" Sobs filled her throat, and tears mingled with the rivulets of rain already streaming down her cheeks.

She plodded on until the sound of rushing water drew her through the trees. The creek. That meant she couldn't be far from town. She could follow it and find her way back. Libby led her horse toward the noise but stopped and gasped.

Dismay flooded through her like the waters flooding the creek before her. Still well below its bank, but rising, the usually docile stream raged and foamed its way between the steep sides. She wrapped Yeller Boy's reins around her hand and stepped closer to search for a way to cross or to follow the banks back to town.

Mud squished around her boots, and she stepped with care along the bank just above the rolling waters. Then her foot slipped, and she plunged downward, hitting her head on a rock. Her vision blurred, but she held firm to the reins. Cold water crept over her ankles, and she yanked on the reins. "Pull me up, Yeller Boy, pull me up."

Her arm seemed to wrench from its socket, and she screamed. The horse stopped and pawed the ground. She peered through the rain to see that her foot had caught under a root protruding from the ground. She wiggled her foot, but it held tight. Maybe if she could reach down far enough, she could unlace it and slip the boot off. Then she looked up at Yeller Boy and realized he stood right on the edge of the bank. If he moved any closer, he'd slide right down with her. When she tried to let go of the reins and free her hand, it had become so entangled that the straps held it secure.

"What else are You going to do to me, God? My head aches, my arm hurts, and my foot feels crushed. Just let me die right here and be done with it."

Yeller Boy stayed still and firm in his spot, as though sensing her predicament and not wanting to injure her further. There she hung, suspended between the horse and the rising water. Then her world went dark as she slipped into unconsciousness.

Cory set off toward the livery to get his horse. What met him along the way sent chills through his bones. Homes had roof damage, and a few had walls missing, exposing the rooms behind them. Trees lay across the road, their roots now exposed, and shattered glass littered the lawns and streets.

Blown-out windows, missing doors, and damaged buildings greeted him when he turned onto Main Street. People came out of the buildings with dazed expressions and some with blood on their faces and bodies. Doc Jensen ran from the infirmary and began leading the wounded back to the hospital. Although Cory felt terrible for not stopping, time was of the essence. He had to find Elizabeth before nightfall.

Cory was relieved to spot the familiar figure of Frank Cahoon standing outside the livery.

"Frank, you're just the one I need to see. Miss Bradley is missing, and I have to go hunt for her."

"Right, deputy."

Cory followed Frank into the livery thankful he'd left his horse here before the storm. In a few minutes the horse was saddled and ready to ride. "Thanks, Frank. Tell Rutherford that I've gone to look for Miss Bradley. I hope I can find her soon."

Frank nodded. "Sure will, deputy, and we'll pray you Godspeed."

On his way back out of town Cory stopped at the boardinghouse for a few supplies. Elizabeth would be hungry when he found her and probably cold if she'd been out in the rain. He found biscuits and some cookies in the kitchen and added them to his bags, along with a canteen of water. Just then Aunt Mae came into the kitchen, and he quickly explained the circumstances. "Aunt Mae, I need a few blankets to take to keep her warm." His aunt hurried to the task, and he thanked her good sense for not delaying him with questions and concern.

He picked up a lantern and packed it as well. There was no telling how long the search would take, and nightfall would be here within a few hours.

Aunt Mae returned and handed him two blankets. She wrapped her arms around him. "Stay safe, Cory, and find her. We'll all be praying she's found and is all right."

He hugged her in return. "Thank you, Aunt Mae. We'll need those prayers." He could always count on his aunt to be praying in any time of emergency, and it filled him with assurance that God would guide him to Elizabeth.

Once in the saddle again, Cory headed west. One thing for certain, she wouldn't have gone back toward Louisiana. When he reached the creek, the high level of rushing water sent alarm signals to his chest. It wasn't at flood stage. However, another rain like today and it would be, and Porterfield would be flooded, since the creek ran only half a mile from the outskirts.

He made the decision to remain on the town side and follow it for a while.

~~~~~

When Libby awoke, she had no idea how much time had passed, but it appeared to be late afternoon. The only sounds were from the water tumbling around her and Yeller Boy's snuffles, which she could barely hear. He'd stayed with her, but then he couldn't leave her because of her hands being curled in the reins and her foot trapped below her.

She shivered and once again tried to pull her foot free, but the pain that shot up her leg stopped her in a hurry. She lifted her free hand and tried to grab hold of the reins to steady herself but couldn't reach them without putting more strain on her foot and ankle. At least the water had risen only to just below her knee, but it could still get deeper.

Next she attempted to gain a little foothold with her free foot to ease the strain on her arm and shoulder, but she couldn't grab hold, as her foot slipped on the slimy mud bank. In addition, the water continued to rise. Cold like she'd never experienced, even on the coldest nights in their cabin without heat, caused her body to shake and tremble like leaves in the wind. Nobody knew where she was, and most likely with that storm no one would come looking for her.

She lifted her face upward, straining to see the sky. "OK, God. Is this how I'm to die? Is this my ultimate punishment for all I've done? I know You must be there, because my ma believed You were, but You don't seem to care about me at all."

Her voice fell silent. God wouldn't hear her anyway. Why waste her breath. He only listened to people like the reverend and Erin. God never intended for her to have any kind of life, so if she died, here no one would care and probably wouldn't even know for several days. Weariness filled her, but her bones ached so much. No way to relax. All she could do was hang there and most likely die from exposure if the water didn't cover her first.

Weary and cold, Cory finally pulled his horse to a stop. The darkness of the forest surrounded him in a thick shroud, and the wet, leaf-covered ground gave no clues as to where Elizabeth could be. With the creek bank steeper along this way, the slightest misstep by Blaze could send them both into the tumbling waters below.

He should be helping folks back in town, and here he sat in his saddle trying to find a girl who most likely didn't want to be found. Why did he even bother? Deep down the reason simmered, just waiting to boil to the surface, but he wouldn't acknowledge it. He couldn't.

Elizabeth had made it clear she didn't like or trust him, and until he could learn the reasons behind her behavior, he wanted just to avoid her. But not helping a female in distress went against everything he'd been taught, so he had no choice. No matter how much she'd wanted to leave Porterfield, he had to find her and take her back to Erin and Ma.

For all he knew, Elizabeth could have been way ahead of the storm and be miles and miles from here by now. If that be true, he'd never catch up to her.

Libby's stomach growled in hunger. The food she'd packed lay just above her, out of reach. She gazed upward at Yeller Boy. The satchel still hung from the saddle, but a lot of good it did her. By cold or hunger, either way she'd die with no one but Yeller Boy by her side.

She blew out her breath and once again tried to swing her

free hand up to grab the reins entangled around her left hand, but pain surged through her. In desperation she tried again and once again failed. Then she tried to lift her left foot and dig her heel into the bank or on a rock, but it only slipped down again in the rushing water.

Somehow Yeller Boy managed to stand fast on the bank and hold her steady in the spot. That root must be big and the space tight since the creek waters hadn't swept her away. In a few minutes, exhaustion and pain caused her to stop her efforts. She gave into both and closed her eyes. Suddenly she jerked against the root binding her foot. The creek level now flowed past her at nearly waist level. Help had to come soon.

It was no use. She had no strength left. This was not the way she wanted to die, but that didn't matter to God. Hunger pangs rumbled again, and despite all the water flowing around and past her, her throat ached with dryness. She scooped a bit of the creek water into her hand and gulped it down. No matter that it tasted like mud; it was wet.

Tears now rolled down her cheeks. As bad as her predicament at the moment, it didn't begin to compare with what she had faced with Pa. Dying here in this spot would be better than going back, but despite her vows to the contrary, she didn't want to die.

After struggling again to get a foothold and to work her foot loose, she finally relaxed and let her body fall limp. Maybe she should sleep. How long would it take to die hanging here? If she died, she wouldn't be going to heaven for sure. Girls like her didn't go to heaven. That's what the women at home told her.

Her eyes closed, and her head nodded. Then Yeller Boy's

neigh shocked her to attention. "What is it, boy? What do you hear?" No telling what hid in these woods.

The bushes trembled, and twigs cracked. Footsteps of something or someone pounded the ground above. Then a voice called out.

"Yeller Boy, it is you. Where's Miss Bradley?"

The deputy's voice. He'd come after her. Then Yeller Boy whinnied.

She strained to see up the bank. "Down here." Her voice came out only in a squeak, but her horse bobbed his head as if telling the deputy to look down.

Then his face appeared over the edge. "Miss Bradley! I'll get you up. Hang on."

Hang on? That's all she could do. "My foot's stuck." Unsure he heard, she called out his name again, this time stronger.

His head appeared again. "OK, I'm coming down."

A few seconds later he slid to a stop by her head. "I have to get you out of here. What were you trying to say about your foot?"

"It's caught under a root, and I can't move it."

He hesitated only a minute then dove into the water. His hands probed her foot and yanked. A few seconds later he popped to the surface.

"It's wedged tight." He whistled up to his horse. "Blaze, come close."

Deputy Muldoon reached up, and the horse shook his reins loose so that they fell to the ground. "Come on, boy, a little closer." A moment later the deputy grabbed the reins. "Good boy. I've got 'em."

He eased back to Libby's side. "Here, hold on to Blaze

with your free hand. He'll stand next to Yeller Boy and help hold you up. I'm going back down to get your foot loose."

He disappeared into the murky waters again. His hands tugged and pulled at her shoe and the root until her foot yanked free. She screamed, but her foot popped free with a pain like she'd never known. It shot up her leg and back again then throbbed with each heartbeat. She understood the reason for both horses holding her as the water pushed her feet out from under her and tugged at her body.

Cory burst up from the water and shook his head, gasping for breath, and grabbed the reins just above her head. He scrambled back up the bank and positioned himself above her then bent down to grab her under her arms. "OK, boys, now help me pull her up."

Even as the deputy eased up her the embankment with the horses' help, she bit her lip against the cries of pain crowding her throat.

When she lay on the bank, he untangled her hands from the reins then cradled her in his arms. She clung to his shirt, as muddy and wet as her own clothes, but she didn't care. Help had come. God listened after all.

CHAPTER
SIXTEEN

*C*ORY USED HIS bandana to wipe the mud from Elizabeth's face. "You're OK. I have you now." He stared down into the incredible blue eyes that swam in tears of thankfulness. Even though her hair was matted on her head with streaks of mud and leaves covering the blonde strands, her beauty shone like a beacon on a dark night.

"I... I was so scared." Her voice trembled then broke into sobs as she reached up and hugged his neck. Then she jerked back with a cry of pain. "My shoulder."

Cory inspected the arm and noted swelling up around the shoulder joint. He remembered her position only a few minutes ago and praised God the arm hadn't been yanked out of its socket. He glanced up at the horses. "Good boys. You did just the right thing."

Yeller Boy tossed his head and mane as though in acceptance of the compliment, and Blaze nickered and pawed the ground. Cory turned back to Elizabeth, his mouth in a grim line. He ran his fingers along her shoulder and upper arm, and she winced but didn't cry out. "Looks like your shoulder is sprained, but I'm not so sure about that ankle. Let me have a look."

He lifted her skirt to find swelling above the laced-up boot. That didn't look good. He unlaced the shoe, only to find even more swelling as he eased it off. When he touched it and moved it only slightly, she screamed out in pain. Cory was no doctor, but that ankle could be broken. He remembered how Abigail's ankle had swollen, and this one was even worse.

"I'm going to lift you up onto my horse. Do you think you can hold on and let me lead us home?"

"Yes, Deputy Muldoon."

His gaze met hers. "Call me Cory. May I call you Elizabeth?"

At her nod, Cory wrapped one of the blankets around her and scooped her up in his arms. He lifted her up to the saddle. "Don't try to put your foot in the stirrup, but just let your feet hang loose." She wavered in the saddle when Cory swung up behind her, and he wrapped his arms around her to steady her. "If you're dizzy, lay your head against my chest and hold on to my shirt."

She simply nodded and relaxed her body into his arms. Cory slipped his hand into the reins and guided the horses out of the woods and back to the road to Porterfield. No telling how many patients Doc Jensen would have in the infirmary, but he had to be able to at least treat Elizabeth. If there were no beds there, Aunt Mae could take care of her. He lifted his head toward the sky, now streaked with the first colors of sunset. *Thank You, Lord, for sparing her life.*

The trip back to town lasted longer than Cory would have

liked, but he didn't rush because of Elizabeth's weakened condition. "Elizabeth, do we need to stop? It's not much farther to town, but we can let you rest if you need it."

She shook her head but didn't lift it and slumped against him, too weak to hold on to him. He tightened his hold on her with one arm and flicked the reins with the other. "All right, Blaze, let's go home."

"So tired. Want sleep." Her words buried themselves in his shirt.

"Sleep, then. We'll have you back in Porterfield, safe in Doc Jensen's care." His heart thumped in his chest when the image of what he'd seen back on that creek bank slipped across his mind. The water had risen so quickly. He'd arrived just in time so he could still get her foot loose.

What if he hadn't heard Yeller Boy in the trees? What if he hadn't followed the creek? The questions rolled through his thoughts in a steady stream. She could have died hanging by one arm like that, and with the water rising, no one would have known for maybe days. Once again God had directed him to find her, just as he had on that first night.

The weight of her head on his chest brought back the memories of his love for Abigail. He'd vowed never to let himself be in that position again, but Elizabeth stirred his emotions and sent the longings once again sweeping through his heart. But he didn't even know who she was.

Until he could learn the complete truth about her, he'd keep all emotion that even hinted at love under careful wraps. He couldn't afford to be hurt again.

Every bone and muscle in her body hurt, but Libby had never felt so safe and secure. Just like the first time he found her, instead of fear, calm assurance filled her. Cory's arms and touch offered only protection and safety. She could trust him to get her back to Erin's.

She had prayed, and God had answered. Did that mean God cared about her and wanted her to stay alive? With all that had happened to her, she found that hard to believe, but the answer had come.

No matter what else she believed, someone had watched over her. Someone had made Yeller Boy stand still and not injure her any more than she already had been. Someone had kept the water from rising higher, and someone had sent Cory to find her in the nick of time. Could that have been God?

Libby squeezed her eyes shut against the tears threatening to spill out. She couldn't have been wrong about God all these years. Plain old luck had sent Cory, and Yeller Boy always knew when she was in trouble. No, God had nothing to do with it.

She listened to the steady beat of Cory's heart. It filled her with a yearning for what she could never hope to have. He simply did his job as deputy and rescued people in distress. He'd never see her as anyone to care about, especially when he learned of her background and the way she'd lived.

Sleep caused her lids to grow heavy, but not before she heard Cory say, "Hang on, Elizabeth. We're almost there."

Elizabeth, her real name. She liked it so much more than what Pa called her. What would it be like to be called that the rest of her life by a man who loved her and wanted only to pro-tect and care for her? She had longed for and dreamed of that years ago, but all hope waned as the years passed with Pa.

As much as she wanted to believe that God could love her, she couldn't wrap her thoughts around the idea. Pa had pointed it out more than once that she was no good for anything but what he wanted her to do. He'd told her that God didn't love her because she was nothing but trash, and the people of God, those Christians, would never allow her in church. And he'd said the words in such a way that Libby could do nothing but believe them.

Cory rode into town and headed straight for the infirmary. He carried Elizabeth inside but found the waiting room already full of people. Some had visible wounds needing treatment; others simply waited with their loved ones.

Doc Jensen came through one of the examining room doors. When he saw Cory, the doc hurried to his side. "What happened here?"

"Her foot was trapped. Now her ankle is swollen and turning colors. Much worse looking than Abigail's was." If it wasn't broken, then it'd be another miracle.

"Let me have a look." Doc Jensen lifted Elizabeth's skirt and examined her foot. His fingers probed with a gentle touch, but Elizabeth flinched and moaned. "Looks broken for sure." He glanced around the room then back to the girl in Cory's arms.

"I don't think any of these out here are seriously injured, and I just cleared a bed in the back room. Take her in there." He turned and spoke to a couple nearby.

Cory wasted no time in getting Elizabeth to the examining room and on the bed there. He grabbed a pillow and
placed it under her head.

Doc Jensen entered the room followed by Kate, who
closed the door behind her. The doctor once again examined
Elizabeth's foot. "I wish I could see inside, under the skin, to
know just where the break is. If I put a cast on it now and the
swelling goes down, the cast will be too big and not do its job.
From the way it's twisted, it's the ankle, but how bad it is or
exactly where I can't tell."

"She hurt her shoulder too. It isn't pulled from the socket,
but came close to it. I found her hanging over the edge of the
creek with her hand twisted in Yeller Boy's reins and her foot
wedged beneath a tree root. I don't know how long she hung
there like that."

Kate unbuttoned Elizabeth's blouse and looked up at her
brother. "Why don't you go home and get into dry clothes
while we examine the shoulder? I have to take her shirtwaist
off, and there's no need for you to see her exposed like that.
Besides, you look like something come up from the swamp."

Heat rose in Cory's face. Trust his sister to speak
plainly. He'd already checked her shoulder himself, but no
need to tell Kate that now. "OK, but you be sure she knows
I'll be right back." Better to do that than to raise questions.
Even though he wore a badge, certain proprieties had to be
observed.

Back in the waiting room he surveyed those sitting or
standing there. Many had head wounds most likely caused by
flying debris or broken windows. None appeared to be serious,
but that was for Doc to decide. Elliot stepped from the front

examining room and called a name. He spotted Cory and walked over to him.

"What in the world happened to you?"

Cory shook his head. "You're not going to believe this." He then proceeded to tell Elliot about the rescue.

Elliot blew out his breath. "That was an ordeal, but God did get you there in time, and for that we can be thankful."

"How are things going here?" Cory asked.

"We've been busy all afternoon. The rooms upstairs are about full. The less seriously injured are being sent home or wherever they can find shelter. The hotel is putting up some of them." He pulled Cory aside and spoke so others could not hear. Cory bent close to listen.

"We have several who are severely injured and one who may not make it through the night. The saloon was heavily hit, and one of the girls was struck by a falling beam. Most of our worst injuries occurred there, although the saloon was closed. The girls and other employees had all gathered there for Sunday evening supper and were there when the storm struck."

Cory furrowed his brow. "Is Marshal Slade still in town? I should go down to the office and check with him if he is." How much more damage had there been that he hadn't seen?

"Yes, and he said he'd be here the rest of the week unless something dire called him away."

"Good." Cory started to walk away but then stopped. "I'm going to change clothes, and then I'll be back to see about Miss Bradley. I can take her to Aunt Mae's and put her in Abigail's room since she won't be needing it." It'd be a far sight more comfortable too, and Elizabeth would have Aunt Mae's expert care along with it.

"That's a good idea. I'm going back to check on Mr. Burns. He's the one who just went into the examining room."

Cory hurried back to Blaze and rode to the boarding-house and changed clothes. He found Aunt Mae in the kitchen preparing a late dinner for her boarders. Cory explained Elizabeth's condition.

His aunt dried her hands on a towel then hugged him. "That's perfect. I'll be glad to have her here where I can take care of her. I'll get the room ready."

Cory squeezed her shoulders. "I knew I could count on you. I'll be back soon as Doc releases her."

He rode back to the infirmary, but weariness filled his bones, and he rolled his shoulders to loosen the tightness binding him in fatigue. He surveyed more of the damage to the buildings along Main Street. Most had roof damage, with the saloon sustaining the brunt of the storm. The sign was gone, and the roof had collapsed into the building with only the staircase to indicate the second floor.

Cory shook his head and waved to people working to pick up the pieces. Tornadoes did strange things to whatever lay in their paths. Whatever the cost, Porterfield would rebuild and recover from this storm. The people here had proved their worth on more than one occasion, and no less would happen now. The work being done now gave more evidence of their strength in times of trouble.

Buildings could be repaired, but what could he do with Elizabeth? No matter how hard his family tried to reach out to her, she shied away and wanted to run. This last attempt almost cost her life. Maybe her injuries would slow her down enough that she could see how much Erin, Kate, and Ma cared about her.

In spite of all that had happened, he'd have a good report for Erin, and he'd tell her after he had Elizabeth settled. He shook his head, with the past few hours whipping through it faster than one of Donavan's hounds after a coon. Less than a day, and so much had happened. No matter what transpired in the next twenty-four hours, they couldn't be as devastating to anyone as the ones just passed.

Libby wakened to find Kate standing beside her with a washcloth in hand. "Welcome back, Elizabeth. You had quite an ordeal out there in the storm."

The storm. That's why her arm and ankle hurt so much. She looked down to see a sling holding her arm against her body. Sheets covered her feet, but the weight on her right one suggested a cast on it. "It was awful, Kate. I thought I'd be jerked in half, but Yeller Boy didn't move. My foot was wedged under that tree root, and I couldn't reach it or get a good hold with my free foot. The water was rising, and I just knew I'd drown or freeze to death…" She let her voice trail off to silence. Kate must think the tree had conked her in the head with way she babbled on.

"I know. Cory told us. You were covered in mud, so I'm cleaning your face. Your clothes are really a mess, but I found a gown for you to wear. We don't have a bed for you, so Cory is taking you down the street to the boardinghouse. Erin and Seth's house had some damage, so it's not fit for you to stay in right now."

Going to Aunt Mae's meant being with all those people who lived there. Being around that many others scared her, but she was in no condition to travel now, or probably for a while. Maybe she could stay in one room and not have to deal with meeting the other boarders. That reporter fellow lived there, and he had already been questioning Erin and Cory about her and where she'd come from.

Kate spoke Elizabeth's name, and she blinked her eyes. "What did you say?"

"I said I don't know what made you take off and run like that, unless you were scared in the storm and thought you could outrun it."

"Oh, I...I...went out for a walk to clear my head. Thought it might help my headache, and then I decided to ride Yeller Boy, and we got caught in the storm." Leastways, it could have happened that way.

Kate laid the cloth on the table by the basin. "I see, and you couldn't get back to town before the storm, so you tried to ride it out by the creek."

"Something like that." That sounded stupid, but it was better than telling the truth. If she did, they'd watch her like a hawk. She had to get away. Pa would be on her trail by now, and eventually he'd make his way to Porterfield. She planned to be long gone by then.

Then she remembered the weight on her foot. A cast put a crimp in her plans, but somehow she'd carry them out.

Doc Jensen walked in and grinned at Libby. "Well now, it's a good thing Cory rescued you when he did. That ankle of yours could have been a lot worse. Looks like your leather boot protected it from more serious damage. There is a break just above the ankle, so that's the reason for the cast."

"How long…how long will I have to wear it?"

"Oh, it'll be awhile before you can walk without crutches. Abigail had to use them last fall when she sprained her ankle, but you'll be using them longer than she did, I'd say at least six weeks."

Six weeks? Libby's insides churned. She may as well plan to return to Louisiana and everything she'd hoped to escape. She picked at the lint on the blanket covering her body. If God saved her life, He'd only made matters worse, especially if she had to go back.

Kate covered Libby's hand. "I'll get your things. Cory will take you down to Aunt Mae's in the wagon. I'm sure she'll try to get your clothes clean enough for you to wear again. Cory went over and told Erin and Seth you're OK, and they'll probably come to see you at Aunt Mae's."

Why were these people being so nice to her? They didn't know her, but they treated her like she was one of their family. Where did people like that come from? She'd never encountered anyone like them.

Kate left and returned a few minutes later with Cory in tow. "Here she is, and she's all ready to go. You'll have to carry her out to the wagon. Think you can do that, big brother?"

The sound of her teasing and Cory's shake of his head warmed Libby's heart. That's the way families should act. Love wrote itself all over their faces and spilled over like the swollen creek, but instead of drowning destruction, their love flooded with a sense of peace she wished she could have.

Cory strode to the bedside. "She's light as a feather." He

scooped her up into his arms then let Kate arrange the skirt of her nightdress over the cast before covering her with a blanket.

Of course, it'd never do for her to be seen riding down Main Street in her nightclothes. If they only knew she had worn clothes that left much more of her exposed than this long-tailed gown. And if they did know, she'd be going somewhere else besides the boardinghouse.

She draped her good arm about Cory's neck. The muscles in his arms rippled as he settled her in position to walk out to the wagon. His strength far out-measured what she remembered from that first time he carried her out of the alley.

The sight of so many injured in the waiting room brought a gasp from Libby. "Are all these people here because of the storm?"

"Yes. Because we had so many broken windows, people were injured by flying glass. They'll all be treated then sent home, if they have a home to go to. The schoolhouse is being set up as a place for those whose homes were too damaged to stay in. What won't fit there will be housed at the two churches in town.

"Here we are, and Aunt Mae sent a pillow to rest your foot on for the few blocks up to her house." He sat her in the wagon bed then helped her lie down and arrange the covers.

She gazed up the street toward the courthouse and shook her head. Debris still littered the streets, and people went about trying to clean up. The noise of hammers hitting nails and wood resounded in the air. "I had no idea there was so much damage. I saw the storm from a distance, but it moved across in front of me and away."

"It's a good thing, or we might not be carting you to a

comfortable bed." He grinned then headed around to climb up on the seat. He clicked his tongue, and the wagon moved down the street.

Lying down she couldn't see any of the buildings, but the sounds of repairs and people picking up the pieces echoed up and down the street. She'd truly been lucky, an unusual thing in her life. She scrunched up the pillow under her head and let tears flow freely.

God, are You really there? Do You really care about me? Why did You let me live? I'm only going to disappoint these wonderful people when they learn the truth. I should have died on that creek bank.

But she hadn't died, and now her plans lay shattered like the glass fragments on the streets. Where was she to go from here? A better question, How was she going to be able to leave here at all with her foot in a cast?

CHAPTER
SEVENTEEN

*L*IBBY SNUGGLED DOWN under the covers and savored the quietness of the room. For two days Aunt Mae had pampered her and made sure everything was as comfortable as it could be. Even Miss Perth and Mrs. Bennett had been in to make sure she had everything she needed. When she had awakened in the night crying and remembering how close she'd come to death, Aunt Mae had come in to wrap her arms around her and fill her with comfort and reassurance.

If the threat of Pa's finding her hadn't filled her with dread, Libby could learn to love the people of Porterfield even more than she did. She'd already made good headway in that direction. Such love and protection could lull her into a state of euphoria and safety that may very well end up costing her freedom—the one thing she must guard against.

Hardening her heart and resisting the charms of Cory grew more difficult with each passing day. She no longer thought of him as the lawman out to get her, and as much as she had loathed the touch of the men in the saloon, she didn't mind Cory's. He'd been so gentle with her at the creek, and his words of comfort and assurance each day at the dinner table gave her the strength she needed to get well.

Someone knocked on her door. Then Erin opened it and poked her head around it. "Hi. We came to see you. Connor's been missing Miss Elizabeth." She held the three-month-old boy in her arms, and he waved his arms and gurgled.

Libby's heart bounced in her chest at the sight, and she held out her arms. "I've been missing him too." She nuzzled his soft hair with her cheek and rocked back and forth with him. She glanced up at Erin. "I'm so sorry to give you such a scare. I didn't realize what a big storm was headed this way."

Erin pulled up a chair and sat beside Libby's bed. "I'm sure you were scared to death." Her fingers flew to her mouth. "Oh, dear, you did almost die. Cory told us how your foot was caught and you couldn't get loose and the water was rising. How awful that must have been. I'm so glad God protected you and sent Cory to find you."

Libby didn't know about God saving her, but Cory had certainly shown up at the right time. God, fate, or luck, she didn't care why he showed up, only that he had saved her. "You have a very good brother. He knew just what to do to get me free."

"Well, I for one am very grateful for him." She leaned forward with hands on her knees. "And I have some good news for you. Doc told me to tell you he's bringing over Abigail's old crutches for you to use. Kate will show you how to balance with your hands and not put a strain on your shoulders, especially since one is so sore."

"That is good news. Henry Wilder has had to carry me to the table the last two evenings before he left, so I'm sure he'll be glad to hear it too." After he set her down, he'd scurried off to see Annie and have supper with her.

Libby placed Connor over her shoulder and patted his back. "Have you noticed how much time Henry is spending with Annie? He hasn't stayed here for supper at all this week, and your aunt tells me he's been skipping noontime too." Libby ate her own noon meal in her room, so she hadn't noticed his absence then.

"Yes, Seth commented about it himself. Since Annie closes after the noon meal, she's been cooking for Henry at her place. She moved into the old Wilson house. It's been vacant since Mrs. Wilson died and he went back to Wichita. Seth thinks there'll be a wedding before too long."

Aunt Mae walked into the room beaming from ear to ear, followed by Kate holding up a pair of crutches.

Aunt Mae picked up Connor from Libby's arms. "Look what Kate brought you. Now you'll be able to come to supper without help."

Kate helped Libby stand to one foot. "If you put your weight on your hands and not slump down on them, your shoulders will be a lot less sore. That's important since your right shoulder is already hurt." She positioned them under Libby's arms. "Now let's see if you can maneuver on them."

She stepped back to let Libby balance herself on the crutches. With her weight on her good foot, she took one step forward. Pain shot through her right upper arm and shoulder, but she bit down on her lip hard. Nothing would distract her from being more mobile.

Libby hobbled her way to the door and back with Kate,

Erin, and Aunt Mae applauding her efforts. "I think I can do this." She glanced at her friends and grinned.

Erin kissed her cheek. "I have to go. Seth is making repairs on the house with Joe Davis's help. Miriam moved over to stay with Rachel and her family since our house was damaged." She winked and nodded toward the crutches. "You'll be an expert in no time."

After Erin left, Kate stayed to make sure Libby used the crutches properly, and Aunt Mae went to finish supper preparation. "It's getting easier." The pain in her shoulder had lessened to a more bearable ache, but that wouldn't hinder her now.

"Good," Kate said. "But still be careful, and don't put your weight on that ankle even with the cast on. We don't want to risk a fall or reinjuring it in any way. I'll check in on you again tomorrow. Now I have to get back to the infirmary. We still have almost a full house with the storm injuries."

Libby sank back onto the bed. That little bit of effort had worn her out much more than she had wanted to let on to Kate. She massaged her aching right shoulder and squeezed back the tears. Every day she spent in this town made it more difficult to leave. She had never had this much attention in her life, not even when Ma was alive and Pa took care of his family.

Even when Pa had been sober and a hardworking man, money had been scarce. He had tried to show his love, but now Libby realized he simply had not known how. She did remember Pa telling her stories by the firelight. Some were so funny she'd giggled and laughed in his lap. He'd tickle her and Jonah and say how he loved them. She'd never forget the tiny cradle he'd made for one of her dolls.

An ache for all that she'd lost after Ma's death throbbed

with dull pain no medication could ease. It surged from her heart to her head then through every muscle and bone in her injured body. She'd loved Pa then as she had her mother and brother. Only after Ma died had Pa taken to drinking and gambling. He had paid so little attention to her, and she'd kept out of the way of everyone so that no one really seemed to notice when she dropped out of school.

Tears flowed freely now that she opened up the old hurts. The horrible memories far outweighed the good ones, and she could never go back to that life. The emptiness in her soul longed for love to fill it again, but that would take a miracle, and she didn't believe in miracles. But she was in this room now because of a miracle, wasn't she?

Confusion joined with exhaustion from the effort with the crutches. Sadness spilled from her heart and soul. Finally she curled up on the bed and let sleep bring relief.

Cory sat at his desk writing a report of all that had happened since Sunday. Even with the steel door separating the cells from the office closed, the voices of prisoners leaked through and reminded Cory of his duties. Three young men tried to steal from Grayson's store in the aftermath of the storm. Each filled a cell, waiting to stand trial.

Although he'd searched through the new batch of wanted notices, none carried the name of Elizabeth Bradley. No word had come from Louisiana and his inquiry about Libby Cantrell. He figured that meant Libby had been found or had nothing to do with Elizabeth.

His heart rejoiced that no criminal activity tainted her

reputation, but his mind grew more curious as to her history. In a little less than four weeks Elizabeth Bradley had worked her way into his life and heart with no effort on her part. Most of the time she shied away from him and barely spoke unless he talked to her first. The only close contact he'd had with her had been during his rescues when she'd been too weak to resist his holding her.

Most young women as pretty as Elizabeth liked to fix themselves up to be even more attractive, but not her. Simple clothes and hairstyles were more in keeping with her, and yet the simplicity added to the intrigue of her past. For all he knew, she could have lied that she wasn't running from an abusive husband, and that was why she flinched when Cory reached out to her.

Daniel Monroe hailed him from the open doorway. "Afternoon, Cory. I just had a wire from the judge, and he'll be here on Friday to conduct a trial for our looters."

"Thanks. That's good to know. I'll be sure to let Rutherford know. He's down at the hotel checking on those who had to stay there because of damage to their homes." Only three ranches had been severely affected by the storm, and Cory offered thanks daily that his family had been spared major damages.

Daniel rolled his hat brim and frowned. "I'm afraid I also have some bad news. Doc just told me that the young woman from the saloon died about an hour ago."

"I'm sorry to hear that. I thought sure we'd get through with no deaths, but now we have four. I suppose that's still a low number, but any death is an unwanted one." Two funerals had been held yesterday, and one more was scheduled for today.

What would the undertaker do about the saloon girl's death? He peered up at Daniel. "The sad thing about that is that I didn't even know her name. Oh, I know what she's called at the saloon, but none of Durand's girls go by their real names."

"Durand probably knows and can give Shoemacher any information about her family. Still, it's a sad thing for her to die alone here with no one to be with her at the end. Kate's feeling bad because the girl never woke up to give Kate a chance to ask the girl about her relationship with God."

"It couldn't have been much to be living like she did." Those girls of Durand's were not the kind he'd befriend or look at more than once… well, maybe twice. As for their dealings with God, he hadn't considered that aspect of it, but that was just the kind of thing to worry Kate.

Daniel turned to leave. "Kate believes everyone should know about God and have a chance to repent." He called back over his shoulder, "Tell Rutherford I'll have everything in order for the trial on Friday."

Cory shrugged and went back to his report. Far as he was concerned, the judge could just pronounce sentence instead of wasting money with a trial. Of course, the law guaranteed one, so a trial the boys would get. Sometimes the rules and regulations were more than he wanted to deal with. How Daniel could remember so many laws and what they meant went beyond his own area of comprehension.

He studied the calendar hanging on the wall amid the wanted posters and other notices pinned there. Easter loomed ahead at the end of the month, and that meant April, with all the beauty of spring, was right behind. Easter meant a time of newness and freshness that blessed his heart and soul whenever the flowers bloomed. That's what this town needed after this storm. Spring would give them hope for rebuilding and starting new.

Already the green shoots of bluebonnets and Indian paint-brushes covered the fields outside town, and in a few weeks a sea of blue would cover the landscape with bright spots of red-dish-orange springing up around and in the midst of the blue.

The meaning of Easter for Christians seeped deep into his heart for the first time in many years. Had he taken the sacrifice for granted for so long that he'd forgotten why Jesus died in the first place? He'd done all the soaking up of God's love, but he sure hadn't been sharing it with anyone. He'd left that job to Ma, Kate, and Erin.

He searched his memory and couldn't come up with one time since he'd become an adult that he'd truly shared his faith with an unbeliever. In church on Sundays he'd enjoyed the sermons, read Scriptures, and prayed, but it had never become a part of his daily life. The image of his mother sitting at the kitchen table reading her Bible by the light of an oil lamp early in the morning had burned into his memory, but it had become lost amid those of outlaws, murderers, and ne'er-do-wells.

Uncertainty colored his thoughts. Did God expect the same dedication from him? As a lawman his job was to capture criminals and see that justice was done. Just like the three men in the cells now, those he dealt with daily had no respect for the law, much less God. Cory reached for his hat. God had made him a deputy sheriff to uphold the law, and that's what he'd do. Sharing Jesus's love and His sacrifice for sins belonged to Seth as a preacher. Let him worry about the souls; Cory would take care of the laws they broke.

CHAPTER
EIGHTEEN

*L*IBBY HAD BEEN able to beg off going to church this morning with the excuse of her ankle and still not feeling up to getting out. The fib ate at her conscience like a dog gnawing a bone, but she couldn't tell Aunt Mae the truth. Anyone who might say they didn't feel like dealing with God that morning would be in for a stern lecture. That kind of reasoning only meant that God wanted to deal with her, but Libby's anger toward God had begun again Wednesday and had festered to the boiling point this morning. After a good nap the anger eased, but not the hurt.

Her shoulder only gave a twinge of pain now and again, but her ankle would take much longer to heal, as it still throbbed off and on. Doc Jensen had given Aunt Mae a vial of medication for the pain, but Libby had restrained from using it as much as possible.

While the others were at church, she had explored other regions of the boardinghouse. Her own room lay between Aunt Mae's and that of Miss Perth on the south side of the house in the back, with Mrs. Bennett's on the east end. Upstairs the men occupied four bedrooms and had a room for bathing and taking care of other needs. Only two were occupied with Cory and Henry Wilder. Mr. Fuller had moved downstairs to live with his new wife, Aunt Mae.

Libby limited her roaming to the more public areas and left the bedrooms alone. The private affairs and belongings of the others didn't hold any interest for her, but the antique furniture and accessories downstairs did. The brocaded fabric of the Victorian furniture in the parlor fascinated Libby. The only furniture in the cabin back home had been made from pine logs, and Pa had built most of it.

Here the sleek mahogany wood gleamed in the sunlight streaming through the window with nary a speck of dust to be seen on a table or chair railing. This is how her own home would look if she ever had one. Hand-painted china lamps sat atop crocheted doilies on tables at the ends of the sofa and between the chairs by the windows that looked up toward the main street of Porterfield.

She sat in one of the chairs and propped her crutches against the table. A book lay on the table by the lamp. Although she had not finished school, reading had been one of her passions, and she'd learned much from books. Libby picked up the book, but instead of reading she found herself gazing up Main Street to the courthouse in the distance.

What a pleasant town Porterfield had turned out to be. She'd been very fortunate to have ended up here instead of somewhere the people would have paid no interest in her at all. Her daydreams still focused on an image of a home, a few children, and a husband. Although she doubted the dream would ever see fulfillment, the longer she dreamed, the more the face of the one in her future resembled Cory's.

This man affected her like no other had in her years as a young woman. She had come to loathe men and their touch. She still flinched and pulled away from Cory, except when she was in danger and he offered her security. If she trusted him in those times, why couldn't she trust him in other situations? The hurt from other men soured her reaction to those who may mean well, so she ended up not trusting any of them.

Voices coming from outside warned her of the boarders' return from church. She grabbed her crutches and hobbled back to her room with long strides. She closed her door at the same time the back door squeaked open and Aunt Mae's voice filled the kitchen.

"All right, everyone, dinner will be on the table directly. Go on and change your clothes and get comfortable. Won't be anybody here but us homefolks today."

Miss Perth and Mrs. Bennett skittered past her room speaking in low tones. Then Cory's voice joined the others as he told Aunt Mae Henry wouldn't be here for dinner. Her heart skipped a beat and thudded against her ribs. Why was he here? He usually spent Sundays with his family out at the ranch. She'd managed to exchange only a few words with him at most meals this week because of his haste to get back to work in the aftermath of the storm. Sunday would be much more leisurely, and with fewer diners, she most likely would have to engage in conversation with him. Why did this scare her so today?

A knock sounded on the door, and Aunt Mae opened it a

crack. "Dinner is on the table if you care to join us. If you need help, I'll get Cory to come help you. Henry isn't here."

"No, I'll be fine, thank you. I'll be out in a minute." Libby didn't have to guess where the reporter would be dining. She'd heard enough talk about Henry and Annie to fill a book these past few days. She reached for her crutches and thumped her way to the dining room.

Cory jumped up and held out a chair for her. She swallowed hard and tried to smile but wasn't sure if her lips responded to her brain's direction. "Thank you, deputy." Her cheeks burned hot as she eased onto the seat. His hand brushed her shoulder, and she reacted out of habit by shrugging away.

The heat remained in her face at his murmured apology, but her throat tightened and her breath caught there, trapped by the innocent touch of his hand that sent shivers to her toes and back. How could she sit next to him and resist the charms of a lawman who would surely reject her if he ever found out who she was and what she'd done?

Conversation flowed like the creek around rocks in its path, but the only thing she noticed sat beside her, the very scent of his cleanliness reminding her of the kind of man he was. When he passed her a dish, his strong hands showed the strength he had exhibited more than once in her presence. When she could no longer bear the nearness of his arm to hers, Libby pushed back her chair and reached for her crutches. "I'm not feeling well. I'm going back to my room."

Cory jumped up from his place and helped her with the crutches. "Can you make it back on your own?"

She dipped her head. If she looked into those green eyes,

she'd never be able to maneuver to the hallway. "Thank you. I have it."

He held the chair out of the way, so she managed to back away from the table without falling. The hum of conversation stopped, as though waiting to see if she would fall or stay upright in her trek to her room. After she shoved the door open, she slumped against the wall and breathed in short spurts then in long deep breaths in an effort to still the pounding in her chest.

Her stomach growled in protest for the uneaten meal back in the dining room. She'd wait a half hour or so for everyone to finish eating and go to their Sunday afternoon rituals. Then she'd head for the kitchen and find a snack to tide her over until supper, which she hoped Aunt Mae would let her take in this room.

After resting and waiting, Libby hopped over to the door on one stocking-clad foot and listened. No sounds came from the other side, so she grabbed her crutches and eased the door open. The hallway rug muffled the sounds of her thumps on the floor. Just as she neared the kitchen, voices in conversation reached her ears. Not sure whether to go on in or to go back to her room, she hesitated. She didn't mind seeing Aunt Mae, but Cory she wanted to avoid.

Then she heard his voice and the word *death*. Who had died? She inched closer to listen. Cory's voice sounded loud and clear.

"Her death gave us another funeral yesterday. I don't think any of the rest of the injured are critical now, so let's hope that's the end of it."

Aunt Mae answered him. "I was really sorry to hear of that

girl's dying. Seems a shame for such a young woman to meet an end like that. I wonder if she knew the Lord."

Cory's laugh had a derisive tone that chilled Libby's blood on the spot.

"I hardly think so. Those girls wouldn't be working at the saloon if they did. They know what they do is against the Bible, but they sit there every night in their skimpy dresses luring the men to spend their money on gambling and whiskey."

Libby's heart jumped in her chest then fell with a thud against her rib cage. She swallowed a cry that filled her throat with pain. What would Cory do if he knew her past was just like that?

"Now, Cory, that girl was one of God's children. Maybe she had no choice in what she had to do. It's a shame they couldn't find any family for her either. At least Mr. Durand made sure she had a nice service and a decent burial plot."

"He did at that, but then he just wanted to look good. She's probably better off dead than working for the likes of Durand."

Libby couldn't stand to hear more. She made her way back to her room as quickly as she could without making any noise. Cory's words burned into her with an all-consuming fire that ate away any shred of self-confidence she may have begun to develop. She was no better than that girl who died, and if Elizabeth Bradley passed on today, no family would mourn her death either. Pa might, but it'd be more because he lost her income and not his daughter.

She closed the door behind her and hobbled to her bed, where she dropped the crutches and threw herself across the quilt. She bit her lips to keep them from quivering then pressed her knuckles against her mouth to keep from sobbing. Christian or not, when it came right down to the gritty facts, they all looked at saloon girls as tramps, worthless and good for nothing.

That saloon girl may have died before her time, but no one truly mourned her passing and probably forgot her, just as they would Libby. How could she have ever believed life would be different if she escaped Pa? Cory would loathe her and what she had been, and the rest would have nothing to do with her after they learned the truth. She must remember this and make her plans to get away as soon as she was able.

In a house full of people, she had never been lonelier than at this moment.

Aunt Mae sat down across from the table from Cory and poured him another cup of coffee. "I don't like to hear you talk that way, my boy. Every life is important to God. If it wasn't, why would Jesus die for us?" She reached across for his hand. "Honey, we're all sinners and need God's love, and sin is sin no matter how it's performed or what it is."

Cory had no answer for her, but he still couldn't help but believe those girls had a choice about the kind of lives they led. He only went to the saloon for business when trouble brewed and Durand needed the law. Otherwise he steered clear of the place. On more than one occasion a saloon girl had sidled up to him and tried to entice him with her womanly charms.

He sipped his coffee. He'd be lying if he said there had been no temptation, but he'd resisted and stayed only long enough to break up a fight or arrest a troublemaker. He had to hand it to Durand, because all of his ladies were pretty, but how much of it was due to the makeup rather than natural beauty?

Aunt Mae drew him back from his thoughts. "You listen to me, and you listen good."

Cory gulped. Here came a lecture, and he wouldn't like what she had to say. He nodded his head. "Yes, ma'am." At least he could be polite, although he most likely wouldn't follow her advice.

"Erin and some of the other ladies in the church have been praying for those girls, and we don't intend to stop. We're praying for God to save their souls and bring them redemption."

"Well, He'll have to bring some new jobs for them along with it. What else are they gonna do?" Saving their souls was one thing, but finding them jobs and a place to live would be something entirely different. No man in his right mind would want to claim one of them for a bride despite the lack of eligible women around here.

"All kinds of things, my boy. Mrs. Bennett can teach them to sew, they could help out at Annie's Kitchen, and I might could even hire one of them to help out around here."

Cory almost choked on his coffee and sloshed it on his hand as he set it down with a thud. What was the woman thinking? "You wouldn't do any such thing. Everyone in town would be talking, and you'd lose some of your best customers."

His aunt planted her hands on her hips and narrowed her eyes. "If that caused them to stop coming here to eat, then good riddance. I'm not going to listen to you or anyone else go on about those girls either. Each one of them is someone's daughter, sister, cousin, or granddaughter. We may not approve of what they do or how they live, but we can't judge them for it, and we have to love them."

She narrowed her eyes at him and pointed her finger at his chest. "I suggest you go read the Book of Hosea, and then maybe you'll see what God's plans are, no matter what one's sins may be."

Cory swallowed the last dregs of his coffee and shoved away from the table. He'd heard all he wanted to hear from Aunt Mae. "I'm going for a walk." He grabbed his hat from the peg by the back door and jammed it on his head. He paused before pushing open the screened door. "All I can say is you won't find me associating with any of them. They made their choice, and now they can live with it. It's not for me to try to change them."

Aunt Mae's gasp and response followed him out the door, but he closed his ears and didn't listen to keep his anger from boiling over and words he didn't want her to hear spewing from his mouth. Right now he wished he'd gone on out to Sarah and Donavan's for dinner. He loved and respected Aunt Mae, but sometimes she expected too much of him and even of God. Reform a saloon girl? Impossible.

CHAPTER
NINETEEN

*L*IBBY POSITIONED HER crutches under her arms and thumped her way to the parlor to meet Aunt Mae and Erin. Doc Jensen wanted to see her today to check on the progress of her ankle, so the three of them decided to include a trip to town to shop. With everyone busy, Aunt Mae planned to have dinner at noon in town with Cyrus at the hotel. Erin chose Annie's Kitchen for her and Libby.

For her first day out and about since the storm, Libby's heart mixed with emotions in a jumble of good and bad. For four days she'd managed to avoid being around Cory any more than absolutely necessary. Of course, he had no clue as to why, and the puzzled expression in his eyes laid guilt in her soul. Even so, that pang of conscience didn't hurt nearly as much as his words had on Sunday.

She counted the days until the cast could be removed and she could make her escape. She'd miss Aunt Mae and Erin, but leaving would be best for all concerned in the long run.

Aunt Mae and Erin waited in the parlor, ready to leave.

Libby smiled and reached for one of baby Connor's hands. "Oh my, Erin, he keeps changing every day."

"I know. He's growing so fast."

Aunt Mae clapped her hands. "Now, come, ladies. Let's not dawdle. Henry brought the carriage around to the front of the house, so we're all ready to go."

Leading the way, Aunt Mae marched out to the driveway with Libby and Erin right behind her. Henry stood by the step up and grinned at Libby. "Thought you might need some help getting up there, young lady, so I waited."

"Why, thank you. That was very thoughtful." She handed Aunt Mae the crutches then held on to the sides as Henry boosted her up into the seat with her good foot on the step. When she settled, the realization hit her with a jolt. Henry's helping lift her up hadn't bothered her. That would be something to think about later, but now they had a trip to town. The other ladies joined her, and Aunt Mae picked up the reins.

In a few minutes they arrived at the infirmary, and Doc Jensen hurried out to assist Libby from the carriage. Then he reached up for Connor and Erin. He grinned and patted Connor's head. "He's as healthy looking as any baby I've seen recently. Keep up the good mothering, Erin."

He helped Libby up the steps and into the waiting area. "Go on along to that room over there, and I'll be in shortly."

Erin sat down in the empty waiting room, but Aunt Mae followed Libby into the examining room. "Let's get you up on that table." She placed her hands on Libby's waist and lifted her just enough to settle her in place. "Now you're all set."

"Yes, she is." Doc Jensen strode into the room and peered at her over his glasses. "I've been told that you've been obeying my orders and staying off that ankle." He reached down and lifted the hem of her skirt just enough to run his hands about the cast.

"Yes, I have. I want it to get better." The sooner it healed, the sooner she could make her escape. That consumed her every thought these days, and the mere idea of the looks on Aunt Mae's and Erin's face when they learned the truth gave her chills to the bone. She wouldn't even let herself think about Cory's reaction.

"Looks good, Elizabeth. Give it another five weeks, and we'll see how it's doing. By then I should be able to remove the cast."

If hearing her real name wasn't enough of a pain, the announcement of five more weeks made it worse. How could she manage to stay out of Cory's way that long? She'd run out of excuses for not eating meals with him at the table. Her rebuffs at other times didn't discourage him from being nice to her, and that hurt as much as the rejection at this point.

A few minutes later Doc Jensen had helped her down, and she and Aunt Mae joined Erin the waiting area.

Out on the boardwalk Aunt Mae folded her arms across her chest. "Now, I'm going to leave you two young ladies on your own and go to the bank to meet Cyrus. Y'all enjoy your shopping and lunch, and I'll catch up with you down at Grayson's Mercantile. Just remember, I'm serving a light supper tonight, so eat hearty at Annie's." With that reminder she swirled around and headed down Main Street toward the bank.

Erin shrugged her shoulders. "I guess that means you and I are on our own for a while. I'd like to stop in at Mrs. Bennett's to see if she's got in any new fabrics and patterns. Come on, let's get the carriage. You certainly can't walk very far with those crutches.

"Now, I'm going to place Connor here on the floor. After you're up and settled in the seat, I'll hand him up to you then climb up myself. You hold him, and I'll handle the reins." Erin reached over to position Connor on the floor of the carriage.

A voice to her side caused Libby to jump. Mayor Tate removed his hat. "If I may be of assistance, Miss Bradley. I'd be happy to help you into the carriage."

For a moment she hesitated, not wanting him to grasp her arm, but Erin intervened. "Why, thank you, Mayor Tate. We appreciate that, don't we, Elizabeth?"

Heat filled Libby's face, but she nodded and let the mayor grasp her waist and lift her so she could pull herself up on her uninjured foot. Again, the expected reaction didn't come as he helped her up, and that unnerved her so that she almost slipped and fell before settling onto the seat.

He let go and stepped back. "Always glad to be of assistance to ladies in need. Enjoy your day." He bowed then turned to cross the street.

Libby breathed in and out slowly to calm her nerves before reaching out to grasp Connor from Erin. The men here meant her no harm. Doc Jensen, the mayor, Rev. Winston, and even Cory had been nothing but gentlemen in their actions toward her, but it would be a long time before she forgot those in her past who hadn't been so kind.

At the dressmaking shop, Mrs. Bennett welcomed them with open arms and a mile-wide smile. "Oh, Erin, I'm so glad you have little Connor with you. He's so precious." The plump little woman tickled the baby's chin, and he actually smiled at her.

"He likes you, Mrs. Bennett, but then who wouldn't." Erin kissed Connor's fuzzy head then gazed around the store. "I saw some hats in your window I think I'd like to try."

"Of course. Let's have a look."

Libby held Connor until Erin tried on a few hats and finally settled on one. She then chose fabric for a new spring dress. She finished her purchases, and they were once again on the board-walk. Erin swayed with the baby. "Let's go on to Annie's. She has a cradle there, so Connor can nap while we're eating."

A few minutes later they were seated in the diner with the baby nestled in a little wooden cradle. After ordering their meals, Libby gazed around at the people gathered there. Henry Wilder waved from his table by the front window. Of course this is where he would be eating. He spent more time here than he ever had at the boardinghouse, and that was probably a good thing for both Henry and Annie. Nothing fancy here, just plain, good food and company. Red-and-white checked curtains on the windows matched the cloths on the tables, and framed proverbs and pictures adorned the walls. Another homey, friendly establishment among the many of Porterfield created remorse in Libby once again. She'd missed out on so much in life. God just wasn't fair about where He put people and what happened to them.

During the meal she didn't say much but let Erin talk about all the things going on at the church and how they were getting ready for Easter a week from Sunday. Kate would sing, and a special group of singers had been formed to sing a few pieces from a great oratorio work that the reverend's aunt had heard in Boston. None of it meant anything to Libby, but she listened.

That was one service Libby wouldn't be able to get out of for certain. Even Pa wanted to attend church at Easter and Christmas—until a few old biddies there had been so insulting, so that last year they'd skipped. Pa said he'd never darken the door of a church again as long as those women were there, only he hadn't called them women.

When they'd finished their meal, Erin went to the counter to pay the check. Guilt again coursed through Libby, but Erin had insisted this was her treat. Somehow, someway, she planned to pay Erin and the reverend back for all their help, and Aunt Mae too with her free room and board this past week.

When Libby turned toward the door, she smacked into a wall of a man, his chest thick and hard. She stepped back, heat rising in her face. With her eyes cast downward, she muttered an apology, but the man grabbed her arms.

"Well, if it isn't Libby Cantrell. So this is where you got to. Your pa's been looking all over for you."

The voice sent cold chills coursing through her veins. He knew her name, and she recognized the voice. She raised her gaze to the man's face and choked back a gasp. This man had been one of them at the saloon. She'd never forget the blood red birthmark that covered one side of his neck. She tried to yank away, but he held her fast.

"You're looking really pretty, but these clothes don't do you justice. Wait till I tell your pa I found you here in Porterfield. He'll be mighty happy to know I found you."

"You've made a mistake. My name is Elizabeth Bradley." From the corner of her eye she noted that Annie sent a message to Henry with her eyes, and he left in a flash. Cory. He was going for Cory. She couldn't let him find her here like this. She tried to wrench away again, but the man just laughed.

Annie stepped up. "Mister, I don't like men man handling my customers. I suggest you take your hands off Miss Bradley." She clenched her hands on her hips and glared at the man.

He laughed again but dropped his grasp. "This gal here isn't Miss Bradley. She's Libby Cantrell, one of the best saloon girls in Louisiana."

Libby heard Erin's gasp behind her and wanted to melt to the floor. Why had she even thought she could be safe for another day, much less several weeks in this place? She wanted to scream, shout, yell, and kick this hateful man, but all she could do was stand there with tears spilling from her eyes.

She lowered her voice in an effort to keep Erin and Annie from hearing her plea. "Please, just go away and leave me alone. If you go back and tell Pa, I'll just be gone by the time he can come here."

This time he grabbed her arm and pulled her to his chest. "Oh no, you won't. I'll take you back myself before I let that happen."

"Take your hands off the lady, slow and easy, then step away from her."

Cory's voice. Now the tears turned to sobs, and Annie grabbed her in a hug as the man let go. She saw the gun in Cory's hand first then looked up to see in his eyes the questions mixed with steely resolve. How could she ever explain this to him?

Annie's voice rang out in the diner. "I believe I asked you to leave, and I don't want to have to do it again. Just leave the lady alone and go on about your business."

The man moved toward the door. "I'm leaving, but don't think that pretty little filly is a lady. She's pulled the wool over your eyes, 'cause she's no lady. She belongs across the street there in that saloon."

With that he settled his hat on his head and sauntered toward the door. Libby collapsed onto the floor. Annie hollered for Henry to run for the doc before everything went black.

❁

Cory made sure the man had left then holstered his gun, thankful he had no need to use it. The man's words began to sink into his brain, but he didn't want to grasp them. Annie hollered at Henry, and Cory turned to see Libby in a heap on the floor. His emotions split him in half, with part of him not wanting to believe what he'd heard, the other realizing that Elizabeth or Libby or whoever had been lying all this time.

Annie grabbed his arm. "Help me get her up on that bench there. Doc will be here in a minute." Her look stabbed him in the gut, and he did as she said, once again scooping her up against his chest. When he held her, he could only think of all she'd said and done these past weeks. No wonder she'd shied away from him and had tried to run away. He laid her on the bench then stepped back, contempt for what she represented filling him with an anger so intense he wanted to smash someone's face.

He turned to find Erin crying and rocking back and forth with Connor close to her chest. He'd let that tramp of a girl live with his sister in the preacher's house, no less. No telling what harm could have come to her and the baby.

"Annie, I have to go take care of some business." He strode for the door, not daring to look back at the girl on the bench. He'd let his heart get ahead of his brain once again.

Once outside he took deep, cleansing breaths to clear his head. He had to think all this through. Ma would tell him to listen to Elizabeth's side of the story. He snorted. Some kind of story that would be.

Aunt Mae ran from down at the hotel and stopped beside Cory. She panted for breath for a few seconds. "Elizabeth...is she OK? I heard some man attacked her in the diner."

Cory steadied his aunt with his hands on her forearms. "No one attacked her. Some man recognized her and called her by another name. Said her pa was looking for her."

"Well, we knew—"

Cory held up his hand. "I know what she told us, but it doesn't change the fact that she lied to us all these weeks. She isn't who she said she was, and from what the man said, she worked in a saloon back in Louisiana."

"Of course she wouldn't tell us about that, Cory Muldoon. Obviously she was running away from that life, or she'd be working at our saloon right this minute. You better find out what really happened to that little thing, and if you don't, I'll have a few choice words for you, my boy."

She was as bad as Ma, but if he didn't do what she asked, he'd be paying for it for quite a while. It wouldn't hurt to hear her side anyway, but as far as he was concerned, the only reason she wasn't working in a saloon now was that she'd fallen amongst good people who housed her and fed her and took care of her. If it weren't for them, she'd be another fast and loose young woman out to entertain the men and entice them to spend their money. He wanted no part of that kind of girl.

CHAPTER
TWENTY

*C*ORY SAT AT his desk with anger, disappointment, and frustration doing battle in his heart and soul. He had found the man, Walt Drury, and asked him about Elizabeth. He had no cause to arrest the man, but he did have questions. The man from Louisiana said that Mr. Cantrell wanted his daughter back home, and he planned to let the man know so he could come after her.

Elizabeth, or Libby, as he supposed he should call her now, had lied to him and to his family. That lodged in his craw, and no amount of reasoning unstuck it. A saloon girl! How could he have been so taken in? He should have stuck to his guns about finding out who she really was, and then so many wouldn't be hurt.

Ma and Kate both said she had scars and signs of long-time abuse on her body. He wanted to believe her to be simply a runaway from an abusive father or husband, but it didn't add up with what Mr. Drury said. Saloon owners he knew may be hard on their girls, but none had been cruel enough to beat them. It may be different in Louisiana, but it still didn't sound right.

Bile rose in his throat at the image of how Libby had lived and worked. Low-cut necklines with skirts up to the knee and fancy feathers or jewels in their hair described the girls at Durand's Saloon. Libby had worn the same. Those innocent blue eyes and blonde curls would tempt any man to give up wages to spend time with her. No matter which way he looked at it, Libby Cantrell worked in a profession he could not condone or forgive. Elizabeth Bradley passed herself off as a frightened young woman on the run from someone she feared, and for that lie he could never forgive her.

Then the memory of Laura Prescott pressed into his soul. She'd been much younger than Libby, but Darnell kidnapped her from her parents and put her to work in his place. The Lord allowed Daniel and him to rescue the girl and get her back to her parents. But what if Darnell had heard of their plans and got Laura out of town before he and Daniel rescued her? She'd still be in that man's clutches and working for him, just like Libby did. Could it be possible that Libby had no control over the situation, like Laura would have had none over hers? The idea sobered Cory. Despite his anger and disappointment, he must find the truth, but could he trust this girl to give it to him?

"Seems to me, Deputy Muldoon, you have some investigating to do."

Cory jerked his head up at Rutherford's statement. He'd echoed the very thoughts running through Cory's mind. Where to go first? He grabbed his hat and headed for the door. "I'll be at the boardinghouse. I aim to get a few answers and hope they won't be more lies."

He grabbed Blaze's reins and swung up onto his back. Someone grabbed at his pants leg. Annie stood there with blood in her eyes. "What is it, Annie?"

"I came to tell you that Miss Bradley is back at your aunt's place. I've never seen anybody so scared of one man as that girl. You let that weasel go 'cause I saw him ride out of town not ten minutes ago. How could you do that after the way he talked to and treated her? I hope you're going after him now and make sure he doesn't cause more mischief."

"No, Annie, I'm going to Aunt Mae's to ask Elizabeth, or whatever her name is, some questions about what happened in your diner."

She narrowed her eyes and crossed her arms over her chest. "You go easy on that child, you hear? She cried buckets after you left, and not one of us could get her to stop. I don't know what happened to her or who did what, but I tell you, you'd better treat her as an innocent victim until something can be proved. You hear, young man?"

"I hear you, Annie. I'll be careful." He pulled the reins and turned Blaze to head down Main Street. He glanced back to find Annie still glaring at him as if she dared him to hurt Elizabeth. He would go easy to a point, but the truth must be told. Whatever it took, he'd do it to find out Elizabeth Bradley's true identity and why she came to Porterfield. One thing for certain, he didn't need Annie and Aunt Mae on his back for not trusting the girl, and knowing his ma, she'd join forces with the other two, and he'd never get a proper investigation done. He set his mouth hard. If that happened, he

might end up arresting all three of them for obstructing justice, and that's one arrest he planned to avoid, if only for his
own safety.

Libby lay on her bed and hiccupped. She'd spent all the tears
stored up for months and now twisted a handkerchief around
her fingers. Her hair hung down the sides of her face, brushing
her cheeks. The front of her dress lay against her chest, damp
with tears. All energy and hope drained from her body, leaving
it cold, empty, and numb.

Erin and Aunt Mae sat on either side of her with their
arms about her shoulders. They had trusted her and taken her
in, and now they knew she'd lied to them. She squeezed her
eyes shut and hung her head low. She didn't have the nerve to
face them.

"Elizabeth," Aunt Mae said, "we love you and can't stand
to see you so hurt. Like I said back at Annie's, we'll get to
the bottom of this yet. We know you've been hurt, beaten so
bad it left scars, and we know there's an explanation for what
you've done. We're here to comfort and help you, but we have
to know the truth."

"So do I." Cory stepped through the open door.

Libby cringed, and her heart plummeted to her shoes.
Cory would never believe her story, especially after what he'd
said only last Sunday. Every shard of hope disappeared. Telling
the truth now meant the whole, sordid story must come out in
the open. The very thought of how these two women might
regard her hurt more than any lash of Pa's. She'd heard all the

names men called girls like her and wanted to hear none of them from Cory.

She raised her eyes to meet Cory's. What blazed there closed her throat and cut off her breath. The flowers on the wallpaper blurred then swam together into one mass that slammed into her head. Her body went limp against Aunt Mae's.

Aunt Mae laid Libby on the bed and shooed Cory from the room. "You can ask your questions later. This poor child needs my care right now. Go check with Henry and see how he's doing with Connor."

The door closed, and the numbness began to lessen with a tingling that increased the ache already building in every fiber of her body. Her heart pounded with the memory of Cory's face as he left to go after that man. Every bit of loathing and venom in his voice last Sunday now burned from his eyes with a fire that ate at her soul.

Erin and Aunt Mae removed her shoes and tucked her feet under the quilt. Erin pulled the quilt up to Libby's chest. "You're shaking like the leaves in a windstorm, and you're cold as ice. Let me get some hot tea and warm you up."

Libby only nodded. Nothing could be hot enough to warm her now. Dying on that creek would have spared her and all of them the disappointment of finding out about her past. Through half-closed lids she watched Aunt Mae bustle about the room pulling down shades, closing curtains, and straightening the covers.

Erin returned with the herb tea and helped Libby sit up. "I sweetened it with a bit of honey to help it soothe your nerves. This has been an ordeal for you, but I want you to know that we'll do everything we can to help you get through this. That brother of mine is a stubborn mule, and his temper is as Irish as they come, but if you tell the truth, he'll listen."

Libby sipped the tea, and it did soothe her throat, but it'd take more than a cup of hot tea to calm her raw nerves. If she told the truth, Cory may listen, but then he'd push her away and send her back to Pa. He wanted nothing to do with the likes of her. She handed the cup back to Erin and reached for the edge of Ma's quilt. She hugged it to her chest. "I hate You, God."

Erin gasped. "What did you say?"

Libby bit her lip. She didn't mean to say that aloud. Now they'd think even worse of her. She turned her face toward the wall. Shame not only for what she'd said but for what the man had said about her coursed through her veins. How could she ever explain something like that?

Weight fell on the mattress beside her, then Aunt Mae's hand reached over and stroked her brow. "Elizabeth, honey, you may mean that, but God doesn't mind. Sometimes His children hurt so bad that they lash out at Him in anger. I did when my Patrick died too young. But God keeps on loving us anyway until we come to see He has a much better plan for us ahead."

A better plan? God had no plans at all for Libby Cantrell but to make her even more miserable than she already felt. Her sins stained her life so ugly that even God would turn His head in disgust.

When Aunt Mae continued to stroke Libby's brow, something inside melted. This wonderful woman deserved to know the truth, but how could she tell her? Libby turned her still damp face to Aunt Mae. "My full name is Elizabeth. My baby brother couldn't say it. He ended up saying 'Libby,' and that's who I became. Bradley was my mother's maiden name, and Cantrell is the name of my father." At least she hadn't lied so much about her name.

"I see, and where are your mother and brother now?"

The room had grown dim with the shades down, so Erin lit the oil lamp beside the bed. In its glow, only compassion and understanding gleamed from Aunt Mae's face. Erin remained standing close by with her eyes closed.

Libby breathed deeply. "My brother died of typhoid, and my mother never got over it. She took sick and died a little over four years ago, when I was fourteen. Pa went crazy. He started drinking and spent all his money playing cards at the saloon. Pa loved me at one time, but I reminded him of what he'd lost, and he just let me be to scrounge around for food. That's...that's when he started hitting me. Not much at first, but it grew worse the past year." Now that she started, her words tumbled over each other as the story unfolded.

Aunt Mae squeezed her hand. "Oh, you poor child, I'm so sorry. Erin, you have to get Cory. He must hear her story."

Libby's heart lurched. "Wait, Erin. I can't tell him. Please, don't get him. I won't say another word if you do."

"But, honey, he has to know. He and Sheriff Rutherford can protect you if your father comes to get you."

"I don't want his protection if I have to tell him everything." He probably knew it all anyway from that man earlier, but she couldn't bear to tell him about how she'd lived. The desire to even tell Aunt Mae and Erin disappeared. Once more the fear of rejection built a cold wall of privacy around her heart. She couldn't trust any of them. They would never see her as the victim but only as the loose woman she became. Hadn't Pa told her often enough that she wasn't worth a thing to decent folks?

"If you don't mind, I'm rather tired now. I'd like to be left alone to think and rest." With her ankle still in a cast, she had no other option but to face these people, who meant so much to her until today. They were entitled to the truth, but telling it would take courage she didn't possess right now.

Aunt Mae hugged Libby. "All right, we'll leave you alone, but Erin and I both will be praying for you to see how we can help you. If you need a lawyer, we have one for you. If you need someone to pray, you got that too. We're going to see you through this."

Libby could only nod as tears filled her eyes and choked her so she couldn't speak. What a horrible mess she'd brought into this home. God should have let her die at the creek.

After the two women closed the door, she curled up into a ball and allowed the sobs she held in check to shake her body. The tears that had drained dry such a short time ago now fell like the rain from the storm-filled clouds she'd endured less than two weeks ago.

The tears washed away all hopes and dreams for a future away from Pa and his beatings. The cast on her ankle may give her a few weeks' reprieve, but then again it might anger him to the point that he'd beat her again because she couldn't earn him money for drinking. Whatever lay ahead, it wouldn't be good.

CHAPTER
TWENTY-ONE

*K*URT COULDN'T BELIEVE what Walt Drury told him. He pondered the words over and over in his mind. Libby had gone only as far as Porterfield, Texas, a day and a half ride away. Why, he could leave now and be there on Monday. With her back here, they could pick up their lives as if she'd never been gone. Working these past few weeks reminded him of how much better it was to have a little money in his pockets. One time in the past he'd worked an honest day's wages and taken care of his family.

With no family left but Libby, life got hard. He didn't like drinking and gambling, but he could escape his troubles through both. Problems came when he ran out of money for the cards. That's where Libby saved the day for him. When she turned seventeen, men began to notice how pretty she had become and started teasing Kurt about her and her womanly charms.

That's when his idea took hold, and the saloon owner decided having Libby around would be good for his business.

Kurt agreed, with the stipulation that part of Libby's earnings would go to him. Then later Kurt figured out a way to use her even more to his advantage. In just the few months men had paid for her services, she'd made him enough to keep up with the card games and whiskey and a little left over for food.

If he brought her back now, he could offer her up without going through the saloon. That would bring in even more money than before, but this time he'd save it for a bigger and better house and fancier clothes for Libby. Then the image of Libby as a child flitted across his mind. What had he done to that girl?

Drury had said Libby lived with a reverend and his wife in Porterfield. That meant she had been well taken care of. He remembered how he and Emma took Libby and Jonah to church when they were little. He'd even tried going with just Libby, but after his drinking and gambling took over, those righteous ladies let him know in not-so-nice terms that neither he nor Libby were welcome. They'd been nice to Libby until she started working in the saloon.

Kurt combed his hair and checked his appearance in the mirror over the washbasin. Without his bloodshot eyes he looked halfway decent. Liquor still pulled him, but having the extra money meant finding Libby faster, and now he even knew where to look. No telling what stories she told the people she met in Porterfield. Drury didn't seem to think she'd told them the truth because of the shocked expressions on the faces of the women with Libby.

When he got to Porterfield, he'd collect his daughter then get on back home in time for the weekend crowd at the Bayou Belle. Satisfied with his plan, Kurt grabbed up his satchel packed with his one decent pair of pants and extra shirt and headed for the livery to rent a horse.

Along the way several good people cast sidelong glances at him, apparently surprised by his appearance. Let them talk behind their hands and condemn him. Today nothing mattered to him but getting his girl back home.

~~~~~※~~~~~

Libby managed to stay in her room after the debacle on Thursday. No matter how Aunt Mae and Erin tried to convince her otherwise, she didn't want to face Cory and his questions. Her heart ached with the thought of the rejection she'd face as well as his scorn for all the lies he'd claim she told.

Reverend Winston had even come to see her with his father, another minister. Both wanted to talk with her, but she'd refused to see them. They'd only condemn her and tell her she had lived a life of sin. As if she didn't know that already.

Her ankle began throbbing again, so she lay back on the pillows and used one to prop her foot up some. If Pa came, she'd have to leave with him and probably get a beating once they left town and traveled far enough away.

She loved this town, and knowing she must leave it sent sharp stabs of pain to her stomach. However, now that people had found out her background, they wouldn't be so nice and friendly to her. The fact that Erin and Aunt Mae both talked to her and took care of her puzzled her. People back home didn't do that once she started working at the saloon. They didn't care one whit about what happened to Libby Cantrell or her pa.

Aunt Mae knocked then entered the room. "I've brought you something to eat. You have to keep up your strength."

Libby's stomach roiled at the mention of food. Although hungry, she'd tried to eat earlier, but nothing had any taste. "Thank you, Aunt Mae, but I don't think I can eat anything."

"Now, this is my famous chicken soup, and it'll cure what ails you in a minute. You can't hide away in your room forever."

"No, you can't." Ada Muldoon popped into the room, removing her gloves and scolding at the same time. "This is no place for you to be. It only makes you more miserable. Doesn't matter what some crazy man says, we know you for who you've shown us."

"She's right. Cantrell, Bradley, Libby, or Elizabeth doesn't make a whit of difference." Aunt Mae set the tray on the bedside table then eased down on the edge of Libby's bed. "We know you've had a rough go of it. Ada and Kate have both seen your scars and bruises, and I did too when I helped you to bed the other night."

"Mr. Muldoon and I came into town for supplies, and Kate told us what happened at Annie's. Whatever that man said doesn't amount to a hill of beans and is worth less."

They didn't know but half the story. If they knew why she had those scars and fresh whelps the first night she'd been here, they'd sing a different song. Drury had hinted at it when he said she had been a saloon girl. If only what he'd said really wasn't worth anything, but she knew the truth. She squeezed her eyes shut to keep the tears from slipping down her cheeks again.

Aunt Mae's hand caressed Libby's forehead, just as she'd

done the other night. "Honey, you told us part of your story, and now you need to tell us the rest."

Libby winced. Yes, she needed to tell them, but she didn't have the courage it took to confess her wrongdoings. After her impulsive actions on Thursday, she'd hardened her resolve not to say anything about the rest. Either Pa would be here soon to take her back home, or she'd make her escape on Yeller Boy again. Whichever happened, her future grew dimmer than her room by candlelight.

Cory sat at his desk tapping a pen on the surface. Libby had remained silent and uncooperative since the incident Thursday. Since Drury had not said where in Louisiana he knew Libby's father was from, Cory had nothing further to go on for an investigation. He'd sent the wire to the town mentioned on the wanted poster but had heard nothing back. Looked like a trip to Bayou Point, Louisiana, would be necessary to find this man Cantrell and make all the connections.

At least Elizabeth was her real name, but she had lied about her last name being Bradley. Aunt Mae told him Libby used the name because she didn't want her father to find her. That's all the information Erin and Aunt managed to get from Elizabeth, or Libby.

He snapped the pencil in half. He didn't even know what to call her. His mind rumbled again with the words Drury had used to condemn her. She lived a life no better than any of the girls at the saloon here in Porterfield. Those girls kept to themselves and didn't mix with the good citizens of the town.

Men visited the saloon for four reasons: whiskey, gambling, women, or all three.

Cory didn't begrudge the decent men in Porterfield a drink or two now and then. That was their business. It became his business only when they caused a fight or other ruckus, and enough of those happened to keep the sheriff and Cory busy on weekends. The girls he couldn't excuse. They chose their way of life and flaunted their looks with low-cut, short-skirted dresses, rouged cheeks and lips, and fancy hairdos with feathers and jewels nestled in the curls. Aunt Mae scolded him for his attitude more than once in the past, but he couldn't condone the sins going on there. But until some kind of law came along to prohibit them, he'd have to live with it in town.

Sheriff Rutherford and Marshal Slade sauntered through the door. Rutherford hung up his hat and unbuckled his gun belt. "Cory, I've been telling Slade about Drury and that Cantrell girl. He knows of a Kurt Cantrell in Louisiana."

Cory leaned forward. "That so? I sent a wire down there weeks ago but never heard back from it. What can you tell me?"

"Nothing good. He does have a daughter, and she worked in the saloon there, but I heard tell that he had a little business going on the side with her. Only time I ever saw him he was drunk and losing money at cards. Saw his daughter only once, and she's a mighty pretty gal."

Cory's heart sank with the news. It filled with dread and lay heavy in his chest. He should never have let himself care about her like he had. He'd let his family take her in and treat her like one of them. She'd touched him with her fear, but it had been a fear of being found out.

"Ma said Elizabeth had welts and scars and bruises on her back and legs."

"That doesn't surprise me. Rumors around town had it that he beat her when she didn't do what he wanted. They lived in a ramshackle cabin on the edge of town. Couldn't arrest him since we had no proof of anything illegal. Nobody would talk, and if a man hits his own children, can't do anything about that either."

No man should ever be allowed to beat up on anyone else, relative or not. Fury boiled in Cory's blood. If he could strangle Cantrell, he would.

"If you can get Libby Cantrell to tell us everything that happened with her father, we might be able to slam him with some charges that might stick. She's the one who'd have to press charges, because you're sure not going to get any of the men using her services to testify. Trouble is, she's over eighteen now, and anything that happened the past year or two I can't do much about."

"What I can't understand is why he didn't answer my wire. If he's so anxious to get his daughter back, you'd think he'd been here by now."

Slade shrugged his shoulders. "When a man like Cantrell is drinking, they don't think straight. He might not have even realized what the wire was about. Now that Drury has found her, he'll let Cantrell know."

Drury hadn't made any bones about what went on, but he still needed to hear Elizabeth's story from her. That didn't seem likely, since she wouldn't even talk to him.

Slade leaned with his palms on Cory's desk. "Look, if you want me to go down there and pick up Cantrell I can, but I don't think it'll do much good, because the laws just don't cover it down there. A small-town saloon isn't considered a brothel and isn't against the law. I'm sorry, but that's the way it is."

It may be the way things were in Louisiana, and even here in Porterfield, but that didn't make it right. Sin was sin, no matter how he looked at it. His emotions swayed back and forth worse than a swing out of control. One minute he hated Elizabeth for what she had done and the way she lived. The next he wanted to cry for her and all the hurt and pain she'd endured.

Cory shook his head. "Picking up Cantrell won't be necessary, Slade. It's only a matter of time before he'll be in town looking for her. He'll have to fight Aunt Mae and Erin and most likely Ma to get to her, and those are three I wouldn't want to tangle with over anything, especially when they're in their protective mode. I guess it'll all depend on much control her pa has over her as to what she'll do."

Cory shoved back from his desk and grabbed his hat. "I'm going out for a while. It's getting too warm in here for me, and I need some fresh air."

His boot spurs jangled with the long strides he took to the door. Outside, he headed down the main street of the town he loved. He breathed in deeply and lifted his gaze to the heavens, now a clear blue that spoke of the new season beginning today— spring, a time of renewal and hope for God's people. Palm Sunday tomorrow would be filled with the story of Jesus's triumphant entry into Jerusalem, and as the week wore on special services would observe the trials and crucifixion of Jesus.

Betrayal ate at his thoughts. Judas betrayed Jesus, and Elizabeth betrayed him with the lies and hiding the truth.

Then his heart ruled once more. He couldn't let her go back to that life. She'd be safer at the ranch.

Lord, I don't know what to do or where to turn. I can't get past the fact that Elizabeth lied to all of us. She's lived a life that is so full of sin, how can she ever be made clean? Why did I let my heart rule over my common sense? Help me, Lord, to learn the truth and to know what You want me to do.

Only one word came to mind. *Forgive.* Impossible. After all he'd said against what she did, how could he now forgive her? He could protect her, because she deserved that from a man who called himself her father but treated her like a slave. But forgiveness? Not likely.

CHAPTER
TWENTY-TWO

*H*IS MIND MADE up, Cory didn't go back for his horse but strode all the way to the boardinghouse. The quicker he moved Elizabeth from town, the safer she'd be. He'd have to sort out all the conflicting emotions later. He burst through the door then stopped short. His mother sat in the parlor with Aunt Mae.

"Ma, what are you doing here?"

"Planning a strategy to keep Elizabeth away from her father, that's what. What has you in such rush? And take your hat off in the house."

He yanked his hat from his head. "I...I..." He shifted his gaze from Ma to Aunt Mae and back again. "I wanted to get Elizabeth out to the ranch. It'd be harder for Cantrell to find her there, and you have all those cowhands out there to protect her."

His ma said nothing, but her mouth worked in a way he knew too well. She had something on her mind, and he'd find out whether he liked it or not. Instead of the tongue lashing he expected, she stood and nodded to Aunt Mae.

"Mae, go get Elizabeth ready to go." Then she pointed a finger at Cory. "We're taking her out to the ranch, but you're gonna get yourself out of here right now. Seeing you will only upset her more. She hasn't left that room since Thursday, and the only way we're going to be able to help her is to move her. Unless you've changed your feelings or your mind, I suggest you go on back and do your job. We'll take care of Elizabeth."

When she crossed her arms over her chest, Cory stepped back. No sense in trying to argue with her in this frame of mind. But then, he didn't even have an argument. They were doing what he wanted them to do and not because he asked them. He shoved his hat back on and strode from the room. Anger and relief fought for attention in his heart. Ma had no cause to dismiss him like that. Or did she?

The way he'd reacted the other night when he tried to see Elizabeth had not been the most polite. In fact, he'd been downright rude, but hearing what Drury had to say tore at his gut like nothing else, not even when Abigail had been taken hostage.

Now he had a long trudge back to the sheriff's office. He should have ridden to the boardinghouse, but he'd been halfway through town by the time he made a decision to pro- tect Elizabeth.

Kate hollered at him from the boardwalk of the infirmary. He stopped to wait for her, and dread filled his soul. Kate knew him better than anyone else, and she'd have a few words to say, no doubt about it.

"Cory Muldoon, I've been looking all over for you." She stood in front of him with her hands on her hips. "We have to do something to protect Elizabeth, whether you like it or not."

He sighed and shook his head. "Ma and Aunt Mae are already taking care of that. She's going out to the ranch with Ma and Pa soon as Pa finishes his business in town."

"Well, thank goodness for that. I've been worried sick about her ever since that awful scene in the diner."

"Kate, you weren't even there."

"I didn't have to be there, big brother. I heard all about it and the way you acted at the boardinghouse later. Then you let that Drury fellow go, and you know he's going straight to her pa and telling him where she is."

"Rutherford said we had nothing to hold him for, so we had to let him go, and yes, I do know her pa will come looking for her. That's why she's going to the ranch. He's less likely to find her out there." Or at least it'd take him a little longer to find her.

"What about you? What are you going to do to protect her when her pa gets to town? He's going to be asking about her, and after what people heard in the diner, they may or may not be willing to spill the beans about her staying at the board-inghouse. What's going to happen when he finds out she's not there?" Anger and concern flashed in her green eyes.

"I don't know, Kate. I'll try to talk with him and find out exactly what he wants and—"

"What he wants? You know exactly what he wants, and you'd better be thinking of what you're going to do and say with that man." She closed her eyes and shuddered. "When I think of what he made her.... Oh, I'd like to string him up by his toes." Her eyes opened wide then narrowed. "All I can say is, you'd better not help him. Understand?"

Oh, he understood all right. All the women in the Muldoon family would be on his back if he did the wrong thing, and maybe even if he did the right thing, whatever that was. "I'll be careful. That's all I can promise."

"Oh, you make me so mad. How can you be so insensitive?" She turned with a swish of her skirts and stomped off down the street.

Cory pushed back the brim of his hat and shook his head. She had no room to talk. She'd been as stubborn and pigheaded when it came to falling in love with Daniel not long ago, and not very sensitive to Daniel's feelings. One thing he couldn't understand about his ma, Erin, Kate, and Aunt Mae: why were they so bent on helping a girl who had done the things Elizabeth had? Better question, why did he want to protect her, feeling like he did about her life? Life should be black and white, without all the little gray areas that kept cropping up to make him question his own motives and behavior.

He'd learned more about the law and brothels and child abuse when they rescued a young prostitute named Laura. The laws hadn't changed, but he had to find a way to keep Cantrell from his daughter or hear every lecture in the book from every woman in his family, as well as a few who were not members. Only one thing to do now. Seek Daniel and get his advice and help.

With fresh resolve he headed toward the courthouse and consultation with Daniel. If anyone could untangle this mess and find a way to put Cantrell away for good, his brother-in-law would find it.

Libby stared at the women standing by her bed. She bit her lip and frowned. "Move to the Circle M? How's that going to protect me?"

Ada patted Libby's arm. "No one is going to know you're with us except Cory, Aunt Mae, and Kate. It'll take a while for him to figure out where you are, and if he comes out there, we have plenty of cowboys who'll protect you."

"But why are you doing this? You heard what that man said. Pa won't stop until he can haul me back to Louisiana." If they knew the whole story, they wouldn't be so eager to protect her, but she couldn't bring herself to tell them, at least not yet.

"Elizabeth, you're just a young girl and a victim of abuse from a man who should be loving you and watching out for you. We love you, and we want to take care of you. It's what God wants us to do."

What God wanted them to do? How could they be so sure of that? If they were determined to help her, she'd let them, whether it was what God wanted or not. "Then I guess we might as well get on with this."

"Good. Let's get you packed and ready to move. Kate's already checked with Doc Jensen this morning, and he's all for the idea."

"That's right. You won't need to come back into town at all. Doc said he'd come out to the ranch and take care of removing the cast when the time comes."

When that time came she could be back in Louisiana or on her way, but perhaps being at the Circle M would give her time to heal and then make her getaway again. "Will you make sure Yeller Boy goes out to ranch with us? I don't want him in town where Pa could find him. He wasn't very kind to that horse either."

Aunt Mae pulled out the satchel and set it on the bed. "Of course you can take him. He's out in our stable with my horse, Danny Boy. I'll get one of the boys to bring her out to you."

That would make escape easier, but only if Pa stayed away long enough. If he came sooner, she would get away, cast or no cast on her ankle. She crossed her arms over her chest and rubbed her forearms and watched Aunt Mae fold a skirt and blouse into the satchel. "I still don't understand why you're helping me at all. I'll just be a burden to everyone."

Aunt Mae picked up a nightdress. "Horsefeathers. You're not a burden to anyone. Besides, like we said before, this is what Jesus would do and what He wants us to do. Now get up and wash your face and get ready to go."

Elizabeth suppressed a grin. When Aunt Mae gave an order, people obeyed, even though her voice carried only concern, determination, and no nonsense. "Yes, ma'am."

Kate headed for the door. "I'm going to find Pa. He should be finished at the bank by now. I saw Jimmy Lowell riding in, so I'll get him to take the horse out to the ranch."

Elizabeth finished washing her face and tackled her matted hair. Lying in bed for hours did nothing to improve it, and now she fought with the tangles.

Ada stepped up from behind and eased the brush from Elizabeth's hands. "Here, let me do that for you." She ran the brush through the snarls with a gentle hand. "You have beautiful hair, dear. It's said to be a woman's crowning glory."

Crowning glory? It certainly didn't look that way now. She winced as the brush untangled the curls and stroked the strands smooth. Ada then pulled back the sides and secured them with a hair clip and a bow. The rest hung free down Elizabeth's back.

"Thank you, Ada. I always hate trying to brush out the mess in the mornings." Because of the fancy hairdos her father insisted she wear, her hair after a busy night always ended up in a mass of tangles and snarls.

Aunt Mae snapped the satchel closed. "Everything you need is right in here."

"Thank you both." Tears threatened to fill her eyes. "No one's taken care of me like this for a long time." She'd enjoy it as long as it lasted, because when Pa arrived and the whole truth came out, things would change.

Kate returned with the news that Mr. Muldoon was out back with the wagon. "The plan is for you to lie down in the back until you're out of town. That way no one will see you leaving. Jimmy will come by and get Yeller Boy and bring him out later. I think he's planning to spend a little time with Jessica Miller today."

Jessica Miller, the school teacher. Libby remembered meeting the young woman at church. Oh, to have the opportunities like that. Teaching school would be such a blessing but probably never even a consideration for her. School teachers had so many rules to follow, and one with a tainted background would never be hired. The possibilities for things she could do if she started a new life grew narrower with each passing day.

"I thank you for doing that. That horse means a lot to me." She picked up the worn quilt. "So does this. Ma made it for me when I was a little girl." It'd seen much better days, but each time she held it, it brought her mother closer.

Kate picked up the satchel and handed Libby the crutches. "Sure you have everything you need to take with you?"

"More than enough, thanks to your ma and Aunt Mae." She had noticed Ada slipping an extra calico print dress into the satchel. Libby started to protest, but since Ada wanted to help, the dress would come in handy at a later time.

The four of them trooped out the back door, with Kate helping Libby get down the steps. Mr. Muldoon jumped down from the wagon seat and lifted Libby onto the wagon bed.

"We're going to get you out to our place without anyone knowing about it here. Stay low until we're out in the country, then you can sit up and be more comfortable." He handed her a folded-up blanket. "Here, you can use this as a pillow of sorts."

His hand touched her as he handed the blanket to her. She waited for the fear to rear its head, but nothing came. She swallowed hard at the realization and placed the blanket under her head then hugged her own quilt to her chest. Was her dread of men helping her truly gone?

Was there no end to the kindness of these people? In her eighteen years...almost nineteen in a few weeks... Realization dawned on her. She didn't have to go back with Pa. She was an adult now and didn't have to be under Pa's thumb. She bit her lip. Still, facing up to him would take a lot of courage, and right now she had very little of that.

CHAPTER
TWENTY-THREE

*K*URT RODE INTO Porterfield a little before noon on Monday and went to the hotel. He'd need a room for only one night, as far as he figured it. He paid the clerk then headed up to his room to shave and change clothes. As long as he looked respectable and acted that way, people would treat him with respect. That he'd learned in the past weeks of being sober.

Hunger rumbled in his belly. He'd spotted a diner not far from the hotel, and it would be a sight cheaper than the hotel dining room. His trousers still held the crease from cleaning last week, and his good shirt fit well since he'd quit drinking and gained a little weight. He wiped the dust from his boots with the towel in his room and pulled them on.

He preened a bit in front of the mirror above the washbasin. No one would know him for the man he'd been a month ago, and he planned to stay that way. He needn't worry about being cheated at cards either. He'd stick strictly to business. The quicker he could find Libby, the quicker he could take her back and start living again.

Across the way at Annie's Kitchen, the menu tempted him to spend money on a good beefsteak, but he had a set amount for this trip, and he wanted to be careful. A bowl of stew and a slab of cornbread ought to hold him over until dinner. Perhaps he'd have Libby to join him by then.

No sooner had a woman taken his order than two men entered the diner and headed straight for him. One wore a badge and the other a fancy suit.

"Are you Kurt Cantrell?" the one with the badge asked.

"Yes, I am. Who wants to know?"

"I'm Deputy Muldoon, and this is Daniel Monroe, our county attorney."

Kurt nodded and smiled. "Nice to know you, but I'm sure you're not here just to welcome me to town."

The deputy held his hat brim with his fingers and peered at Kurt through narrowed eyes. "No, we need to talk to you about your daughter."

He should have known. "Ah, yes, Libby. Can you tell me where she is?"

The deputy shook his head. "No, I can't, but you'd be doing us all a favor if you'd just leave town and not attempt to see her."

Kurt's stew arrived, along with the cornbread and more coffee, giving him time to tamp down his temper and pretend to be reasonable. "If you care to sit, we can discuss this while I eat my meal. I've had a hard day of travel to get here."

The deputy nodded to the lawyer, and they both took a seat. A woman hurried over to their table. "Anything I can get for you, deputy, or you, Mr. Monroe?"

"Sweet tea would be fine, Annie. What about you, Daniel?"

"Same for me. I'm eating with Kate later."

Deputy Muldoon leaned his arms on the table and stared straight into Kurt's face. "Why are you looking for your daughter?"

Kurt eyed the two men. They were sharp and wouldn't take to his lies. "Well, you see, deputy, she ran off with my only horse and my money."

Muldoon's eyes narrowed. "You have a horse you rode in on and money for your meal, so it couldn't have hurt you much. Besides, she's nearing nineteen and can't be hauled back just like that. She has a say in her own life."

Kurt swallowed hard and waited to speak until the serving girl had placed the glasses of tea on the table. "Now, don't you think that's something between a father and his daughter?"

"Not if that daughter is afraid of the father and has bruises and scars that speak of a severe beating a time or two."

Kurt clenched his teeth. "I don't know what lies that girl's been telling you, but you can't believe anything she says. Isn't anyone else's business how a man disciplines a daughter who lies, disobeys, and steals. She cheated me out of an income and took my only means of transportation. All I want to do is take her home where she belongs." These men had no right to refuse him getting his daughter. He hadn't broken any laws. What Libby had done recently was as an adult and no crime the last time he'd looked.

The lawyer spoke up. "We made some laws here in our community against the beating of children, no matter what their age. Drury told us he'd used her 'services' before and that she'd been entertainment for him. Is that why you're so anxious to find her and take her home?"

Fury spread across the deputy's face, and red blotches appeared on his cheeks. Something else was going on here, not just protecting Libby, but something that had the deputy riled. "As I said, she was—is—my means of a livelihood, and she works for me."

Again the deputy sat silent and let the lawyer do the talking. "If you mean selling her to the highest bidder for the evening, then we plan to keep her here in jail on prostitution charges, and while we're at it, we can charge you too." He stood. "In fact, when you're finished here, we're taking a little trip to the sheriff's office and see what he has to say about this."

Kurt threw down his napkin and stood to his full height. "You're not taking me anywhere but to find my daughter. Like you said, she's of age, so she can consent to do anything she wants to. Besides, the last time I looked, prostitution wasn't a crime."

The deputy stood and had a good three inches on Kurt, but he refused to back down. He placed a hand on Kurt's arm. "Not if it's against our laws. We don't allow prostitution."

Kurt jerked away from the hold. "I haven't broken any laws here."

The deputy clenched his teeth and narrowed his eyes. "If you don't want to be charged with resisting arrest, I suggest you come along with us. We can discuss this further down at the jail."

Kurt stood his ground a moment then swallowed hard. He didn't need the extra trouble a ruckus with the sheriff could bring. "All right, I'll come with you, but I still say you have no cause to hold me."

Cory slammed the door between the cells and the office with a bang. "Do you think he bought into your story about the law?"

Daniel shrugged. "Even if he did, it won't take him long to find out we're bluffing—about the prostitution part, not the beating. We have to get Elizabeth to testify that he's been beating and using her since she was underage. If he didn't start until she was eighteen, we can't do much about the prostitution, especially if she consented."

Cory slumped into his chair and rubbed his hands across his jaw. If she'd given her consent, then she really was no better than those girls at the saloon. Did it really matter one way or the other? She was soiled goods. No telling how many men she'd been with. He couldn't do anything about that, but he could not shake the feeling that he must do something about her going back.

The front office door slammed back against the wall, and Aunt Mae and Kate stormed into the room. Didn't take brains to see the thunderclouds following those two women. Daniel jumped up from his chair.

"Kate, what are you doing here? We're supposed to meet at the hotel for dinner."

"We heard from Annie that you have Elizabeth's father here. Is that right?"

"Well, yes, it is, but you can't—"

"Don't tell me what we can or can't do, Daniel Monroe. Elizabeth's life is at stake."

Cory had seen Kate riled up like this once before, and then it had been Darnell getting the brunt end of her anger.

That man went to prison, but this time Kate's anger would do no good. Daniel shook his head and turned to Cory.

"Tell her she can't go back there, Cory. She doesn't need to be around the likes of Cantrell."

Before he could speak, Cory noticed the smirk on Kate's face. He turned just in time to see Aunt Mae had snagged the keys from the hook and already had the door to the cells open. Kate had been the diversion. He raced after Aunt Mae with Kate and Daniel right behind him.

Aunt Mae stood in front of the jail cell with clenched hands on her hips and fire in her eyes. "You call yourself a father, Kurt Cantrell? You're the poorest excuse for a father I've ever seen or heard tell of. You have the sweetest little gal for a daughter, and everyone here in town loves her. I've seen the welts and scars and bruises on that poor child. It takes a coward to hit a woman, much less a child."

Cory reached out to stop Aunt Mae but pulled his hand back. Let his aunt rant and rave all she wanted. Cantrell deserved every word.

"Furthermore, a man has no right to use a young girl the way you have Elizabeth. She's frightened to death of you and most men at an age when she should be thinking about a husband and a family."

Cantrell grabbed the bars and glared at Cory. "Are you going to stand there and let her talk to me like that?"

Cory shrugged and hid a grin. "It's a free country, and the lady can say what she likes."

"I'll turn you in for harassing a prisoner. I'm a victim here."

"Do what you want, but she's not the law and can rant on all she wants." Cory waved a hand toward his aunt.

"Thank you, son." She turned back to Cantrell and got within inches of his face. "You're nothing but the scum of the earth, and if you don't turn from your evil ways you're going to rot in…in…in that place with the devil. And I just might help get you there quicker."

Cory had to hide his smile. Even in anger Aunt Mae couldn't bring herself to utter the word.

She turned to Kate. "Anything you want to add?"

Kate stepped up to the cell. "Mr. Cantrell, all we're trying to do is save Elizabeth. What you've done to her is terrible. If you could only see how we love her and want to take care of her. She's not the same terrified girl who ran away from you last month." She took a step back and linked arms with Daniel. "That's all I have to say to you. Please just go back to your home and leave Elizabeth here with us."

Daniel led Kate from the cells, with Aunt Mae following. Cory turned back to Cantrell. "You'll do well to listen to what those women had to say. They can make your life miserable if you don't."

He stepped back into the office and closed the door behind the women. He shook his head and hung the keys back on the hook. "You two women are going to be the death of me yet. Whose idea was this to come in here and get my attention away so you could get into the cell block?"

The two women glanced at each then cast their gazes to the floor. Neither one would own up to the idea, but it didn't really matter. It had worked, and now Cantrell at least had an idea about what everyone thought about Elizabeth. She needed someone to defend her, and in her good fortune it happened to be two of the most influential women in town.

Daniel wrapped his arm around Kate. "I think you've done enough here today. Come on. Let's go get something to eat. You too, Aunt Mae." He escorted the women from the office. At the door he turned back to Cory and shrugged as if to say, "He's all yours now."

Kurt sat on the cot with his head between his hands. The truth of what the two women said hit him hard. If he'd really looked at Libby, he could have seen how unhappy she was, but all he'd been interested in had been making money for his whiskey and cards. Over half the time he didn't even remember hitting her, much less beating her.

Was it too late to do anything right? He'd come into town with so much confidence in seeing Libby and taking her home, but now he sat in defeat. He had no legal bindings on Libby, and she could do what she wanted. Maybe if he could see her one more time he could convince her to come with him. He was still her pa, and she'd loved him at one time in her life.

He held out his hands. The shaking had stopped days ago, and seeing them firm and steady now renewed his hope that somehow he could break the habit. Cards he didn't need. He'd proved that in the past few weeks too. The look on the faces of those he'd worked for gave him courage to keep sober. Even now when he wanted a shot of whiskey so bad he could taste it he wouldn't drink it.

God had no use for the likes of him, but if he stayed sober and worked hard, he might just be able to win back Libby's love and respect. He shook his head. Who was he trying to fool? It'd take a lot more than words and promises to make up for all that he'd done the past few years. Maybe he should do as the deputy suggested and just leave town.

The door from the office swung open, and the deputy returned to stand at the cell door.

He leaned toward the cell bars with his hands gripping them. "Can you tell me why you're just now coming to get her when I sent a wire a few weeks ago inquiring about a Libby Cantrell and that wanted poster you made?"

Kurt's head jerked back. He didn't know of any wire. "I don't know what you're talking about. I never heard from nobody about those papers I sent around." If he had, he'd have been here long before now.

The deputy frowned and shook his head. "Then can you give me one good reason for what you did to Elizabeth?"

Cantrell dropped his chin to his chest. The concern in the deputy's eyes led Kurt to believe more was involved than just the man's curiosity about Libby's past. Being a lawman made him a hard man, but if he was a Christian and could forgive, he needed to hear the truth. "No, but I want to tell you the whole story. I think you will understand a little more about Libby and who she is. And when I'm finished, I have one small request to make."

CHAPTER
TWENTY-FOUR

ADA SAT DOWN across the table from Libby and poured them both cups of tea. "Now that we have morning chores done and cleaned up after dinner, we need to have a little serious woman-to-woman talk this afternoon. With all the family around yesterday and my being so busy, we haven't had a chance to chat."

Libby bit her lip. This family had taken her in as one of their own despite what Drury had said about her. Maybe if she told Ada everything, she'd have good advice on what to do. She stirred her tea to cool it and tried to decide how to begin. Finally she laid the spoon against the saucer and plunged ahead.

"I've already told you some of what happened. It really wasn't Pa's fault. I just think he didn't know what to do with a daughter. If it'd been my brother who'd survived, Pa would have put him to work with him on the farm. Pa didn't think I'd know about running a farm, and then he took to drinking. That's when we moved into that shack in town."

Ada sipped her tea. "I can understand his confusion and his deep sorrow, but there's a better way to handle our problems. His drinking didn't solve anything. It only created more problems."

"I know, but I was too young to know how to help him." Now came the hard part. "When I was seventeen, Pa noticed how all the men looked at me with lust in their eyes. It scared me, and I tried to stay away from town and men as much as possible. Then one night Pa brought home some fancy clothes and told me to put them on. I refused, and that's the first time he beat me. He said I was a disobedient, ungrateful girl."

Ada's eyes misted over. "You poor child." She reached across and grasped Elizabeth's hands. "That's when you decided to go along with his demands?"

The strength in Ada's hands transferred courage into Elizabeth. "Yes, for the last four years I've been doing whatever Pa told me to do. At seventeen I started working in the saloon. All the money I made went to Pa. Whenever I disobeyed Pa or things weren't just right, he'd beat me. I deserved what he gave, because I couldn't do things right."

Now tears streamed from Ada's eyes, and the rest of the story spilled forth.

"Then last fall Pa realized I could make him even more money if he offered me to them for the evening. That's when it really got bad. I ran away because I couldn't take it any longer."

By the time she finished, both she and Ada were crying. Ada wrapped her arms around Elizabeth's shoulders. "You didn't deserve any of it, and there's no way Callum and I will let you go back to that way of life."

Elizabeth sat back and swiped at her cheeks with her fingers. "I don't want to either, but it's all I know, Ada. The people at our church let us know we weren't welcome in our parish after I started working at the saloon. I'm a tainted woman, and no one will think of me as anything else."

"Elizabeth, listen to me. God loves you. You are still His child, no matter what was done to you."

"I believed in Him once. Ma and Pa and my brother and I all went to church. It was fun, and we heard wonderful stories about Jesus, but the preacher also said God hates sins and sinners. When they turned Pa and me out of the church, I figured God didn't love me anymore because I was such a sinner."

"Honey, Jesus had something to say about that in Luke 17. He said that things that cause people to sin are bound to come, but woe to the person through whom they come! He said it would be better for that person to be thrown into the sea with a millstone tied around his neck than to cause a young person to sin. Your father, who was charged to bring you up in the Lord, led you down the road to destruction."

Libby chewed on the corner of her lip. Instead of condemning her, Ada was telling her that the greater part of the fault lay with her father. It sounded good, but how could it be true? "But I sinned too. I don't understand. Sinners deserve punishment." That's the only message anyone ever gave her.

"Yes, they do, if they don't repent. That *if* is a very big little word. If you truly repent deep down in your heart and don't plan to ever sin like that again, you are forgiven, and your sins forgotten."

The memory of the preacher once saying Jesus died for all sinners flashed across her mind. Could it really be possible?

Could she put the past behind her and look ahead to a new life? Then a memory she'd completely forgotten surfaced. "I want to be believe that just like I believed it when I was twelve and told the preacher that I did. Does what you're saying mean He still loves me and forgives me?"

Ada hugged her again. "Yes, it does, and that's the reason we're celebrating this week. It's the last week of Jesus's life, when He was betrayed, taken prisoner, accused, and then put to death."

She'd loved Easter as a child because of the beautiful story of Jesus coming out of the tomb alive. She'd drawn pictures of it in school at Easter time. The church had been decorated with white flowers and candles and was always the beginning of spring.

"Oh, Ada, I remember all that now, and I do believe God forgives me. I believe it with all my heart, but I must go to a place where no one knows me, and then I can get a fresh start as Elizabeth Bradley and not Libby Cantrell." God may forgive her, but the people here in Porterfield wouldn't. The look of contempt and disappointment in Cory's eyes told her all she needed to know about her chances of happiness in this town.

Ada shook her head. "No, you don't need to go anywhere. You can stay right here, hold your head high, and let people see the new you. In Christ, the old is taken away, and new life is given. That's what you have right here…new life."

How she wanted to believe that, but too many bad experiences from the past kept her shackled to it. The only way to freedom had to be in starting over completely.

Libby looked down at her hands, fear still filling her heart. The one person she wanted to see her as a new person never would. She raised her eyes to Ada and once again bit her lip, hesitating. "What about…Deputy Muldoon? Your son? You've seen how he looks at me now with such distaste. He'll never accept me for who I am because of who I was."

Ada's eyes lit up, but then a frown turned her lips down. "So, it's that youngest son of mine that has you ready to leave and go somewhere else."

Heat rose in Libby's face. She should never have admitted that to Ada. It was one thing to forgive a person and let her live her own life, but it was entirely different when that life involved a member of the family. Still, Ada had been understanding so far, and since it had now come to light, she might as well share everything.

"Yes, I admire Deputy Muldoon. I think his approval would mean more to me than just about anybody else's. His kindness and courage touched my heart." She blinked and swallowed hard.

"And…?" Ada's gentle prodding and kind, glowing eyes said she guessed the rest.

Then a dam burst within Libby, and she spilled the last deeply held secret in a rush. "I care a great deal about him, but I care too much for him to expect him to carry the burden of my life with his."

Ada's mouth firmed, and her eyes took on a look of understanding and resolve. "Don't you think he should have some say about that?"

"Ada, you know how he feels about women like me. I even heard him tell Aunt Mae there was no excuse for being in that kind of work." Even now the words she'd heard cut to the quick and sliced her heart into a million pieces. As kind as he'd been to her at the river and just after, he'd changed since Drury's outburst, and that hurt even more.

Ada said nothing but appeared to be thinking deeply about what Libby had just said. Finally she pushed back from the table and stood. "That boy will come to his senses. I've seen the look in his eyes when he's around you. True, he didn't come out here yesterday, but again, I think that was for your protection in case your pa came into town. Don't do anything you'll regret before giving him a chance."

She pulled out a skillet and mixing bowl. "Now let's start thinking about supper this evening."

How easy for Ada to talk. She'd never had to face the trials and troubles of a fallen woman. Ada had a family who loved her and did her bidding. If anything, Libby would regret leaving behind Ada most of all when the time came to leave Porterfield. "Ada, if you don't mind, I'm going to my room to rest a bit. I need to sort through a lot of things."

"All right, dear. You just remember how much you're loved by our family and how much God loves you. You're no longer burdened by that old life. You're a new creature in Christ."

Libby hobbled to her room then collapsed onto her bed, Ada's words ringing in her ears. A new creature in Christ. That's what she wanted to be. Tears flowed from her eyes like cleansing rain. God forgave all those past sins, and she would do everything she could from now on to live a life that would reflect that love and the new person she had become. She might never win the affections of a man like Cory, but now that she had her heavenly Father's love, she could face whatever came into her path as Elizabeth Cantrell and not Libby.

Cory listened to Kurt Cantrell's story. In reality it was Elizabeth's story, but he still had to hear it. The darker the picture Cantrell painted of his daughter, the more the bile rose in Cory's throat at the image of all the girl had done. Everything he'd ever blamed the girls here in Darnell's and The Ruby Slipper saloons belonged to Elizabeth, including how she dressed. Everything he'd loathed, everything he'd condemned in the past, Kurt now threw back at Cory.

When Kurt finished, the man still sat with his head in his hands, staring at the floor. He lifted misty eyes to Cory. "I did my baby girl wrong. Those women were right. I have no right to call myself her father. A father protects and looks after his children, and I did none of those with Libby. She didn't want to do those things, but I beat her if she didn't."

The words slammed into Cory's chest. Cantrell used her for gain to feed his own greedy nature. No matter why, Elizabeth had still done those things and lived in a way he couldn't fathom or stomach. To think he'd almost given his heart to her.

"You were and are a sorry excuse for a father. One thing I can tell you for sure is that you won't be taking her back with you. You'll have to go through some mighty tough women to get to her." Why they even bothered he couldn't understand, but he didn't plan to stand in their way.

"Son, I don't think I really want to even try. Just let me go, and I'll go on back to Louisiana and leave her here, but I want to see her one last time."

"You what? After what you told me, how could I let you

see her again? We're looking into the other charges, so you can just sit tight for now."

Cory slammed the door shut with a clang that shook the wall of the office. His anger almost equaled that of his aunt and sister earlier. He couldn't hold Cantrell much longer, because despite the big talk earlier he had no real grounds to keep the man here in Porterfield.

He collapsed into his chair. Rutherford and Slade glanced his way but continued their conversation without speaking to him. Just as well, since he didn't care to talk with anyone. He'd really like to ram his fist through the wall and release some of the anger building up in him. Anger at Cantrell, anger at his aunt and sister, and anger over his own reactions all rose up to boil in his gut.

Finally his emotions built to the point he had to get out of the office. He shoved his hat onto his head, buckled on his gun, and strode through the door. This time he mounted his horse and trotted down Main Street. Where he headed, he had no idea, but wherever it was, he needed time to think.

His head distracted by all he'd heard and seen, he didn't watch where Blaze took him until he looked up and found himself in front of the church.

Maybe this was a time he needed to talk to God again. The answers hadn't been good before, but maybe now they'd make some sense. He dismounted, hitched Blaze to a rail, and entered the dim interior of the church.

In the quiet of the cool sanctuary Cory lifted his eyes to the ceiling.

Lord, I don't know what to do or where to go. I've never been this angry with anyone as I am with Cantrell. Even

Darnell didn't raise my wrath this way. Why can't I get it out of my mind? Why do I keep thinking about Elizabeth, and why do I keep calling her that? "Libby" suits her just fine for what she is. For all I know she may even want to go back with him.

Cory cringed at those words. They couldn't be true, because he'd seen the fear in her eyes and remembered how hard she tried to run away. He sat in silence for a moment before his eyes focused on the cross behind the pulpit. Draped in black today and through the week, next Sunday it would be draped with royal purple and gold. The cross, the symbol of the greatest sacrifice known to man, reminded him of exactly what the Easter season meant to Christians everywhere.

I love you with an everlasting love. I loved you enough to die for you to pay for your sins.

In the quiet of the moment, the words became clear and sank deep into his soul. What he had to do fought a battle with everything he'd said and believed to this point. The only way to win would be by making the right decision. A decision he couldn't bring himself to admit even now.

CHAPTER
TWENTY-FIVE

ORY WALKED THE distance to the jail on Wednesday morning. For a day and a half he fought with his conscience about letting Kurt see Elizabeth. Sheriff Rutherford and Marshal Slade had gone over to Dallas yesterday and left Cory in charge. He used that as an excuse not to take Kurt to see his daughter.

This morning he'd have to think of something else, because they'd held Cantrell as long as they legally could. Daniel met him on the way into town. "You're not riding Blaze. Eat too big a breakfast at Aunt Mae's?"

"Something like that. What's your excuse?" He and Daniel had walked into town together many days before he married Kate.

"I need the exercise. I've been lazy lately and put on a little weight."

"Not from my sister's cooking."

Daniel laughed and shook his head. "Not hardly, though

she is getting better. No, I think it's from being behind a desk so much."

Neither one said anything else but greeted the few people who wished them a good morning. Finally Daniel voiced Cory's concerns. "You know, you can't keep Cantrell from seeing his daughter, and you do have to set him free this morning. Actually, you're a little over the limit for keeping him, but I don't think he'll complain."

"There's nothing you can do about the other charges?" If only they could find a way to punish Cantrell for what he'd done.

"Not here in Texas, and unless Elizabeth wants to go back to Louisiana and bring charges or testify against him, nothing will be done there either."

Cory's fingers curled into fists at his side. How he'd like to smash one of them into Cantrell's face. But that would only bring more problems, and he had enough to face as it stood.

"One more thing I need to tell you. Cantrell asked for a lawyer, and Nathan will be waiting to visit with him today."

"Nathan Reed? But why would he want to help Cantrell? What did Rachel have to say about that?"

"I don't know, but every man is entitled to representation, and as county attorney I had to make sure he got it. I chose Nathan instead of a stranger from another town because I know he'll be fair and not let Cantrell do anything to hurt Elizabeth or anyone else."

"Maybe so." But he still didn't have to like it.

When they reached the courthouse, Nathan waited for them on the steps. "Good morning, Cory. I can tell by the storm on your face that you're not happy to see me. Believe me, I don't like to represent scum like him, but like Daniel has probably told you, it's the law."

"Yeah, he told me, but that doesn't mean I have to like it."

Daniel turned and headed to his own office without saying anything else to Cory. Nathan followed Cory into the office. "If you'll allow me to see my client, I'll explain what he needs to do."

Cory pulled the keys from his pocket and unlocked the door to the cells. Nathan went into to visit with Cantrell, but Cory remained in the outer office. He didn't need to hear what was said, and by law the prisoner did have right to private counsel. The paperwork for Cantrell's release had to be done, but Cory didn't want to do it.

After a few minutes he picked up his pen and began filling in the information. After his stop at the church on Monday evening, Cory wrestled more with his emotions in that one night than he had in all the days he'd been living. All he could see in his mind's eye was Elizabeth, or Libby, in the clothes and makeup she had to wear at the saloon. The fact that she'd run away from it did not alter the facts of the way she had lived.

Nathan stepped through the door. "Cory, Cantrell wants to see his daughter before he goes back to Louisiana. I'm going to take him by the hotel and let him clean up. Then I have to ask you to take us where she is. I suspect she's out at the ranch, and if you don't take us, I'll have to do it alone. I just thought you might want to be there."

"All right, but wait until this afternoon. I'll go out and tell Ma he's coming so she can prepare Elizabeth to see him." As much as he hated the thought of facing Elizabeth, he'd rather she be warned first. He could probably send someone else, but Ma and Aunt Mae would be on his case about not doing it himself.

Cory released Cantrell to Nathan and waited for them to leave. He didn't like the way this day was headed, but he could do nothing to stop it.

When Rutherford and Slade returned, Cory filled them in on Cantrell's release and his request.

Rutherford hung up his gun belt and faced Cory. "It may not seem like a good idea to you now, but it's the best way in the long run."

"He's right. Of course, she has the right to refuse to see him. That's a whole different issue." Marshal Slade shrugged his shoulders and nodded to the sheriff. "I'll check back with you two later. I'm headed over to Carthage to take care of a prisoner there."

When he left, Cory remained at his desk a few minutes. Of course, Elizabeth could refuse to see him, and he could come back here and tell Cantrell that before Nathan could take him out to the ranch.

He grabbed up his hat and gun belt. "I'm going to talk with Elizabeth and let her know her pa wants to see her. If she says no, then I'm coming back and stopping him from riding out there."

When he reached the boardinghouse, Aunt Mae waved at him from the porch. He waved back and headed on to the stables for Blaze.

"Cory Muldoon, you bring yourself over here. I have a few things to say to you."

He winced at the tone of her voice. He'd heard it often

enough to know she meant what she said. He had no choice but to obey. He strode over to the porch. "What is it, Aunt Mae? I'm on my way out to the ranch to talk with Ma."

His aunt balanced the broom against the porch railing. "I hear tell that Kurt Cantrell wants to go out and see his daughter."

Small towns and their news systems. "You heard right. That's why I'm going to the ranch. Elizabeth needs to know and have the chance to say no."

"She does at that, and I wouldn't blame her none if she does refuse, but don't you go meddling and trying to control things."

"Aunt Mae, I honestly don't know what I want. I know he has the right, but after what he's done, I figured you'd be against it too."

"Does that mean you don't blame her for all that's happened?"

Cory frowned and stepped back. "I . . . I . . . of course I don't blame her."

She narrowed her eyes at him and clenched her hands on her hips. "Does that also mean you accept her as she is?"

Heat rose in Cory's face. He'd been battling that for three days now, and he still didn't know if he could accept her. The things she had done, even against her will, filled him with revulsion. "I . . . never mind. I'm going now." He turned and with long strides made it to the barn before his emotions could get the best of him. Once inside he slammed his fist against the stall, causing Blaze and Danny Boy both to jump and whinny.

"It's OK, boys." He reached up and brushed back Blaze's forelock. "Didn't mean to startle you, but I had to let off some steam." He threw his saddle across the stallion's back and tightened the cinch strap. A few minutes later he dug in his heels and headed for the ranch.

⚜

Libby sat at the kitchen table and watched Ada set jars of green beans and carrots on the counter. "I've never seen so many vegetables. When did you put these up?"

"Me and the girls do a lot of canning every summer. We're getting to the end of last year's stash, and then we'll do it all over again."

"I've never canned or done much in the kitchen. I had to do with whatever I could manage to get with the money Pa gave me, and that wasn't much." To have fresh meat and vegetables at dinner and eggs and biscuits at breakfast would have been extravagant with her means. She'd dreamed of someday living like this but never dreamed it would come this way.

"Then I guess I'm going to have to teach you." Ada poured herself a cup of tea and sat across from Libby. "Doc said he'd be out to check your ankle on Friday. I don't think he'll take the cast off yet, but he may let you start putting weight on it, so you can put aside those crutches."

"That would be wonderful." Libby nibbled on a cookie. "Ada, I've been thinking about Pa. He wasn't always like he is now. I remember sitting in his lap while he read stories to me and my little brother. He made me a doll out of corn husks one time when we didn't have much money for Christmas and then a cradle for it out of some scrap wood he had. It's those things I want to remember about him, not these past four years. Ever since you told me about how God could forgive my sins, I've wondered if He would forgive Pa too."

Ada reached across for Libby's hand. "You have grown so much in the few weeks you've been in Porterfield. You would never have considered your pa even a week ago. I take it you're not afraid of him any longer."

"No, I'm not." And the weird thing was, she meant it. Her heart held only pity for the man who had lost so much and didn't know what to do about it. Her own newfound faith made such a difference in her life, and she wanted that for Pa too. Would either one of them ever be able to earn the respect of the people of Porterfield? Probably not, but she wanted to try.

"Ada, do you think I can ever live a normal life now?"

At first Ada laughed, but then her faced sobered. "Normal is what we make it. No, if *normal* means you never expect people to talk or make comments. Yes, if you mean as a child of God with a new heart. You see, now it doesn't matter what people think or say about your past; that's not who you are."

"I want to believe that with all my heart. I love Porterfield and the people here, but some are not going to accept me, no matter what I do in the future." Of course, the main person she had in mind would never accept her past. How could he?

"There's one other thing I need to know," Ada said firmly. "Would you prefer to be Libby, or do you mind if we keep calling you Elizabeth?"

Joy bubbled up in her heart. She wanted to be Elizabeth, the girl they'd found and rescued. Libby was now buried in the past, and Elizabeth had become her new name in Christ. "I'm Elizabeth Cantrell, and I'm a new child of the King."

Now she'd said it aloud, and it hadn't been as hard as she'd feared.

Ada wrapped her arms around Libby—now Elizabeth. "That's my girl. I'm so glad Cory found you in that alley and not some ne'er-do-well who would have hurt you even more." She sat back in her chair. "Speaking of my son, what are we going to do about him?"

Elizabeth gasped, and her hands clenched in her lap. "Ada, what do you mean?"

"You know exactly what I mean. That boy cares about you. He just doesn't realize how much yet."

At Ada's words hope blossomed in her heart, but quickly she moved to squelch it. "But knowing who I was, he'll never accept me." That was more than she could even begin to hope for.

"Don't you worry about that. Cory may be stubborn and have a touch of my Irish temper, but he loves God—"

Cory burst through the door. He stopped short when he saw them sitting at the table.

"What in the world has you so fired up to come busting in here like that?" Ada demanded.

He snatched off his hat and grew red in the face. "I came out here to warn you. Cantrell's been released from jail, and he wants to see Elizabeth, I mean Libby."

"Her name is Elizabeth, and is he on his way now?"

"No, but Nathan is going to bring him out here." He turned his gaze to Elizabeth then cut away to stare at a place on the wall behind her. "That is, unless you don't want to see him."

"Honey, it's your choice." Ada grasped Elizabeth's hand. "You don't have to do this."

Elizabeth bit her lip. She had to believe that God would see her through whatever came her way. "Yes, I need to see him. He must know that I will never go back with him. He's still my father, and I do love him in spite of all the horrible things he did, but I have to stand firm in what I now believe. I will forgive him, but he will no longer have any control over me. Jesus has that control now."

Cory's mouth dropped open then clamped shut. The veins in his neck stood out, and his jaw clenched. His hands curled around the brim of his hat. "I can't believe I heard you right. After all that's happened, you still love him and want to see him?"

Their eyes met in one heart-stopping moment. "Yes, I do. I hope you understand. I have to confront him." Fear niggled its way to her heart. Not fear of seeing her father, but fear of complete rejection from Cory.

His eyes dropped. "No, I don't understand." He turned and stomped from the house.

Tears filled Elizabeth's eyes. Whether her pa loved her now or not didn't make any difference, because the man she wanted to love her either couldn't or wouldn't, and that did make a difference.

CHAPTER
TWENTY-SIX

*C*ORY MET NATHAN and Kurt on his way back to town. "You didn't waste any time, did you?"

Kurt actually looked like a decent man with his hair combed, chin shaved, and suit pressed. Looks could be deceiving, as he'd learned with Elizabeth. Finery and cleanliness didn't make up for or cover evil deeds.

Kurt leaned forward with both hands on his saddle horn. A light shone in his eyes that hadn't been there before. "What did my daughter say?"

Cory dismissed the man's appearance and ignored the question, addressing Nathan instead. "You're really going through with this. Despite all the harm he's caused, you're going to take him out there and dredge it all up again."

"I'm sorry you don't approve, but unless she outright refused, you can't stop us. Did she refuse?" Nathan stared at him with narrowed eyes and firm mouth.

"No, she didn't. She's ready to see him, although I can't see any rhyme or reason for it." He glared at Kurt, hoping he'd get the message.

"Are you coming back with us?" Nathan moved his horse forward and motioned for Kurt to follow him.

Cory hesitated. He didn't really want to see a reunion between this man and his daughter. It could well mean that she'd be willing to go back and live with him again, even if she said she wouldn't. If that happened, he'd wash his hands of women. All they ever did turned out to be disappointing or heart-breaking. He could live without that.

Then a strong desire to see exactly what would transpire overrode his disapproval, and he turned his horse back to the ranch. Better to be with them in case Kurt caused any trouble than to let Nathan handle the man alone. Of course Nathan could take care of himself since he was almost the same size as Cory, but it might take both of them to control Kurt if anything went wrong.

At the house Ma waited at the door and stepped back to allow the men to enter. Elizabeth stood in the middle of the room near the sofa. Her blonde hair hung down her back in curls held in place by a hair clip he recognized as his ma's. Her face bore a scrubbed-clean look of innocence that caused his heart to jump in his chest. Her blue eyes, the same shade as her dress, sparkled with moisture.

Cory bit his lip. He hadn't really looked at Elizabeth since Drury had spilled his tale. Earlier he'd avoided looking at her as much as possible, but now she drew him as a moth to flame. He gulped and turned away.

Kurt walked to stand in front of her. Cory stopped, his curiosity getting the better of him. Kurt lifted his fingers to touch Elizabeth's cheeks. She flinched just a hair, but enough for Cory to see and realize that beneath her serenity lay a deep-seated fear.

"Before you say anything, Pa, I want you to know that I can't and won't go back to Louisiana with you. My life is not what it used to be, and I no longer want to live like we did."

"You look just like your ma when we first met. She was a beautiful woman, just as you are. I see the same kindness in your eyes that I saw in hers." He dropped his hand and shook his head. "I didn't come to ask you to go back with me."

The softly spoken words ate at Cory. Cantrell couldn't fool him. Surely Elizabeth could see through him too. The scene caused his stomach to churn with anger and resentment.

Elizabeth's eyes misted over. "What are you saying, Pa?"

"I'm so sorry, Elizabeth, for all I've done to you. You didn't deserve to be treated like that, and you don't deserve a father like me. Please forgive me. I prayed with Nathan Reed here and asked the Lord to forgive me, but if you can't, I understand."

The gall of the man. Cory shot daggers at Nathan, but he only shook his head and turned away. How could Nathan have done such a thing? The man deserved to be punished not forgiven.

Elizabeth's eyes now spilled their tears. She sniffed and swallowed hard. "Pa, I asked God to forgive me for all the things I've done, even though He knows I didn't want to do them. I'm a new creation in Christ now, and all that stuff from the past is gone and buried. I forgive you because God forgives us." She took a step forward, and Kurt wrapped his arms around her. She hugged him back, and both sobbed.

Cory had enough. These people were crazy. He loved God,

and God loved him, but since God hated sin, how could He love Elizabeth and Kurt? They had sinned in the worst ways. He strode from the room and climbed atop Blaze. The quicker he got back to town, the quicker he could put all this behind him. He'd forget Elizabeth and go on with his life like he'd planned in the first place.

⁓⁂⁓

Elizabeth opened her eyes to see Cory's back just before he slammed the door behind him. He'd ruined this moment with her father, and she almost hated him for it but then recognized her own deceit had led him to this place, and she held some responsibility for his attitude.

Ada grasped Nathan's arm. "Let's you and I go into the kitchen. I have apple pie and some coffee waiting." She patted Elizabeth's shoulder as she walked past. "You two can join us whenever you feel ready."

"Thank you, Ada. We have much to discuss." From the sparkle in her father's eyes, he didn't want her to return to her old way of life. "Pa, if only you had come to this decision four years ago. Think how different things would be."

"Yes, they would, but we'd still be poor and looked down on by the people in town because of it. Nobody wanted to hire me then."

"What about now?" Had he really given up drinking and cards?

"That's up to you, Elizabeth, and I like your name. It's always suited you better than Libby."

"It's the name Ma gave me, and I like it too. But what do you mean it's up to me?"

"I like what I've seen of Porterfield. The people have treated you well, and I don't want you to give up your new-found friends. If I get a job around here, do you think we could stay on in Porterfield?"

That worried Elizabeth more than any other thing. Ada and some of the others had been forgiving and encouraged her to stay, but what about those like Cory who condemned her for the kind of life she'd had?

"I…I don't know, Pa. I love the people I've met and who've taken care of me, but once they find out who we really are, I'm not so sure they'll be as forgiving." Especially Cory, and he mattered more to her than anyone else.

She grabbed his arm. "I know what. We'll ask Ada and Nathan. They're smart people, and they'll help us. Mr. Muldoon is a wonderful man too."

Pa followed her into the kitchen, where Nathan and Ada sat eating the pie and drinking coffee. Elizabeth hugged her pa's arm close. "We have a great favor to ask of you, or we at least need your advice."

"Sit down, you two, and I'll get pie and coffee for you." Ada bustled about to get the refreshments then sat back down. "All right, what is it you need?"

Elizabeth sat with her father next to her. She breathed deeply then plunged ahead. "Pa wants to stay here in Porterfield, and so do I, but I'm worried about what the people in town will think after what they heard in the diner. I don't want to cause you or any of your family trouble with our reputations."

Ada studied first Elizabeth then her father, as though weighing the sincerity of their words. She glanced at Nathan then back at Elizabeth. "I, for one, don't have any problem with your staying here. As for what others will say, you can't let that bother you. Now that you've started on a new road in life, you'll have bumps and dips along the way, but as long as you keep your faith in God, He'll take you along the right path."

Pa placed his hat on the table. "That's kind of you, Mrs. Muldoon. What about you, Mr. Reed? You're my lawyer. What is your advice?"

"My first inclination is to say leave and start over elsewhere, but Elizabeth has made friends here. I'd hate to see her leave them, and I'm sure they'd rather she stay too. My wife's father is a wise man, and he once told me that if I could face up to my sins, confess them, and then face whatever consequences came from them, I'd be a better man in the long run."

Pa nodded his head and appeared to be considering what Nathan had said. Finally he spoke. "If I can get a good job here and Elizabeth is happy, then what more can I ask than that?"

Ada lifted her cup. "Sounds like a smart choice to me. As for what the townspeople will say, let them say it, get it out their systems, and as they get to know you, they'll see you for what you are now and not what you were."

Elizabeth wanted to believe that with all her heart, but what did it matter if she gained the admiration of the entire town and still didn't have Cory's?

Ada leaned forward and grasped Elizabeth's arm. "Sunday is Easter, the day of resurrection to new life. What better day for you and your pa to join the church and make your declarations of faith before the entire congregation? Looks like God had plans more far-reaching than we could ever imagine."

Elizabeth nodded, but a lump formed in her throat. If only those plans could include Cory, then all would be perfect.

~~~~~~

Cory avoided the boardinghouse when he returned to town. He needed no lectures from Aunt Mae or anyone else. When he passed the infirmary, he looked the other way in hopes Kate wouldn't come out to meet him. His hopes dashed when the door burst open and Kate barreled into the street, followed by Rachel Reed.

Kate grabbed Blaze's harness. "Whoa, you stop right there, big brother, and tell me what's going on. Rachel said Nathan is Mr. Cantrell's lawyer."

Cory tried to jerk the horse away from Kate, but she held firm. Rachel stood beside her with as determined a scowl as that worn by Kate. Unless he wanted to create a scene here in the middle of the street, he'd better get inside where they could have a little privacy.

"All right, I'll tell you, but first simmer down." He slapped Blaze's reins around the hitching post and marched up the steps to the infirmary. He shoved open the door then stepped aside to allow Kate and Rachel to enter.

"Have a seat, and I'll tell you what's happened so far." When they were seated in the empty waiting room, he removed his hat and paced the floor.

"Nathan did take Mr. Cantrell's case, and since we didn't have anything we could hold him on here in Texas and he's not a fugitive from Louisiana, I had to let him go free. He told me the whole sordid story of what he'd done to Elizabeth and then had the nerve to ask me to let him see her."

Kate's face clouded over, and a scowl furrowed her brown. "Well, did you? Let him go see Elizabeth?"

"Didn't have much choice. I went out and asked her if she wanted see him, and she said she did, so Nathan took him out there."

"Well, what happened? Were you there? What did Ma do?" Kate's voice held as much agitation as roiled in his own heart, but hers came from curiosity and wanting to know, while his came from already knowing.

"They welcomed each other with open arms. Seems Mr. Cantrell had some crazy story about talking with Nathan about God and God forgiving all his sins. He asked God to forgive him, so now he was asking Elizabeth to forgive him." It still made no sense how two people with such evil in their lives could change just like that, in the snap of the fingers.

Rachel and Kate hugged and both women cried. Rachel dabbed at her cheeks with a handkerchief. "Nathan told me he thought all Mr. Cantrell needed was a good talking to about God. Looks like he was right. Wait until Papa hears about this. He'll be so proud of Nathan."

Kate and Rachel continued to exclaim and talk about a miracle. All Nathan had done meant nothing to Cory. Who was Nathan to say that God had actually forgiven Kurt or that Kurt wasn't lying about wanting to repent? Men like Cantrell couldn't be trusted, and neither could Elizabeth. They'd probably go right back to their old ways soon enough.

Then the image of the frightened girl he'd found in the alley rose before him, and the haunted look in her eyes in the days that followed. Elizabeth had been scared and tried to get away. If she was so frightened then, why wasn't she now?

How could she accept back into her life the man who caused so much damage?

Kate slapped his arm and jerked him back to attention. "You're not listening to me, Cory Muldoon."

"I'm sorry. What did you say?"

"I said we need to go tell the others so they can rejoice with us. I bet Erin and Seth will be absolutely delighted to know about this turn in events." Then she peered at him and leaned forward.

"I don't like what I see in your eyes, Mr. Muldoon. I don't see joy or relief or any of the things you should be showing. Are you still angry with Elizabeth?"

Cory clenched and unclenched his fists. His hat dropped to the floor, and he bent to retrieve it to keep from looking directly at Kate. "Suppose I am. I have every right to be. I went out of my way to protect her and even left the town right after a huge storm to go find her. All for nothing but—" He turned on his heel to leave, but Kate and Rachel both grabbed him by the arm.

"Oh, no, you don't, big brother. You're going to stay right here and listen to what I have to say, and Rachel will probably have a few choice words of her own." She pushed him back into a chair and pointed her finger at his chest.

Cory leaned back away from her. The fire in her eyes let him know he had a good tongue-lashing coming, one he didn't want to hear. He steeled himself for the lambaste.

"You listen to me, and you listen good. God is in the forgiving business, and whenever He forgives a person, it's all the way. Everything is wiped clean. Elizabeth and her father are new creatures in Christ Jesus. They have a chance at a new life and a new relationship, and that's what they'll get. You may think they don't deserve it, but does any one of us deserve God's love and forgiveness? The Bible says we've all sinned and fall short of the glory of God, and that includes you, Mr. High-and-Mighty."

Rachel nodded and added her opinion. "Nathan's father did some horrible things, and so did Nathan when he rejected his mother and cursed God for allowing him to be born. God forgave Nathan, and Nathan forgave his father. It takes a heap of character to be able to forgive another person who has hurt you and disappointed you, but God did that with you, so how can you do less with Elizabeth and her father?"

Cory's hardened heart didn't want to hear any of what they said, much less act on it, but the words rang in his ears and hung in the air. "Is that all you have to say?"

The two women looked at each other and shook their heads. Kate gave one last parting shot. "All I can do for you is to pray for God to open your eyes to see the miracle He has given us." She grabbed Rachel's arm, and the two strode from the building, leaving him sitting in the growing dusk, the silence roaring in his ears even louder than their words only moments earlier.

CHAPTER
TWENTY-SEVEN

*W*HEN NATHAN RODE back into town and told Cory that Kurt had been offered a job at the ranch and Elizabeth planned to come back to town and stay at the boardinghouse until the repairs on the parsonage were complete, anger, frustration, and disappointment rolled together into one cannonball that threatened to explode and spew out words that wouldn't be pretty.

After clearing it with the sheriff, Cory took time off and rode out into the country to get away from his family and friends. For four nights and three days he fought with his conscience in a tremendous debate over Elizabeth and her father. Every time he remembered her blue eyes as she gazed at her father, he couldn't understand how she could forgive the man for what he'd done to her. No matter how she tugged at Cory's heart, the memory of her past snuffed out the attraction. It was all well and good for the women to accept Elizabeth as she was. If he were a woman he would too. If he were a man with no feelings for her, he could also accept her.

But he was a man, and he did have feelings for her. And there he came to the heart of the matter: he loved her. And he wanted to love her as only a husband could and should. But something evil, something beastly and horrific, had stolen into what should have been a place of infinite joy and pleasure. And he didn't know if he had the strength or the wherewithal to ever set that aside.

He rode back into Porterfield just before dawn on Sunday. Pink and lavender painted the clouds with a promise of a sunny spring day to celebrate the resurrection of Christ. Seth would be leading the sunrise service, started last year in partnership with the other church in town. Baptists and Methodists came together to celebrate the new life Christians have in Christ.

That meant the boardinghouse would be quiet, and he could slip in and clean up before the regular services later in the morning. He weighed everything he'd ever been taught about the life of Jesus, but doubt and anger kept him in turmoil. No matter which way he turned, he couldn't bring himself to the ultimate step he'd have to take if he were to ever have peace again.

He bathed then dressed in the stillness. A door banged, and voices drifted up the stairs. They were back from the service, and now Aunt Mae would prepare breakfast for the boarders. He slumped onto his bed and let his hands fall between his knees. In a few moments the aroma of frying bacon and biscuits in the oven wafted up to his room. His mouth watered, and his stomach rumbled. Biscuits, egg, and bacon would taste mighty good after three days of beans and jerky.

He reached for the Bible on his night table. He'd purposely left it behind, because he didn't want to read the truth.

Now it was all he had left. The truth. He loved Elizabeth, and that hurt.

Someone knocked, and he turned to see Aunt Mae at the door. "May I come in? I saw Blaze out at the barn and knew you'd come home."

He simply nodded, and she came to sit beside him. "You're hurting. I can see that, and so could everyone else the days before you left." She slipped her arm around his shoulders. "How I wish I could pull you up onto my lap like I did when you were a little boy and tell you everything will be all right."

His throat tightened, but he would not let her see any tears in his eyes. She'd always been a solid rock of faith like his ma. They'd been through a lot in their lives, but their faith held fast. Why couldn't his?

How could he accept Elizabeth and her past without ruining everything he'd worked so hard to build? Would people understand that he could forgive that which he had condemned? He stared at the Bible in his hands. One verse kept running through his mind. *Ye shall know the truth, and the truth will make you free.*

He knew the truth, but it hadn't set him free.

"Cory, you love that girl. I've seen it in the misery in your eyes. Misery because you want to care, but your condemnation of everything she represents stands in the way. All these years you've fought to keep that kind of thing out of Porterfield, and here she brings it right to your doorstep. Is it so hard to admit you've been wrong? People aren't going to think any less of you if you accept Elizabeth and forgive her father like she has. As a matter of fact, they will probably think more highly of you."

He hung his head. He didn't worry about his reputation, but Aunt Mae didn't know that. His heart caused the problem. He had seen himself in a new light while in the country alone. Fresh misery overwhelmed him, because his family had seen his sin before he had. He was someone who condemned too quickly and who divided people into two camps: law abiders and lawbreakers. Someone so proud to uphold the law that he could show no mercy to those who broke it.

That is what he'd become, and he didn't like it. He'd always thought that he shouldn't marry because he didn't want his wife to be put in danger. Could it be he'd used that as an excuse not to marry so he was free to continue a life he loved—with no sacrifice and no compromise and no fear of hurting anyone, including himself?

Aunt Mae stood and placed her hand on his shoulder. "You still have some thinking to do. Just remember what today represents. Think on what Jesus did for us, and then consider what you have to do for Elizabeth." Her skirts swished as she left the room.

Alone once again he let his thoughts roam over all the teachings and verses he'd learned over the years. He opened his Bible and began reading. Then the fourteenth and fifteenth verses in the sixth chapter of Matthew jumped out at him: "For if ye forgive men their trespasses, your heavenly Father will also forgive you: But if ye forgive not men their trespasses, neither will your Father forgive your trespasses."

How many times had he read those verses in his lifetime? Too many to count, but today they stabbed at his heart like never before. God told him last week he had to accept Elizabeth for who she was now, and he had to forgive her father. But he hadn't wanted to forgive or accept. Instead he'd used his self-righteous anger to protect himself, and in so doing hurt Elizabeth once again. *He* had sinned just as much as Mr. Cantrell. His heart ached with the truth, but the Bible spoke only truth, and only one Person could set him free.

Until he could forgive Mr. Cantrell for what he'd done to Elizabeth, there would be no future for him and the girl he loved.

He fell to his knees beside his bed. "Father, You've told me over and over this is what I have to do, but I hardened my heart against Your voice. How can I change now? How can I go to her and admit the truth? And how will I ever get over what happened to her and what her father did to her?"

Because she is a new creature in Christ, and you both are My children, just as her father is My child.

Yes, she was a new creature and a new child of God, and so was Mr. Cantrell. She looked nothing like the terrified and ill young woman he'd picked up in the alleyway. If God had shown her how to break free from her past, could He not do the same for Cory? Could they not be a new creation—together?

Peace filled his soul, and love filled his heart. Why had it taken so long for God to shine a light on the Scripture and make it clear? Because in his fear of being hurt, he'd refused to listen or look for the truth. Only one thing left to be done, but did he have the courage needed to make that first step toward showing Elizabeth his love and forgiving her father? It was time to find out.

Elizabeth sat proudly beside her father as they rode into town in the Muldoons' surrey. All of the family had come to the ranch last night and heard what happened with Elizabeth and her pa. The women had been quick with their love and support, but the men had been more skeptical until afterward when the children came in and gathered around Elizabeth and loved her with their hugs and kisses.

Donavan had wrapped his arm around his wife, Sarah, and said, "Children are a pretty good judge of character. With God's forgiving love and mercy, we all must accept Elizabeth and Mr. Cantrell for who they are in Christ."

After that the evening turned into one of joyous celebration that led to her decision to attend church today and stand before the congregation and tell their story. At first Pa had been reluctant to bare his soul like that, but finally agreed after urging from Ada and Callum.

Ada turned back to face Elizabeth and her father. "Not everyone will be as accepting of you as we have been, but remember they are only human and reacting the only way they know. Don't let their words or attitude determine what you do or where you go."

"Thank you. I'll try to do that." Facing the people of the church would be hard, but with so much love supporting them, they could do it.

When they arrived at the church, Rev. Winston greeted them. "I've set aside a time just before my message for you and your pa to speak. This is a courageous thing you're doing."

Elizabeth didn't know about courageous at the moment, as

her knees shook. Even the support of the one crutch she now used didn't help. Before the address to the congregation, Rev. Winston announced the special music by the music ensemble and Kate Monroe.

The organ and piano began the melody, one Elizabeth had never heard before. Kate's clear voice rang out in the small church. "If God be for us, who can be against us?"

As she sang, Elizabeth's heart became lighter and lighter, and her soul filled with peace. Then as Kate concluded, the choir picked up the words, "Worthy is the lamb that was slain, and hath redeemed us by his own blood."

That's what Christ did for her and for all sinners, including Pa. Only He is worthy of all honor and blessing and glory. As the choir sang, Elizabeth reached over and squeezed her father's hand and noticed the tear in the corner of his eye. The music touched him as it had her. It truly meant redemption for them both.

After the music faded away, the congregation sat in silence as the elder Rev. Winston prayed. Elizabeth didn't catch all his words, but the last few words gripped her.

"May whatever we hear today be heard in the light of the words from this great music and from the Lord Himself. May we see the resurrected Christ as He opens His arms for all sinners to come to redemption and become children of the King."

He spoke those words for her and for Pa. He prepared the way for them to speak. As the prayer ended and the people settled back in the pews, the younger Rev. Winston stood at the front behind the pulpit and introduced them.

"You've heard rumors and tales all week about two of our special guests today. In order for all that be put to rest, they will tell you their story in their own words." He held out his hand toward them. "Welcome, Elizabeth and Kurt Cantrell."

Elizabeth's knees wobbled, and she held firm to her father's arm. When they turned to face the crowd, both smiles and curious stares greeted them. Her heart pounded when she locked gazes with Cory seated on the back row. He had come. Now he had to listen and hear from her lips the events of the past years and few days.

Pa cleared his throat and began his story. Some scowls appeared as he came to a close, but no one got up to leave. Then it came her turn. She turned a steady gaze to Cory, who looked down, but she would not turn away from him. Elizabeth silently prayed for courage as she began. Her voice remained steady throughout the testimony of her life with Pa.

When she reached the end, to her amazement she heard a few sobs and noted tears in many an eye. Cory's face remained unreadable, and the joy from a few moments ago deflated. She returned to the pew with Pa, where Ada and Kate greeted her with a hug. They sat down, and Rev. Winston continued on with his sermon on God's redeeming love. If she hadn't believed before now, she would certainly have done so after his message.

At the conclusion the ensemble sang "Hallelujah" from the same oratorio as the other music. What a joyous sound filled the small church as members stood while the voices carried the message of the King of kings and Lord of lords.

Just as she expected, many members left without speaking to Elizabeth or her father, but many others rushed to their sides and followed them outdoors. Her gaze immediately sought out Cory. He lounged against a tree at the edge of the church yard observing what happened on the church lawn.

Erin wrapped an arm around Elizabeth's waist. "You see how people respond when they know the truth? Not all understood or agreed, but those who do will love you and help you and your pa have a good life here."

"I wouldn't have believed it a few days ago, but it truly is a miracle." All the while she talked with Erin, her gaze darted to Cory. When he finally straightened up and headed her way, her heart nearly jumped into her throat. It pounded harder with each step he took toward her.

Conversation stopped among the few people left. Even Pa and Mr. Muldoon ceased their talk. Cory stood before her and removed his hat. "I think we have a few things we need to clear up, Miss Bradley, or should I say Miss Cantrell." He held out his hand to her.

She grasped it, and the warmth shot straight to her soul. His eyes no longer held condemnation, and what she saw gave her the first glimmer of hope.

He glanced at his parents and then the others. Then he stretched out his hand to her father. "Mr. Cantrell, it took courage to do what you did today, and I want you to know I admire you for it. Forgive me for the way I've acted this past week. I've been a self-righteous idiot, but no more."

Pa pumped Cory's hand. "Of course I forgive you. You did what you had to do to protect my daughter."

Cory grinned. "Then if you'll excuse us, I have a few private words I need to speak to your daughter."

Elizabeth's heart threatened to jump right out of her chest. Could her dream be coming true? When Pa nodded his approval, Cory slipped her hand onto his arm and led her away from the crowd.

A few minutes later he stopped and took both her hands into his. "Elizabeth, I've been fighting and wrestling with the Lord for weeks. I didn't want to care so much about you, especially after Mr. Drury arrived. What you had done represented everything I've fought against in this town for the past five years."

If not for the tone of his words, soft and blameless, her heart would have been once again crushed in defeat. Instead, that flame of hope began to burn brighter. "I'm so sorry I lied to you, Cory. I was so ashamed of the truth and couldn't bear to tell anyone. Please forgive me for that."

"Shh, I know that now. There's nothing to forgive you for. You did what you had to do for survival. I set myself as judge and jury and did exactly what the Bible warned against so many times. We are not to judge, lest we be judged, and that's what happened. I judged you and your father, and God judged me as an unforgiving sinner who hurt one of His precious children with his words and actions. When you forgave your father, I couldn't understand how you could still love him, but now I do."

He shook his head and frowned. "What I'm trying to say is, can you forgive me? It took a great deal of courage for you to forgive your father and then to stand with him before the church and give your testimony. Can you forgive me like you did your pa?"

She wanted to throw her arms around his neck and hug him, but she restrained her happiness to a smile. "Of course I forgive you. And does that mean you truly forgive Pa too?"

"Yes. It took a while, but I can honestly say I have. But can you find it in your heart to care about me after the way I've treated you the past weeks? I mean, is there a chance for us to get to know each other without all the baggage of the past and start all over in our relationship?"

Was there a chance? That's all she had ever hoped and prayed for. She bit her lip to keep from crying and nodded her head.

When he pulled her to his chest, cheering went up from behind them. Cory wrapped his arms around her and grinned. "Sounds like they approve. What do you suppose they'll think if I kiss you right here in the church yard?"

With his arms around her, the safety and security she had sought enveloped her. Never again would she be afraid of rejection. God loved her, and Cory did too. She lifted her gaze to his. "I don't know, but I'd like to find out."

He bent his head and pressed his lips to hers. Then his hold tightened, and she allowed every ounce of love she had for him to flow through that kiss. Never had she experienced anything quite like it.

Their road would not be an easy one, but then, no one had the promise of an uneventful journey. The hope of the spring season ahead embraced her with the assurance that her future with Cory would be one based on truth, not lies, for she had come to know the truth, and it had set her free.

Coming in 2013 from Martha Rogers...

Love Comes Home

CHAPTER ONE

Point Lookout, Maryland
Monday, April 10, 1865

COLD AIR CHILLED his arms, and something poked at his cheek. Manfred Logan reached down to pull a ragged blanket up over his arms and brushed away the straw scratching his face. A few moments later a sudden brightness aroused him again. His lids opened to find slivers of sunlight peeking through the cracks in the wall and dispersing the shadows of the night.

He shut his eyes against the sun's rays, but sleep would not return. He lay still in the quiet of the new morning and sensed a difference in the air that settled over him like a cloak of peace. That sense of something different caused him to raise his head and glance around the room. The same familiar stench of wounds, dirty hay, unwashed bodies, and death permeated the air, but in it all, the difference vibrated. Something had happened to change the day, but he couldn't determine what. His heart beat rapidly, and his palms were sweating even in the cool of the morning.

Manfred peered over at the pallet next to him where his younger brother Edward lay sleeping. He could see nothing different in him or in any of the others in the room, but the aura persisted. There was no use in trying to sleep now. He pulled a worn journal from beneath his dirty mat.

The almost ragged book, his lifeline for the past three years, fell open, and he tried to read about the past, but the foreboding in his heart returned him to the present and the new dawning day. Manfred wrote.

April 10, 1865

Three more died during the night. The near full moon shining through the cracks gave me light to see. I took one man's shoes. He won't need them, but I will. Took his socks and another man's for me and Edward. God, I never dreamed I would do such a thing, but we are desperately in need. Please forgive me. Help Edward and me to get out of here and get home safely. I so desperately need to see Sally and my family.

The scrape of wood against wood sounded, and Manfred shoved the journal under his mat. No sense chancing the guard taking it from him. Manfred turned on his side once again to feign sleep. The door thudded against the wall, and the guards' shoes clomped on the wooden floors. Union soldiers made their usual morning inspection looking for any who may have died during the night.

The blunt toe of the sergeant's boot kicked Manfred's hip and sent a sharp pain through his leg. He grunted in response and raised his head to let the sergeant know he was alive. When the man passed, Manfred sat up on his mat and stretched his legs out in front of him to relieve the expected early morning stiffness. Others awakened, and their groans filled the air as they rose to sit on their bedding. They waited for breakfast, not knowing if they would even get rations this morning. The guards exited carrying the bodies of the three souls who didn't make it through the night.

Manfred voiced a silent prayer for the boys and their families who would receive the news of the death of their loved ones. He bit his lip. He and Edward had to survive. They had too much life to live, but then so had the three just taken away. What if God chose not to spare him or Edward? No, he wouldn't think of that. His mind filled instead with Scripture verses memorized as a child and young boy. With no Bible, God's Word stored in his heart gave him the comfort and hope he needed for his future.

A few moments later the guards returned with what passed for a meal. Manfred accepted the cup of what the men called "slop water" coffee and a hard biscuit that would have to suffice until they bought a lunch of greasy water soup. Months ago the putrid smells of death, the filth in the barracks, and the food sickened him, but now he barely noticed. It may have been Monday on the calendar, but the day began and would end like every other day they'd been here.

Manfred took a few sips from his cup then leaned toward

the man on his right. "Here, James. You take the rest of mine. You need it more than I do."

The man clasped a trembling hand around the cup then reached for the biscuit. A few drops sloshed over the rim. "Thank you, Manfred. You're a true friend." He stuffed the biscuit into his mouth then gulped down the last dregs of liquid. With a nod to Manfred, the young soldier set the cup on the hay and lay back on his pallet.

Manfred breathed deeply then almost choked on the rancid air. The men were so weak. When would this nightmare come to an end? This question had gone unanswered for these five long months. Too many lay ill and dying.

His brother rested next to him on a mat to Manfred's left. Edward cushioned his head on his crossed palms with his eyes closed. Manfred reached over to touch the boy's shoulder. "You all right, little brother?"

Edward didn't open his eyes. "Yeah. I'm OK. Just hungry. I dreamed of home last night and Flossie's cooking. When I close my eyes, I can see her and Momma in the kitchen. Flossie up to her elbows in flour making biscuits, and Momma stirring the fire and making grits."

"Shh, brother, you're making me hungry too." Manfred pulled what was left of his jacket tighter about his thin body. "We've been here near five months, but it seems a lifetime. Home, our parents, and my dear Sally may as well be a million miles away."

Edward sat up and pounded his fist into the straw. "Yeah, and sometimes I think we'll never get back there." He stretched his legs out on his mat, hugging what passed for a pillow. "I sure pray I'll get to see Peggy again soon."

Manfred positioned his body to sit squarely on his mat. "Soon as we're home, I'm asking Mr. Delaney for Sally's hand in marriage. That is, if she still wants me. No telling who she's met since I've been gone."

"I wouldn't worry about that if I were you, big brother. Sally loves you." He smacked his fist into the open palm of his other hand. "I just want to be out of here and out there where the action is, fighting with Lee."

Manfred sighed and pulled his knees to his chest. He felt the same, but they could do nothing but sit here and wait. He clenched his hands about his legs. What he wouldn't give for a bath, shave, and haircut. A good meal wouldn't hurt anything either. If only he could somehow communicate with Sally and let her know he was alive.

Almost a year since he'd seen her and six months since the last letter.

He reached into his pocket now for the folded piece of paper containing her words to him. She had written from her grandfather's home. He prayed her family had stayed there and were safe in St. Francisville. He held the worn paper to his lips. With God's help he'd get home to his love and claim her for his bride.

Once again a strange sensation of something about to happen settled over Manfred. The hair on the back of neck bristled, and goose bumps popped out on his arms. Whatever loomed in the future, it would change his life. His bones told him so.

The doors grated against the floor and swung open again. The guards returned to collect the tin cups and utensils from breakfast. Sometimes Manfred wanted to throw the slop passed off as food right back into the corporal's face. But anger would get him nowhere—except maybe dead. He stuffed the letter back into his pocket.

When they were once again alone, Edward sat cross-legged on his mat and leaned toward Manfred. "You know, they told us the Yanks are fighting Lee in Virginy, and that's just across the river. Lee has to beat them Yanks. We'll be hearing about it any day now. I just know it."

Manfred simply nodded. The foreboding feeling wouldn't leave and swept over him now even stronger, as though he sat on the edge of something powerful about to happen. When Edward closed his eyes, Manfred picked up his journal again, but he sensed movement near him. He raised his head to find Luke Grayson standing near.

"Manfred, Edward. How's it going this morning?" Luke twiddled a piece of straw in his hands.

"Same as usual." Manfred moved over and made room for the fair-haired young man to sit on the mat. Although Luke had only been there a little over two months, his body told the same tale of lack of food as those who had been here longer.

Manfred gazed around at the damp, filthy structure that had served as both prison and home for the past four months since his capture in Nashville. At least they were in a shack and not one of the tents on the grounds. Clumps of straw covered with moth-eaten blankets and rag sheets served as beds. None of them had any more than the clothes on their backs and a few personal items in knapsacks or small packets.

His gaze shifted from Luke to Edward. Both were too young to be away from home. Luke's blue eyes were as sunken into his face as Edward's brown ones. Their matted and dirty hair needed a good washing and cutting. But at least they were alive.

Luke reached across to touch Edward's arm. "And how is your healing coming along?"

The young man popped open his eyes and rubbed his shoulder. "I'm getting better. The pain's almost gone. How about you?"

"I'm fine. But I want to get home. It's so close—just across the river there in Virginia. About a day or so walk from the river to Grayson Farms. If I could get out of here, I'd be home in a couple or three days. That is, if there's anything left. No telling what those Yanks have done." Luke's hands dropped into his lap, and his chin sagged to rest on his chest.

Edward sat cross-legged with fists clenched between his knees. "We have to believe we'll get home. I hate sitting around here all day rotting with nothing to do."

Manfred shook his head. "No, but we can plan, hope, and dream about the future. I believe God will see us through this."

He stood and stretched. The stiffness in his knees reminded him of his lack of exercise the past months. How he longed to run free. "We heard about Port Hudson being cap-tured when we were home last. That's only a ways down the big river from our home in Bayou Sara. In Ma's last letter she said they'd had some damage, but she reported nothing else. I've worried about them ever since."

Manfred sat back down. He wiggled a toe peeking through a hole in his sock and reached over for the pair confiscated the night before. "Don't suppose we'll find much of the South the same. It's all been touched in some way by the looting and burning of property. But something's up. I can feel it." He removed the tattered sock and pulled the better one up over his foot.

Edward unwound his legs then rolled over on his stomach and rested his forehead on his hands. "Can't come too soon for me." He closed his eyes.

Luke squatted with his elbows resting on his knees. "Saw you reading while ago. What was it?"

"Just my journal and Bible." Manfred patted the straw where he had stowed the two books. "They help me keep my sanity."

"Good reading, the Bible. Looks like Edward has the right idea." He nodded toward Edward, now asleep. "Think I'll get on back to my little space." He shuffled down the narrow aisle to his blanket.

Manfred's gaze rested on his younger brother. Barely seventeen, he had joined the Fourth Louisiana unit a few weeks after his birthday. He had served with Manfred while their three brothers joined up and fought in other areas. The image of home brought a smile to Manfred's lips as he remembered Sally, his sweetheart. She lived with her family in Pineville, over the Louisiana state line and into Mississippi, and a little over half a day's ride up the road from his home.

He reached into his pocket and removed Sally's letter once again. No need to open it; he'd memorized every word. As long as he believed them and held on to them, he'd get home and see Sally and fulfill his dream of becoming a doctor. He wanted to heal people, not hurt them.

Sally Delaney sat at her dressing table running a brush through her mass of tangled curls. Tears blurred her image in the mirror, and she grimaced as the bristles caught in another snarl. She dropped the brush onto her lap.

"Lettie, what am I to do? Not knowing about Manfred is too painful to bear." She sobbed and scrunched a handful of auburn hair against her head. "Nothing's going right. I can't even brush my hair. I hate the war and..." Her voice trailed off, and she dropped her gaze to the floor before turning toward Lettie. "What am I to do?"

The housemaid clucked her tongue and fluffed the pillows on the walnut four-poster bed. "I don't know, Miss Sally. I hates the war too. Too many is dyin' out there."

Lettie's skirt swished as she crossed the room. She picked up the discarded brush and began smoothing out the mass of curls. "You know, Miss Sally, you have the prettiest red hair in all of Louisiana."

Sally lifted her tear-stained eyes and found Lettie's reflection in the mirror staring back.

"You got to have courage. I'm worried about my Burt off fightin' in the war too, but I know God is takin' care of both him and Mr. Manfred."

"I know, Lettie, but the waiting is so hard." Sally swiped her fingers across her wet cheeks. "I mustn't let Mama see me crying."

Mama had enough worries of her own without fretting about her children. Besides, so many others, Lettie included, loved men off fighting for the South. Lettie's strong young man had joined the Rebels only a few months ago and gone off with others from Louisiana. Last they'd heard he was one of the soldiers at Vicksburg, but they'd heard nothing since then. Lettie missed him as much as she missed Manfred.

His letter a few months ago placed him near the battle for Nashville. Stories coming back from that area spoke of the volumes of soldiers killed at Franklin and then up at Nashville. Reports stated that the surviving young men had been taken prisoners, but no one knew which prison they were in. She prayed every night that Manfred lay captive somewhere and not buried on the battlefield.

She pushed the thoughts from her head. If she let her imagination take over, she'd be in no shape to go down to breakfast. "Lettie, we both have to believe our men will be coming home soon."

"Yes, Miss Sally, we do, and when they come, we'll be ready and waitin'." In a few minutes Lettie's skilled fingers had tamed the unruly ringlets and secured them with a silver clasp at Sally's neck.

"Thank you, Lettie. I'm all out of sorts this morning. Here it is April, and I haven't heard a word since November." Her fears tumbled back into her mind. "I want this war to be over. Too many have died, and I don't want Manfred or Burt…" She couldn't utter the words. Saying them might make them true. She pressed her lips together and pushed a few stray tendrils from her face. She had to get her fears under control. God had promised peace when she offered her prayers, but so far that peace eluded her.

Lettie secured the wayward strands with the others under the clips. "Now, Miss Sally, I done told you we got to believe they're alive and comin' home. We can't do nothin' about the war. Your momma and grandma need you to be strong. When Mr. Manfred gets home, you'll have a weddin'. You'll see."

Sally turned and wrapped her arms around the dark-skinned girl's thin waist. "I want you to have a wedding too, Lettie." She blinked her eyes to clear them and stared into the dark brown eyes of her friend. Lettie had been with Sally since childhood, and they shared so much life with other. If it had not been for Lettie and her mother, Nellie, Sally might never have recovered from the incident in Mississippi that brought them all to St. Francisville. Lettie had become her friend and confidante, not just another servant.

The young woman's brow furrowed, and she pursed her lips. "Are you thinking about what happened back home?"

How well Lettie knew her. Sally blinked her eyes and nodded.

"Then you best stop it. What you did had to be done, and we both know it. You saved all our lives."

No matter that Lettie spoke true. The images of war could not be erased from Sally's mind. "I just want this war to end."

"Well now, I want that too, but it's all in God's hand. But just think how Mr. Charles, Mr. Henry, and Mr. Theo got back without any harm."

True. Of the five Logan brothers, only Edward and Manfred remained out on the battle field. Henry and Charles Logan had even been prisoners themselves, but they were now safe at home. She must have hope for Manfred, Edward, and Burt.

Lettie lifted the edge of her white apron and patted Sally's cheeks dry. "There now, Miss Sally. It's all goin' to be fine. It'll all be over soon. I just know it. I feel it in my bones. Besides, Easter's a comin', and that means a new season, new life, and new hope."

"You and Mama, the eternal optimists, but I love you for it. You always know how to make me feel better." Sally breathed deeply and reached for a green ribbon to secure in her hair.

She would get through this day just as she had all the ones since Manfred left. Then the memory of what she overheard between her father and mother last night drained away her determination. She peered up at Lettie. "I need to tell you something." Sally squeezed the hand now clasped in hers.

At Lettie's solemn nod Sally took a deep breath and revealed her worry. "Last night I couldn't sleep, and I heard Papa come in from his trip to Pineville. I sneaked downstairs to see him, but he was in the parlor talking to Grandpa."

Sally's lips trembled. "Our house in Pineville is ruined. The Yanks took everything they could carry out and left the rest in a shambles. Mama's beautiful things. Oh, Lettie, it's just terrible."

Lettie pressed her hands against her cheeks, her eyes open wide. "Oh, I'm sorry. Your poor Mama. It's so sad. No wonder you're feelin' blue this morning."

Sally squeezed Lettie's hand again and for the next few moments sat in silence. Lettie understood her better than anyone else. The servant girl knew her deepest secrets and could be trusted to keep them.

"You are such a comfort. I don't know how I'd get through these days without you to share my feelings."

Lettie patted Sally's hand. "We've been together too long and been through too much for me not to be with you. My Burt's out there somewhere, and so is your Manfred. We have to wait and pray they'll be home soon." She stepped back. "Come, now let's get you dressed. Your family will be waitin', and you know your grandpa doesn't like tardy children or cold eggs even if you is his favorite."

Sally had to smile at that. She did love Grandpa Woodruff, but he could be gruff when the occasion arose. She hastened over to a bench by the bed and picked up a green and white print cotton dress. Lettie grasped it and gathered it up to slip over Sally's head.

She held her arms up and bent toward Lettie. "I believe Mamma invited the Logan family for supper one night this week. I'm anxious to speak to Manfred's mother. Perhaps she's heard from him."

The dress billowed about her as the full skirt fell down over her hips and the myriad number of petticoats. At least Mamma and Grandma didn't require her to wear hoops with her day dresses, nor a corset. Lettie's nimble fingers went to work on the buttons lined up the back.

"I think you lost more weight, missy. This dress is looser than it was last week. You sure don't even need your corset. You have to eat more." She peered over Sally's shoulder into the mirror and shook her head. She shoved the last button in the hole.

Looking over her shoulder, Sally smoothed the dress around her waist. She gathered the wrinkles from the excess fabric. "It is big, but I'm just not hungry." At Lettie's stern gaze she added, "But I'll try to eat more."

Lettie sniffed the air. "If that aroma coming from the kitchen is what I think it is, my mammy's ham and eggs should do the trick. She'll have biscuits and gravy too."

Sally nodded. "I promise I'll eat some of everything this morning." This was a promise she would try to keep, especially with her grandmother's and Nellie's cooking being so delicious.

The two girls locked arms and resolutely walked down the stairs to the dining room. Sally forced a smile to her lips and went in to join her family for breakfast.